Escape to Love

They were alone on the side of the cliff, hidden now from the eyes of the world. Paul dropped down on the grass and put an arm across Celia's shoulders, forgetting for a moment the difference in their stations. They were just boy and girl, on equal terms, and the young Frenchman drew her into his embrace. He whispered in her ear, passionately—

"Celia, adorée, belle amie, I won't let them force you into marriage."

"Oh, Paul," she sighed, and put her cheek against his. They lay like that, close clasped, until suddenly, as though by mutual consent, they turned their heads and their lips joined in a kiss which bound them irrevocably and for always.

The first kiss of real love that Paul had ever given, the first she had ever received. A strong glad ecstasy surged through her and lifted her to heights way beyond fear or suffering.

Now the child Celia was wholly woman and wholly his. . . .

Escape to Love

DENISE ROBINS

AVON
PUBLISHERS OF BARD, CAMELOT, DISCUS, EQUINOX AND FLARE BOOKS

AVON BOOKS
A division of
The Hearst Corporation
959 Eighth Avenue
New York, New York, 10019

ISBN: 0-380-00657-X

First Avon Printing, July, 1976

AVON TRADEMARK REG. U.S. PAT. OFF. AND
FOREIGN COUNTRIES REGISTERED TRADEMARK—
MARCA REGISTRADA, HECHO EN CHICAGO, U.S.A.

Printed in the U.S.A.

PART ONE

1

One evening early in September in the year 1934, a Jaguar saloon driven by a chauffeur in blue uniform rounded a bend in the road that led from Helston to Ruthlyn Cove.

In the back of the car sat a man and a woman. The man was aged about forty, smartly dressed. He was gazing upon landscape familiar to him, for this was his home, and although for the last eleven years he had been living most of the year round in London, he was a Cornishman who had been born and bred here. For centuries back the Trevarwiths had been owners of the land across which the car was now moving, and of that tall grey Castle which had just come within view.

Francis Trevarwith leaned forward and looked with a slight flicker of interest at his ancestral home, then turned to the woman beside him.

"There you are, my dear . . . Storm Castle!" he announced with a touch of pride in his tired voice.

The woman, younger than him by ten years or more, and who had been married to him only three weeks ago, let down the window of the car and peered out.

"Oh, how grand," she exclaimed.

She spoke with a touch of excitement. Her husband took one of her hands and pressed it. He was as much in love with Isobel as any man of his quiet and unimpassioned nature could be. She looked particularly handsome this evening, dressed becomingly in grey tweeds with silver-fox-ties and a pale grey chiffon scarf swathed around her turban hat and under her chin, concealing the burning red of her hair. She had a very white skin, darkly-lashed blue eyes and a red, narrow little mouth. Her figure was perfect. She had a strong attraction for most men, and Francis Trevarwith, who had imagined himself dead to all passions and who had forsworn the love of women after the death of his first wife eleven years ago, was desperately in love with her. From the moment of their first kiss she had stirred up long-buried and forgotten emotions in him. Apart from the physical attraction of her wonderful red hair, her camellia skin and beautiful body, she had a bright amusing tongue, and a certain coyness which appealed to a man of his age. He knew little about her beyond the fact that she used to work for a T.V. studio and that she came from simple ordinary stock . . . people who had no pretensions to the aristocratic breeding of the Trevarwiths. But when Francis had first met her (it had been at a race-meeting to which she had come with a man who knew him) she had appeared to him as a pathetic creature as lonely and unsatisfied as himself— hating her job and longing for a home of her own. He had gone away haunted by the memory of her very blue eyes and a trick which she had of looking through her lashes at him and saying:

"I'd like Mr. Trevarwith's opinion. I'm sure *he* knows . . ."

It was flattering to have a pretty woman, still a girl, take so much interest in a man of his age. He had seen to it that he met the lovely Isobel again. A couple of months later he had, to his own astonishment, asked her to marry him.

Now, after three weeks' honeymoon in the south of France, they had come down to the Cornish home which Isobel had, so far, not visited. She was not really fond of the country—London was more her mark— and she had enjoyed herself to the full at Monte Carlo and Cannes, where it had amused Francis to let her gamble and spend a lot of money on clothes. But the Côte d'Azur bored Francis. He was a man who preferred living in his own country. In actual fact he preferred Cornwall to any other place in the world. But the tragedy which had befallen him here in this very place eleven years ago had driven him away from Ruthlyn all this while. Only now, when he had this new attractive, high-spirited wife, did he feel compelled to return and take up residence at the Castle again.

Isobel was looking with interested, slightly amused eyes at the Castle which they were now rapidly approaching. An historic-looking building. Its old grey lichened walls looked as though they had withstood the buffeting of the storms throughout the centuries. The grounds were bare, well-kept lawns, walled-in gardens with formal flower-beds, fruit trees and flowering bushes. But there was an absence of trees which gave it a stark unfriendly aspect.

Isobel was longing to see the interior. Three-quarters of the place was closed down and the family lived in one wing. Francis admitted that it was not very up to date, but Isobel had already made secret plans to modernize the whole place and fill it with young amusing people. She could twist Francis around her little finger and she was going to do it to her own advantage in the future.

The one fly in the ointment so far as she was concerned was the presence in that Castle of the little girl who was Francis Trevarwith's daughter by his first wife. The child whose birth had caused the death of the first Mrs. Trevarwith. Isobel was not by nature at all maternal. She did not want children of her own, although she had secretly decided that it might be a feather in her cap if she could produce a son and heir for the Trevarwiths. She had no wish, certainly, to play the mother to somebody else's child. The existence of Celia Trevarwith was definitely a bore. But at least she felt that she had no cause to be jealous, because Francis Trevarwith seemed to have no particular affection for his small daughter. Her existence was also a bore to him. He was a queer man. Isobel could not yet quite fathom him. But she had gathered from what he had told her that he had adored Angela, his first wife. She, too, had come from this part of the Cornish coast. They had known and loved each other for years before they married. Isobel had seen a photograph of Angela . . . a slender, wistful-eyed girl. What Isobel would call "mushy."

Something had gone wrong when her baby had been born. Possibly a muddle-headed country practitioner who failed to understand the case. A specialist summoned from Truro was too late and the first Mrs. Trevarwith had breathed her last there in the great Castle and left Francis alone in the world except for his small daughter. Instead of him turning to the child and lavishing his devotion upon her, he had conceived what Isobel thought a rather curious bitterness against Celia. He seemed to blame the poor little creature for the death of his adored wife. He had handed Celia Angela Trevarwith over to the care of nurses, and later to a succession of governesses, who all found it lonely and dreary in the big Castle which had no mistress and which rarely saw its master these days.

Mr. Trevarwith had taken himself to London and thrown himself into his job as a stockbroker. He lived more or less the life of a recluse at his Club when he was not working. He carried out only his bare duty toward the unhappy little daughter, visiting her occasionally and making sure she was well cared for.

But she had grown into the living image of her mother and that stabbed him every time he looked at her face, so he curtailed his visits.

A strange, hard man. But Isobel had changed all that. He had become flesh and blood again with her and she had felt proud of her achievement. It was pretty good work on her part to find herself the wife of a wealthy man with a Castle for her home.

She gave an exclamation as they drew nearer yet to the place. It looked magnificent. To the right, in the distance, the faint shadow of Land's End. But her thrill lay only in the size and splendour of the Castle itself.

"Oh, Francis!" she said, pressing her husband's fingers, "what a place!"

"It's very fine," he admitted, "but I hope you won't

find it too lonely down here. If you do, we will move back to town."

"Oh, no," said Isobel gaily, "I've had enough of London, and as we own this place, I think we ought to live here. What marvellous parties we can have."

He winced a little at that thought. But his young wife's childish enthusiasm warmed his blood. He had lived alone far too long. He realized that now. His honeymoon with Isobel had shocked him a little. But he liked being shocked. And he liked the idea of coming down here and chasing away the ghosts of the past with his red-haired charmer at his side.

"Won't your little girl be excited to see us!" observed Isobel.

Francis Trevarwith frowned. The memory of Celia generally evoked a frown. He was a little sorry that she must be here this evening. He would have preferred to be alone with Isobel. It would be so embarrassing to see a replica of Angela about the place. Besides, the child was intensely shy, and—in his opinion—difficult, although those who looked after her always said she was "as good as gold."

Totally lacking in interest in her, having no sense of sympathy or compassion, he was anxious only to please his bride. He said:

"If Celia irritates you at all, we can send her to boarding school, my dear."

"Oh," said Isobel loftily, "I'll manage her. I can make her like me. She'll do what I tell her."

"I'm sure she will," said Francis Trevarwith, and then, slipping an arm about his wife's supple waist, added: "I always do what you tell me, don't I, my darling?"

She raised her mouth for his kiss and then, with one of her pretty coy movements, wiped his mouth with her handkerchief.

"Can't have Mr. Trevarwith entering the ancestral home with Isobel's lipstick all over his face," she said merrily.

He clasped her closer, more in love with her this eve-

11

ning than he had ever been. As the car turned through the gates and up the gravel drive which led to the door of Storm Castle, he was haunted just a trifle by the memory of that other bride whom he had driven down this same road in a less up-to-date car and with more financial worries than he had today.

How sweet and gentle Angela had been! He remembered how he had raved and cursed when they had told him that she was dead . . . cursed himself for having allowed her to bear a child, and recoiled in horror and loathing from the innocent cause of her death.

He drew away from the warm vital body of Isobel, and, taking out a handkerchief, wiped his forehead.

"It's warm, isn't it," he murmured. "We get lovely Septembers here, as you will see."

"I'm going to adore it," exclaimed Isobel.

But Francis Trevarwith wished that there was no Celia waiting inside those Castle walls. Unwittingly she had been the cause of all his agony and desolation in the past, and somehow he had a strange premonition that she might be the cause of trouble in the future— trouble between himself and Isobel.

2

Upstairs in the west wing of the Castle in the big room which had at one time been Angela Trevarwith's boudoir, and which was now the schoolroom, Celia Trevarwith waited for the arrival of her father and his new wife.

It was half-past six and she was eating her supper, carefully spreading a piece of bread and butter with honey. Opposite her sat Miss Ellis, the last of a long line of governesses who could not stand the complete isolation which went with this job. Miss Ellis was more likely to stay than the rest . . . for she was old and really past the age when she should be the constant companion for a quick-minded child of eleven. And she was a settled spinster who did not require much amusement. So, as she had told Celia herself one morning, she intended to remain here until Celia went to school . . . a fact which had caused the child a pang because she found Miss Ellis very dull, also very set in her ideas, and out of date. Celia loved to run barefoot on the grass or down on the beach with her hair streaming in the wind and her face wet from the salt of the sea, or the rain. She longed to be given the little shirts and shorts which she saw advertised in magazines for modern children. She longed to have other children to play with.

Celia waited for the arrival of her father and his wife without a trace of excitement, which Miss Ellis thought unnatural. Miss Ellis could not understand why Celia seemed quieter than usual—even sad.

Inwardly, the child was a bundle of nerves and repressed emotions.

Deep down within her, she was highly sensitive. She devoured as many books as she was allowed to read.

Celia could not be fond of her own father who had so little interest in her and who came so rarely to see her. When he did come, she was nervous and ill at ease with him. But the memory of her own mother she worshipped.

Now she had been told that she was to have a stepmother. But that did not excite or interest her to any degree. She was afraid of her father. How could she ever love his wife? And why should somebody be put in her darling mother's shoes? It seemed wrong to Celia that there should be a new Mrs. Trevarwith.

She finished her supper in silence.

"Now please may I go to bed?" she asked.

"Certainly not, Celia. You are to put on that blue dress that is on your bed and your black slippers, and run down to the hall to wait for your father—and his—er—and Mrs. Trevarwith."

"Must I?" said Celia.

Miss Ellis looked at her over the rim of her glasses.

"Now don't be foolish, my dear. What would your father think if he arrived and found you in bed? You don't feel sick or anything?"

"No," said Celia dejectedly, and then wondered if she could possibly make herself sick so that she could stay up in her bedroom and not have to meet Mrs. Trevarwith.

"Run along then, and get dressed," said Miss Ellis, and then added in a kinder voice: "And cheer up, my dear. You'll probably like your stepmother very much and she'll take your own mother's place in your heart."

A wave of red spread across the little girl's thin face, which was brown from the sun but delicate-looking in spite of its tan.

"No, never, *never!*" she said in a passionate voice and turned and ran out of the room.

Upstairs in the turret room which she had occupied

ever since she could remember, Celia stood trembling a little, trying to fight her fears.

She looked at her row of books on the mantelpiece, then at the shabby doll which leaned against her pillow. Miss Ellis disapproved of that doll because it was old and worn. It encouraged germs, she said, but Edith, the cook, had given it to her three years ago and Celia loved it and called it "Gretel" after the little girl in *Hansel and Gretel*. She spent hours dressing and undressing it, giving it the time and affection she had never herself received.

"I shall love you all the more now that father has come home with a new wife," she whispered to the smiling painted face, "and you will hate my stepmother, too, won't you?"

Half an hour later she was dressed and on her way downstairs to the big hall where a log-fire had been lighted in the huge open fire-place. Big yellow and red chrysanthemums mixed with autumn leaves nodded from great stone jars. Celia, herself, had in fact superintended these decorations because she loved to arrange flowers. But neither the fire nor the flowers could make the place look really bright. The curtains and covers were of sombre hue, expensive but shabby. A great deal of the furniture was marquetry, handsome in a fashion but overpowering. It had been collected by the Trevarwiths for years. Everything was on a big scale, and the place was ill-lighted and draughty despite the huge red damask curtains across the windows, and one or two heavy Spanish leather screens.

At this precise moment that Celia walked solemnly and nervously down the wide staircase, the front door opened and Francis Trevarwith ushered his bride into the Castle.

On the bottom step Celia stood rooted, her small thin hands clasped nervously behind her back. She cast a quick glance at the figure of her father and then at the woman who had been put in her mother's place. Isobel Trevarwith, with a theatrical gesture, swept off her hat and shook back the magnificent red curls of which she

15

was justly proud. She looked gay and animated in this moment, but to the child her beauty was at once repellent, if not evil. She was like the red-haired witch in her fairy book. She had bewitched Father, and now she was coming to the Castle to put everybody under her spell.

Isobel's first impression of Celia was that the child was an insignificant plain little thing, but at a second glance her shrewd gaze detected promise of future beauty in the slight graceful body and the large blue-green eyes. She had very lovely fair hair with a natural kink in it, but Miss Ellis had drawn it tightly back, plaited it and tied it with a ridiculous bow. The blue dress was unbecoming.

"What a funny little thing," thought Isobel.

Francis Trevarwith took off his hat and coat and said:

"Well, Celia, and how are you?"

"Good evening, Mr. Trevarwith, and welcome to Storm Castle, Mrs. Trevarwith," Miss Ellis said, having carefully rehearsed this greeting.

Francis Trevarwith murmured a reply. Isobel ignored it rather rudely. She could not be bothered with that silly-looking old fossil. And now her quick bright eyes were searching around inquisitively, taking in everything. What a barn of a place. Nothing like so imposing inside as outside. It would be perishing in the winter despite those radiators. She hated the old-fashioned furnishings. Even if it cost Francis a packet she must bring the Castle up to date.

She supposed she had better do the heavy stepmother act, and advanced upon Celia with her most charming smile.

"Well, dear, and how are you going to like having me for your mother?" She put out a hand and drew the child toward her.

Immediately Celia drew a sharp breath and recoiled, her cheeks burning, her large eyes dilated.

"You can't be my mother. My mother is dead and buried in St. Ruthlyn churchyard. Nobody can take her place!" she said breathlessly.

16

Isobel coloured, then shrugged her shoulders, and turned to her husband.

"What a quaint child!" she said.

Francis Trevarwith frowned and approached his small daughter.

"Celia! What are you thinking of? Kiss your stepmother at once and behave yourself."

The child looked at her father with an appealing expression which he did not notice, and had he done so he would not have understood it. She had always been a thorn in his flesh and tonight she was more—she was a definite menace to his new-found happiness. She said:

"Father, I . . . she *can't* be my mother. I can't have two mothers, can I? My darling mother is buried in . . ."

"Oh, for heaven's sake, be quiet," broke in Mr. Trevarwith harshly. "Isobel is your stepmother. Don't stand there gaping at me like an imbecile. Kiss her at once and make friends."

But Isobel's interest in her husband's young daughter had passed. She made a mental note of the fact that she and Celia would come to grips very shortly and she would soon teach her how to behave. The whole place needed pepping up. She'd sack that genteel old hag of a governess and get the kid into a modern boarding school. The sooner the better.

"Don't worry about Celia, Francis," she said to her husband, "I'm tired and it's chilly. Isn't there another cosier sort of room we can sit in?"

Francis Trevarwith looked vaguely around him. Elspeth, the little hunch-backed maid, in fresh white overall, had appeared on the scene. He said:

"Have you lighted the fire in the small drawing-room?"

"Yes, and so is the fire in missus's bedroom, sir."

"Come along then," said Mr. Trevarwith, taking his wife's arm. "We'll go upstairs. After dinner you'll find the drawing-room smaller and more to your taste, my dearest."

They walked up the stairs together. Celia stood motionless watching them go. She was trembling.

"Tck . . . tck . . . you didn't do *anything* that I asked you, Celia. You were so rude and unkind to Mrs. Trevarwith, and you've displeased your father," said Miss Ellis.

"But she isn't my mother and she never will be," said the child passionately. "She is a witch and I don't like her."

"You read too many stupid fairy tales," said Miss Ellis crossly.

Celia burst into tears.

She wept until she was sick and blind with misery. The harassed Miss Ellis took her off to bed. She did not see her father or stepmother again that night.

3

In the morning when Celia was in the middle of her history lesson in the schoolroom, which was full of the bright September sunlight, her stepmother visited her.

Isobel was not in a particularly good mood. She had come to the conclusion that life at Storm Castle was not going to be all honey, and she had learned, for the first time, that most of the money which she had thought Francis Trevarwith's had belonged to his first wife and was held in trust for Celia. That put a different complexion on many things. Francis was, himself, moderately well off, but by no means a man of unlimited means as she had fondly imagined. He had already told her that although she could go ahead with certain redecorations and furnishings, she could not turn the place into the sumptuous film set which she had hoped for.

Indifference to her stepdaughter had given place to decided resentment. It was a damned shame that this nervous stupid child should, when she was twenty-one, inherit all that money. Even if she, Isobel, produced a son and heir for Francis now, he could only have the Castle and estates for what they were worth. The bulk of the money would always remain Celia's.

Francis had said he would give her everything within reason and that he hoped she would find friends in the district and be amused. Well, thank goodness, she knew of one man who lived not more than ten miles away, Fulke Withers, who was an engineer from Kyland and ran a flourishing business in these parts. Fulke was often in London and belonged to a set in which Isobel used to move when she was at the studios—a crowd mad about horse-racing and cards. She had been with Fulke that day at Newmarket when she had met Francis. She must look Fulke up and get him to organize some parties down here for her.

But first and foremost she decided that she must deal with the child who had been so unpleasant last night. Reminding her father of his first wife . . . the brat! Francis had seemed depressed for the rest of the evening. No, it wouldn't do to have Celia hanging about the place.

Isobel advanced smilingly into the schoolroom and put an end to Celia's lessons.

"You can run along, Miss Ellis, and do something else. I must get to know my new stepdaughter," she said brightly.

Miss Ellis rose. She looked with surprise and some alarm at Mrs. Trevarwith. She was not used to being told to "run along," and she resented this intrusion upon little Celia's history of the Wars of the Roses.

"I . . . Celia generally works until twelve, Mrs. Trevarwith, and—er——" she began.

"That's all right. I shall be making a number of alterations now that I am here," interrupted Isobel.

Miss Ellis coughed, glanced at Celia, then picked up a book and walked sedately and with an injured air into the adjoining room.

"I will get on with some needlework," she announced primly as she departed.

Isobel seated herself on the edge of the schoolroom table, and taking a cigarette from her case, lit it. She flung the burnt match into the grate. Celia sat still as a mouse in her chair, her pencil still suspended in her hand. She regarded her stepmother with faint astonishment. Celia promptly labelled her as a very untidy person. It was a reputation which stuck, for in the years to come Celia was always to associate Isobel with complete disorder in the rooms she occupied . . . with burnt matches, cigarette-ends and half-emptied glasses and library books lying with crumpled pages or stained

20

covers, and a continual search through the Castle for things which she had lost.

Isobel said:

"Well, what are you thinking about?"

"I—I don't know."

"What do you think of your new mother?"

Celia's sensitive face flushed.

"I . . . you're not . . ." she began.

"Now, now," broke in Isobel in a warning voice, "we mustn't have that nonsense again. Your father will be very upset if you upset *me,* so remember. I *am* your new mother, and that is that."

Celia did not answer.

Isobel repeated sharply:

"Do you hear?"

"Yes," said Celia in a whisper.

"Say 'Yes, Auntie Isobel.' I don't particularly want a kid your age to call me 'Mummy,' but you can call me Auntie Isobel."

Celia's blue-green eyes stared again at the woman.

"But you aren't my auntie."

Isobel slid off the table on to her feet and jerked her shoulders irritably.

"Oh, don't be so difficult."

Celia lapsed back into silence and looked down at her exercise book. Her own big unformed handwriting was blurred by a mist of tears. She did not like to be spoken to so sharply and crossly and did not see what she had done to deserve it. This red-haired witch wanted such unreasonable things. Why call herself "auntie" when she was a stranger? Why say that she was her new mother when she did not wish to be called "Mummy"? Not that Celia wanted it either.

Isobel looked frowningly around the schoolroom, then walked to the window and eyed the sunlit cliffs and the blue shining sea. It was a splendid scene. But Isobel was more interested in her powers of control over the Castle and all who were in it. She turned back to the little girl.

"Stand up! You haven't given me much of a welcome so far, you know. Why don't you offer to take me round and show me the place?"

Celia obediently rose.

"I'll take you," she said.

"You aren't much like your father, I must say."

"No—I'm like my mother," said the child gravely.

"Hadn't she got better manners than you?"

Celia flushed again and bit her lip nervously.

"I—I'm sorry."

"Loopy, more likely," was Isobel's private opinion. She had never met a more awkward kid. The way she stared with those big sad eyes.

It seemed to Isobel that only two courses were open to her. She might "take the child up" in a big way and amuse herself by dressing her and turning her into something good. Or send her away to boarding school as Francis suggested. The latter course would certainly be less trouble.

Isobel said:

"Have you always lived in the Castle? Don't you ever go away?"

"Oh, yes, my father sends me with Miss Ellis to a farm near Redruth for a fortnight every summer," said Celia.

"Well, that's very nice, isn't it?"

"It would be if I could make friends with all the animals, but I'm never allowed to," said the little girl sadly. "Miss Burton who used to be here and Miss Ellis, too, think you get diseases from animals. And I have never had a dog or kitty of my own. I wish I had."

Isobel puffed at her cigarette. What a life the kid appeared to have had! Francis just ignored her, except for doing his bare duty. No wonder Celia was half-witted. She had been imprisoned in this great barracks of a place since she was born. Not that Isobel blamed Francis. What the devil could a mere male do with a small daughter left on his hands? He wasn't the paternal kind, anyway.

"Ever been to the cinema and seen a film?" she asked the child curiously.

"No."

"What games do you play?"

"Miss Ellis and I play draughts, and she is teaching me chess, and we have a game called Ludo and sometimes Elspeth plays snakes and ladders with me."

Isobel grimaced to herself. The child depressed her.

"What you want, my dear, is pepping up," she said. "You'll be covered with lichen like the walls if you go on this way."

Celia did not quite understand this. She continued to look at her stepmother with her great grave eyes. Isobel then flung a half-finished cigarette into the grate and said:

"Let's see your bedroom."

Celia took the woman into the adjoining room. Isobel looked around. On the mantelpiece she saw the photograph of a sweet-faced girl in evening-dress. She picked it up. Celia said quickly:

"Please put that down. It's my mother."

"All right. All right. Can't I look at it?"

Celia bit her lip. She did not like Isobel to touch that photograph. Isobel eyed the gentle face of her predecessor with some interest and then, with a shrug, replaced the photograph on the mantelpiece.

Her gaze now fell upon the dilapidated doll upon Celia's bed. Idly she picked that up and turned it over in her fingers. Celia watched this handling of her precious Gretel with agony. Isobel's long red-pointed nails were hurting darling Gretel, she was sure.

"What's this monstrosity?" inquired Isobel.

"It isn't a mon . . . monstrosity," said Celia indignantly. "It's my darling Gretel."

And she tried to take the doll from the woman, who held it high above her head where she could not reach it.

"Not so fast. Don't be so rude. Does Miss Ellis allow you to snatch?"

Celia's eyes were lifted to Gretel. Her lower lip quivered.

"Please may I have it?"

23

"In good time. What's all this fuss about? You're out of date, my child. You ought to have a real modern baby doll. It gives me the creeps to see the way you are shaping."

Celia did not understand half that Isobel was saying. She only knew that Isobel disliked Gretel and, out of spite, was keeping her away.

"Please may I have Gretel?" she repeated patiently.

"Auntie Isobel is my name."

Something spirited and stubborn in the child refused to allow herself to be bullied like this. She said sullenly:

"You aren't my Auntie Isobel."

Something equally stubborn in Isobel Trevarwith made her want to be cruel just because the little girl defied her.

"Then you can't have your doll," she said. "I'm going to teach you manners, my dear."

Celia began to breathe very fast. She was used to neglect, to solitude, to discipline from women like Miss Ellis, but not to deliberate bullying. It frightened and upset her. She was appalled at the thought that Isobel was going to take the doll away from her altogether. Gretel was her dearest friend. The person she loved and cuddled and spoke to when she was in bed at night. She said breathlessly:

"I want Gretel."

"You want a lot of things, but you are not going to defy me," said Isobel. "It's just as well you should learn that right from the start, my young girl. I'm in your mother's place now and I'm going to bring you up the way you should go."

She marched out of the bedroom with the doll tucked under her arm.

In a flash the child was after her, pulling at that arm.

"Please let me have my doll."

"When you learn to call me Auntie and behave yourself."

Celia's enormous eyes stared incredulously at the woman. And then she lost her childish control. She burst into tears and said through her teeth:

24

"I hate you. You're a witch. I hate you."

Isobel, her face as red as her hair, shook the child off and called for Miss Ellis.

"Come and take this little fiend away. She can go to bed until she learns how to treat her stepmother."

Miss Ellis came hurrying into the room. In her fashion she loved Celia, and she was shocked by this unusual demonstration from the child which she realized must have been brought on by some acute injustice.

"Now, now, what is it, Celia?" she began.

Celia, with the tears pouring down her cheeks, looked with anguish at Gretel, who was still hanging ignominiously from beneath Isobel's arm.

"She's taken Gretel from me. She's a cruel witch and I hate her."

"Oh, Celia," began Miss Ellis nervously, "you must be polite to Mrs. Trevarwith and not call her——"

"I don't care what she calls me," broke in Isobel sharply. "And I can see I am only wasting my time. As for you, Miss Ellis, you had better take a month's notice. It is Mr. Trevarwith's wish that Celia should go to boarding-school immediately."

So saying, she walked out and slammed the door.

Miss Ellis blinked. Celia was sobbing bitterly. The governess found her own lips trembling.

Never before in her monotonous life had she been spoken to so impolitely. She at once formed the opinion in her mind that the new Mrs. Trevarwith might be smart and pretty but she was *not* a lady. Poor Mr. Trevarwith had been "caught". And poor little Celia . . . a pang of genuine pity and affection shot through the woman as she turned her blurred gaze to the sobbing child. She wiped her own eyes, then gathered Celia into a rare embrace.

"Never mind, dearie, maybe it is all for the best. It is too lonely for you here. You'll like boarding-school."

"Oh, Miss Ellis, I wish I was dead! I wish I could be with my mother," said Celia passionately, flinging her arms around the governess.

Miss Ellis was shocked at such a display of grief. It

25

seemed to her wrong that anybody so young as Celia should feel so intensely about anything.

"Now, now, pull yourself together, dear, and let us face this matter calmly," she said, patting the child's head.

"I hate my stepmother."

Miss Ellis coughed.

"You must do as your dear father would wish and learn to be pleasant to her, Celia."

"But she isn't pleasant to me, and she has taken Gretel away."

"Oh, dear!" sighed Miss Ellis.

Celia stopped crying, although her thin body still jerked with spasmodic sobs. She stared blindly at her governess.

"What will boarding-school be like, Miss Ellis?"

"Very nice I'm sure. There will be lots of little girls of your own age for you to play with."

Celia reflected upon this in silence for a few moments. She had never had anyone of her own age to play with. Storm Castle was the only home she had ever known, and although she had had little of love or happiness in it, it was familiar to her, and the idea of being sent away to the unknown was not a little frightening.

"Oh, Miss Ellis, I don't want to go. I want to stay here with you and Elspeth."

Miss Ellis sighed. She was just beginning to realize that she had been given notice, which meant a search for a new job. Positions with good families were not easy to get, and she was fond of Celia and used to Storm Castle.

"Oh well, you'll have to make the best of it and so will I," she said. "Now dry your eyes and let me take you down to Mrs. Trevarwith to apologize for being so difficult."

Celia bit her lip. All the colour had left her small face.

"Do you think she will give me back my Gretel if I do?"

"I'm sure she will."

But when Celia and the governess got downstairs they found that Isobel Trevarwith, in a fit of temper, had marched into the kitchen and burned the child's doll in the kitchen grate. An act greatly deplored by Edith, the cook, and by old Elspeth, who loved Miss Celia. An act which Celia, in the years to come, remembered and was never able to forgive.

For the rest of that month Celia was docile and polite. She did exactly what Isobel told her. In deference to Miss Ellis's wishes she made no further reference to her own mother. And she accepted a severe lecture from her father without explaining her own point of view.

Isobel thought that she had conquered. She was blind to the child's state of mind, and to the look of utter misery stamped upon that small face. It mattered not to her, in any case, if Celia looked with dread at the prospect of being sent away to the care of strangers. Isobel found what she considered a suitable school in Truro, and was glad to be getting rid of Celia. Francis approved of St. Wilfred's. The headmistress had sent them a list of parents who could recommend it and there seemed to be several well-known names to satisfy the most snobbish. There were over a hundred girls there and the school buildings were modern and stood in open country. It amused Isobel to drive into Truro and see St. Wilfred's for herself and ape the gracious and kindly lady anxious for her little stepdaughter's welfare.

Miss MacMaster, the Scottish Head, thought Mrs. Trevarwith "a charming girl" and was surprised when Isobel suggested that little Celia had been so rude and difficult. She promised Mrs. Trevarwith that Celia would soon have some sense knocked into her. They encouraged good sense, good manners and a keen spirit at St. Wilfred's.

Isobel further endeared herself to Francis by volunteering to supervise Celia's outfit for the school. (Isobel, in Francis' opinion, was being wonderful with the

27

child.) A new trunk was purchased. Celia was duly fitted out and turned into one of a pattern. Dark green tunic and purple blazer, felt hat with the St. Wilfred's badge, hockey-stick—all the stereotype school paraphernalia, which left Celia completely bewildered and more frightened than ever.

The last two days before she left Storm Castle to start the winter term at the school, she crept about the place with red-rimmed, swollen eyes and such a white face that even her father noticed it and questioned Miss Ellis.

"There is nothing wrong with the child, is there?" he asked anxiously. He did not want anything to go wrong with Celia's health, not only for her own sake, but also because he was looking forward to the time when she would be installed in the school and he would be alone with his pretty, gay young wife.

Miss Ellis, now that she was leaving Storm Castle in two days' time and had a written reference from Mr. Trevarwith safely in her bag, answered rather testily.

Nobody seemed to realize except herself, she told him, that Celia was an extremely sensitive, highly strung little girl. This was the first time in the eleven years of her life that she had ever been away from the Castle except for her brief fortnight's summer holiday. It was upsetting her badly. She hadn't slept properly or eaten much for a week, and she was a bundle of nerves.

Mr. Trevarwith felt a slight pang of pity for the child and remorse, perhaps, at the thought of what Angela would have said could she have seen such wretchedness as he had just noticed on the face of their small daughter.

He pulled a pound note from his pocket and pressed it into Miss Ellis's hand.

"Give her that from me and tell her to cheer up and buy something that she wants. And—er—I'm sure she will settle down at school and be very happy."

Miss Ellis gave the pound to Celia, and the message.

Celia eyed the money indifferently, and with a quivering underlip said:

"But I can't buy Gretel back, can I, Miss Ellis?"

Then the good woman burst out crying and for a moment governess and child wept together.

It was the last time that Celia was given a chance to weep in any arms so friendly. With a swiftness that appalled her, the day came when Miss Ellis and her luggage departed for ever from Storm Castle, and she, Celia, was driven by Isobel into Truro to her school.

Edith, the cook, shed a few tears that night when she discussed things with old Elspeth.

"It fair broke my heart to see her poor lil face," said Edith. "Her poor mother would have turned in her grave if she could have seen the way the present Mrs. T. went on at that child this last month. And always so sweet and smarmy when Mr. T. was present. Reckon he'm made a fool of himself and he'll find it out."

Elspeth agreed, but she had no intention of handing in *her* notice. The poor little creature with her deformed back stood no chance of getting married and she had worked in the Castle since she was sixteen. She had served not only Celia's mother but the old Trevarwiths before that. This was her home now and she must stick it, no matter what the new Mrs. Trevarwith did or said. But, like Edith, she hated Isobel and pitied Celia with all her heart.

4

That first term at St. Wilfred's was a long-drawn-out agony to Celia Trevarwith. An agony neither understood nor shared by her companions, who, for the most part, were normal healthy young creatures, full of animal vigour, with their mischievous pranks, schoolgirl slang, and care-free attitude to life. All with normal happy homes, and loving parents behind them.

Celia arrived at the school a mass of inhibitions and repressions caused by her peculiar upbringing. Because she was so painfully shy, and also bewildered by this sudden "vortex" of school life into which she had been flung, she was not popular. The mistresses were inclined to think her affected. In the private reports of the pupils it was said that "Celia Trevarwith was inclined to pose." Her companions thought her not only affected but—to use their own terms—"snooty."

The trouble was that Celia did not know how to make friends, because she had never before had a companion of her own age. She was not particularly good at games. (To be good at hockey meant that you were "someone" at St. Wilfred's.) She was also a nuisance to the matron because she suffered so severely from colds, coughs and chilblains.

She was good only at music and poetry, but St. Wilfred's was not a school that encouraged either of these subjects to any degree.

During that unhappy term, Celia not only endured the miseries of the average homesick schoolgirl, but received none of the comforts. She watched the others rush for their parcels and letters from home, receiving none herself. She heard continually the words "Mummy and Daddy". But for her they had no meaning. Mr. Trevarwith seldom wrote to her. Her stepmother sent a scrappy note only once or twice during the term.

Celia was homesick only for Storm Castle, for the friendly cove, and for the Cornish people who knew and loved her, for the sea and the cliffs and the walks she knew. And perhaps for Miss Ellis who had been kind to her. She wrote to Miss Ellis, the only person to whom she could pour out her starved young heart. It was towards the end of that first term that Celia received two of her own letters to Miss Ellis sent back by the old lady concerned. Across one of them was scrawled the words: *"Miss Ellis passed away last night from a heart attack."*

Celia wept with genuine grief for the old governess. There was now nobody to whom she could write. Nothing left but the duty letters which the headmistress ordered her to send to her stepmother.

Meanwhile at Storm Castle events were momentous. Isobel Trevarwith was going to have a child.

"It must be a son for you and for Storm Castle," she assured Francis Trevarwith.

He, remembering the fact that he had lost his first wife in childbirth, was full of fears and as concerned about Isobel's health as she could wish any man to be. He was ready to obey her slightest wish. When she said that she wanted to be warm, he took her at once to Italy. They stayed there until Easter. When the Easter holidays came round, Celia Trevarwith spent her vacation at St. Wilfred's with two other children who had no relatives in this country.

It was not until she had spent almost a year at school that she was allowed to return home.

During this time she had seen her stepmother not at all, and her father had called only once or twice at the school. Each visit had been embarrassing both to him and the little girl. They had nothing to say to each other. Mr. Trevarwith took Celia out to lunch and a cinema, then departed hastily. The fact that Celia was

31

so grave for her years, so thin and big-eyed, escaped him. So far as he could see, she was well enough, and Miss MacMaster said she had "settled down".

The only time that he bothered to communicate with his young daughter was in that June, when he sent her a telegram announcing that a son had been born to Isobel, that mother and child were well, and that the boy was to be christened Anthony Francis.

At the end of July, full of tremendous excitement, Celia returned home for the summer holidays. Not only was it a thrill seeing her old home again after a year's absence, but she had a stepbrother now, a little brother whom she could perhaps love, and who might love her. She arrived at the Castle full of passionate intentions to be the best sister in the world to Anthony Francis.

She found that Isobel had grown a little plump and discontented, but was still the spoiled and pampered wife. Much had been done by Francis Trevarwith to modernize one wing of the Castle for his wife. Beautiful new nurseries had been made for Anthony. An expensive nurse had been installed. In fact the whole place revolved around Anthony. Nobody really noticed the lonely little schoolgirl who, in her ugly uniform, arrived home so full of anticipation and goodwill.

Isobel's first words upon greeting Celia were scarcely in the form of a welcome.

"Gracious, you've grown plain and gawky! If you don't look better than this in a few years' time we'll never get you married!"

Celia flushed and said:

"Please may I see my little brother."

"Aunt Isobel is my name," said the woman in a slightly threatening voice.

"Aunt Isobel," repeated Celia, and flushed still deeper. The memory of their feud of a year ago returned all too sharply. But Celia was older now and had learned discipline and obedience. It was obvious to Isobel that she would be no trouble. It was equally obvious to Celia that she need never expect affection or understanding from her stepmother.

She was taken to the nursery to see Anthony. A fine baby with curls as red as his mother's and bright blue eyes. Celia was enchanted with him.

"Oh, I shall love him," she exclaimed. "Please may I hold him and play with him?"

But the nurse would not allow Anthony to be touched and the nursery was forbidden to Celia.

"I'm not going to have Nannie worried by you," said her stepmother. "If you want to stay here for the holidays you must amuse yourself."

So once again Celia was thrown back upon herself, and allowed only to adore her small stepbrother from a distance. Being a year older, she was even more conscious than before that she was unwanted in this house. Her father and stepmother entertained their friends and had little time to give her. They seemed to find her always in the way. But Celia was not unhappy running wild that summer. She had many friends among the villagers, and she found plenty of time in which to read, which was her favourite pastime.

There was a new-comer to Storm Castle whose visits Celia dreaded. He was an old friend of Isobel's from Kyland House—Fulke Withers by name. He belonged to a gay, racing crowd which Isobel liked and which her elderly husband tolerated only for her sake. Even though she was only twelve, Celia learned to dislike this man, Withers. As soon as she saw his car coming she made herself scarce. He was a big, fair-haired man, with a red face and a loud laugh. When he had first been introduced to Celia he had pulled her into his arms and kissed her and said:

"I say! I say! Here's a little beauty. What eyelashes! Think I'll stay a bachelor until you're grown up, Celia. We might hit it off, eh? What do you say?"

He had let her go, still laughing, but the touch of his moustache against her cheek had repelled Celia. She ran away, her face burning, and decided that she had no use at all for Mr. Withers.

So that summer holiday ended. Celia returned to her school. By this time she had grown used to St. Wilfred's, and was not quite so unhappy. She looked upon life with a certain patience and resignation which should never have been the portion of one so young.

They were qualities, however, which it was as well for Celia Trevarwith to encourage within herself, for she had to make good use of them during the five years which followed. Years of study and discipline at St. Wilfred's and of indifferent holidays at Storm Castle where she had always to find her own amusement and take a back seat to her small stepbrother.

As Anthony grew into a healthy little boy, and Celia saw more of him, she lavished her devotion upon him. He was a tyrant demanding a love that must be completely unselfish; but she gave it, ever ready to read to him the books he liked, play the games he chose, and obey his slightest command. In return he gave her a selfish kind of affection, but at least it *was* affection, and this was more than she ever received from his mother. Isobel continued to be totally disinterested in Celia, and Francis Trevarwith, forced to recognize the fact that his daughter was fast developing into a young woman who could no longer be pushed away in the background, had no more liking for her because of this fact.

It was not until Celia was sixteen and with only one more year in front of her at St. Wilfred's, that Francis Trevarwith's infatuation for his second wife died a somewhat sordid and miserable death.

By the time Anthony was four, Isobel had had enough of her elderly husband who lacked humour and had no real interest in any of the things which she, personally, enjoyed. Lately he had started to accuse her of being extravagant and of inviting the wrong people to Storm Castle. She called him mean and a "killjoy."

War clouds were threatening Europe, and Francis Trevarwith was financially harassed and a worried man. Besides which, his health had become very poor. His heart was giving him trouble, and the doctor had warned him that unless he "went slow" the results might be fatal. He received scant sympathy from Isobel when he broke this news to her, and he began to see her as she really was—a selfish, spoiled young woman to whom he had given everything and from whom he had received little in return. True, she had presented him with a son and heir, but heir to what? Most of the money in the family had belonged to his first wife and although she had left it to him unconditionally, he had at least done the right thing by Angela and their daughter. He had not touched a penny of Angela's money. It was left in his Will solely to Celia.

Isobel was soon to realize that the son she had so proudly brought into the world was heir to nothing much but a large castle. Because Francis would not use his first wife's money upon her, Isobel, and her son, she raved and ranted at him. In a short time he grew old, tired and bitterly disillusioned. Failing in health and spirits, his thoughts harped back to his first marriage and that gentle tender wife who lay buried in St. Ruthlyn churchyard. He knew that he was a dying man and would soon lie buried beside her. And now conscience really awoke within the man. He saw how miserably he had failed Angela's child and how wrong he had been to allow Angela's death, when Celia was born, to embitter him so against the unfortunate child herself.

Towards the beginning of September 1939, Storm Castle lay under a sinister cloud. Celia's father was desperately ill, chained to his bedroom, in the charge of a hospital nurse. Isobel went about the place like a bear with a sore head, or spent her time out at parties given by Fulke Withers and his crowd. When she was at home she remained mostly in the schoolroom with her small son. For reasons which Celia could not understand she seemed to bear her, personally, a new grudge. The servants whispered about jealousy and "financial difficulties." But Celia was ignorant of all that was happening. She was alarmed and miserable.

Francis Trevarwith died the week after Great Britain declared war against Germany.

Celia never forgot that day. Isobel, reduced to hysteria, retired to her bed. It was Celia who sat with her father until he drew his last breath.

She was now a tall, slim girl with honey-coloured hair falling to her shoulders, and a grave face out of which shone amazingly beautiful eyes. She was still very much a schoolgirl, but with a sadness about her that was all too mature.

Confined as she had been to school and to this lonely home, she had no real knowledge of life and its realities. But one thing was very real—this war which had come upon Britain. The planes in the sky, the muffled sound of guns at sea, the ominous warnings on the radio.

War had come even to Ruthlyn Cove. And Francis Trevarwith lay dying, holding the slender hand of his young daughter . . . the only hand offered to him in comfort . . . the hand that he had rejected for so many wasted years.

Celia watched him. He seemed a stranger to her. She had never been allowed to love him, and now that she was losing him she could not pretend that it would be a loss of any magnitude. But he was her father, and when he had gone there would only be the hated Isobel left . . . and little Anthony. She would be more alone than ever.

In the presence of death she felt no great fear, only awe and a natural melancholy.

The nurse had drawn the curtains aside. It was a September evening. Soon it would be black-out time. *"Black-out"* sounded so strange. It was a new shadow over all the homes in Great Britain. Danger lurked in the skies. No more lights could shine from the windows of Storm Castle, or any of the cottages down there in the Cove.

It was a warm, still evening. The gulls cried plaintively down on the rocks. Celia, motionless, watched her father, not knowing what the future held for her, wondering if she would ever be as happy as other girls . . . wondering if when she left school she would be al-

36

lowed to go out into the world and find some kind of personal happiness for herself.

Then suddenly she felt a slight pressure on her hand and saw her father's eyes open. He was trying to speak. Quickly she bent down to hear.

Francis Trevarwith whispered:

"Celia . . . forgive me . . . I wish I had been . . . kinder to you."

"Oh, Father, it's quite all right, really," she said with deep embarrassment, and added: "Would you like to see Anthony now and . . . Aunt Isobel?"

But Francis Trevarwith never spoke again. That apology to his young daughter were the last words he uttered. The nurse came forward and gently unclasped Celia's fingers from her father's. He was dead.

In the days that followed it was Celia who took upon her shoulders the full burden of responsibility. Isobel stayed in bed and kept the hospital nurse on to look after her, although she was not really ill. The only member of the family to follow the hearse to the little churchyard of St. Ruthlyn's was Celia herself. And the villagers who came to mourn with her eyed the young girl who looked so thin and desolate in her black dress, with deep pity.

She was no longer a schoolgirl. She had grown up. She was Miss Trevarwith of Storm Castle.

So Francis Trevarwith was buried beside his first wife, and Celia returned to the Castle, there to be summoned almost at once to her stepmother's bedroom, and to receive a storm of grievances.

"Your father has left precious little money for me to live on. Barely enough to run this great barracks of a place," Isobel snarled at the girl. "And now there is this rotten war and air raids and I daren't go back to London. For Anthony's sake as well as economy I'll have to stay down here. You'll have to leave school and help me. Nannie will have to go and you can help me look after Anthony and run the place."

Celia looked uneasily at the red-haired woman.

"Oh, must I stay here?" she asked timidly. "I was hoping I might go away and do some war work and . . ."

"Slip out and leave me to do all the work down here?" broke in Isobel. "Not on your life, my dear Celia! Just you sit down and write to Miss MacMaster and tell her that you won't be going back to St. Wilfred's next term. Your place is with me now, and here you stay."

Slowly Celia turned and walked from the room. She was not particularly sorry to leave her school. She had many friends there nowadays, but no one in particular. Neither did she mind being asked to look after Anthony, who still held a large portion of her affections. But she had wanted freedom . . . she had hoped and believed that with the death of her father she would be allowed to go free and make her own life. She could not bear the thought of many more years with Isobel.

Later that evening she made one more feeble effort to break away. But she was up against more than she realized. Isobel Trevarwith was not merely anxious to make use of her young stepdaughter for economical reasons, but determined to keep an eye on her from now onwards. In four years' time Celia would inherit her mother's money. Grudgingly Isobel had to admit to herself that Celia promised to be very beautiful. It wouldn't be difficult, therefore, in a year or two's time to marry her off. And if Isobel had anything to do with it, she meant to see that Celia's marriage would be to one of Isobel's own particular friends.

She wanted money not only for herself but for her son. That old fool Francis had cheated them both. Thank heaven, at least, he had died before he could get his lawyer down from London to change his Will, which she knew he had intended to do. She, Isobel, was still one of the executors with Mr. Forbes, the family solicitor. That gave her some control over Celia and Celia's money—for the time being. Nothing would induce her to let Celia out of her sight now.

That evening while Celia went out in the darkness for

a long walk along the cliffs, brooding over the strangeness of life, Isobel Trevarwith lay in bed telephoning to Fulke Withers. He was her best friend. She was going to get him to help her "arrange" Celia's future.

PART TWO

1

Every morning for the last two weeks Paul had seen her sitting there on the ledge of the big rock which jutted out over the tiny harbour of Ruthlyn Cove.

Every morning Paul and Will Hoskins, the fisherman, went out with their boat and fishing nets, rowing away from the little curved wharf. Out beyond to the shining sea, and back again with a haul of shining fish that leapt and squirmed, flashing silver in the sun, while the strong-winged seagulls wheeled and cried shrilly and greedily overhead.

Moving in and out of the harbour, Paul never failed to look toward the rock and the girl who lay there, often with a book, often with her gaze fixed on the sea. Whether she ever saw him or not he could not tell because he could not see that far, but he did know that she was young and beautiful, for once, when he was walking up the path up the winding cliff, he met her face to face. He knew that she was still in her teens and was small and slender, with hair so fair that it was almost the silver of his leaping fish, only it turned to gold when she moved her head in the sun. And she had a thin, pale face that did not seem to tan, and enormous eyes, the same colour as the water down there in the harbour—translucent, grey and green, and with a touch of the sea's sadness. She had flung him a shy look and murmured: "Good morning," and he had responded in his native tongue: *"Bon jour, Mademoiselle."* For although he had lived a long time in England he could never forget the familiar formality of that greeting. Besides, he was not likely to forget his native tongue, for he was one of a colony of French and Belgian fishermen who had come over on one of the little ships from Dunkirk and had settled here on the south coast of Cornwall.

They were needed because so many of the young, strong Cornishmen had gone into the Services. Paul, too, had wanted to join the Free French Forces. But he had been prevented from doing so, first of all because it had been pointed out that there must still be men at home to catch the fish, and secondly, because of a slight limp due to an accident in his childhood and which would prevent him from marching as a soldier should.

At first, when Paul had come to Ruthlyn Cove, he had been desperately homesick and lonely. He had wondered how he could stand the complete separation from his beloved France, his home. But after a year in Cornwall he had settled down to his new life. Without knowing whether his parents were dead or alive—but always sure that they would remain patriots and wait for their liberation—he was content to work on English soil and wait for the day when he could return to his people.

Because he was young and handsome with his black curly hair, his brilliant dark eyes which were set narrowly in a tanned eager face, and because his body was tall and slim, he was a great favourite with the girls.

Will Hoskins was his English friend, and Paul and another French boy lived in one of those white-washed little old houses on the quayside that braved all weathers, was gay with climbing roses in the summer-time, and warmed by wood fires and lamplight in the winter. He enjoyed home-life there with Will and Edith, his wife, a good-looking Cornish woman who wanted the handsome Paul to take a wife from one of her friends. But although he had a gay word for everybody, the Frenchman's genius for saying the right thing and making an easy conquest, so far he had found nobody whom he wished to marry.

There were times when Paul craved for a life other

than this one he led in the fishing colony. Since his arrival in England he had spent much of his spare time (particularly during the long winter evenings) learning English and reading books. This surprised Will Hoskins and his wife.

"Paul's a bit queer," they said in the village.

But Paul was not like his peasant-born mother. He was an artist.

It was the artist and the dreamer in him which made him think so much about this lovely girl who came regularly to sit and sun herself on the rocks. And one morning he was tempted to ask Will if he knew anything about her.

Will said:

"Oh yes, that be little Miss Trevarwith from Storm Castle. She's a purty creature, but there be strange stories about the Trevarwiths. Edie, she'll tell you more, for she was cook to Mrs. Trevarwith before she married."

So, that evening, Paul Manton learned from Mrs. Hoskins something about the intriguing young girl, and it was a story which fired his imagination as already it had been fired by the Castle.

Paul learned that the most recent owner of the Castle, Francis Trevarwith, lay buried in St. Ruthlyn churchyard. It was his first wife, Angela, whom Edith Hoskins had served as cook, eighteen years ago. The poor lady, Edith told Paul, died when her daughter Celia was born, and the father turned against the little baby because he had adored his wife.

Paul thought this very sad. Perhaps, he suggested to the Hoskins, the *"pauvre petite"* would have a happy marriage to make up for it. But Edith had more to say on that subject. Her friend, Mrs. Trenown, was cook at the Castle now, and she heard a lot of the goings-on up there. She said that Mrs. Trevarwith was determined that Celia should marry a man of her choosing. In other words she wanted to keep the money "in the family," and Mrs. Trenown said there had been a scene one night, and she heard Miss Celia crying and the mistress telling her that she had no right to her money and that it should have been left to Master Anthony, which was a shame.

When Paul asked how Miss Celia got on with her stepbrother, Edith said that her devotion to the little boy was pathetic because he abused her kindness and was led on by his mother to make her life more difficult —he was so spoiled and exacting.

"But I see her always alone," said Paul.

"That," said Mrs. Hoskins, "is because the family be away in London at the moment."

That next morning when Paul went out in his boat, he was thinking of the lonely girl living up there in the great castle with her stepmother.

It was when he brought his boat back again and was helping Will hoist the big nets of shining fish up the wet stone steps that Paul lifted his eyes and suddenly saw Celia Trevarwith standing there watching him. At first he glimpsed the small sunbrowned feet in sandal shoes . . . then slim tanned ankles . . . and jeans upwards to a face which he was never afterwards able to forget. Small, pale with haunting eyes, fair hair floating to her shoulders.

She looked young for her age.

Just that one look . . . and Paul Manton knew that his life was never to be the same again. His brown cheeks flushed. His dark inquisitive eyes gleamed at her. He pulled off his beret and said:

"Bon jour, Mademoiselle."

"Bon jour," she replied shyly in his own language. Then it was as though his blood turned to water and his knees trembled under him and he could hardly walk up the steps on to the quayside. Paul Manton, who had never known the word fear, was afraid this morning, because of the effect this girl had upon him. She was truly adorable.

"We have guests at the Castle tonight returning with my stepmother, so I have come to ask for the fish."

Paul stammered in English because he was proud of it:

"We have a big catch this morning. You can have many fish."

She smiled, and now he saw how exquisite she could be when she looked happy.

He turned to the nets.

"I will bring them myself to the Castle now."

"If you wish," said Celia. "Thank you very much."

2

Celia watched the young Frenchman's brown slender fingers picking out the best fish and laying them aside, gazed at the bent, dark curly head and thought how handsome he was, this young fisherman. She did not meet any attractive young men in the Castle.

As Celia waited for Paul to collect the fish she thought in a troubled way about her stepmother's attitude toward Fulke Withers. She knew that Isobel wanted her to marry him. Whenever Fulke came to the Castle he eyed Celia in a way which she could not bear.

Celia had always had a secret hope that Isobel would marry again and go away and that she would not want to take her, Celia, with her. That might also have been Isobel's secret hope, but there were not so many men wanting to marry a woman with a son to whom she was guardian and who was to inherit a castle and big estates which they could barely afford to run. Added to which, perhaps the men whom Isobel gathered around her were scarcely the marrying kind. They liked to have a good time at her expense. Such visits as these held no pleasure for Celia, who spent most of the time in the kitchen helping with the meals and lying awake at night listening to dance music and loud laughter, and knowing that she and Elspeth would have to clear away a lot of empty bottles and dirty glasses in the morning —to say nothing of looking for cigarette burns on the furniture and alcohol stains on the lovely rugs.

These last two years had been no happier for Celia than the former ones. Nobody in the district who might have been of help or interest bothered to call these days at Storm Castle, and the only young girl in the neighbourhood—a doctor's daughter who had struck up a friendship with Celia after her father's death—had now left. She had joined the W.R.N.S. at Plymouth.

Celia envied this girl and all the girls who were in the Services.

Isobel kept her nose to the grindstone. Celia was virtually a slave to Isobel's whims these days . . . to her domestic duties and her job of looking after Anthony. The young girl waited on Isobel as no modern servant would have done. She performed menial tasks that Isobel was too lazy to carry out . . . her shopping, her sewing, the care of her clothes; a dozen other thankless tasks.

Celia had spirit and a determination of her own. But Isobel crushed them. She had a vile temper and an acid tongue. She bullied Celia mercilessly. Anthony was fast growing into the image of his mother. He, too, was a bully. He wore Celia out with his demands on her time and care.

For the last week, Mrs. Trevarwith and Anthony had been in London, and it was a week which had meant happiness for Celia. There had been nobody up at Storm Castle to give her orders or forbid her doing what she desired to do. And that was how Paul had come to see her every morning, lying on the rocks with her book or watching the sea. She loved the sea. She felt that its underlying sadness and its varying moods were in tune with her yearning soul.

But this morning her thoughts turned in a less spiritual direction to the personal charms of this very attractive young fisherman. He looked like the heroes of the many romantic novels she had read. And he spoke French, which she adored. At St. Wilfred's she had had an excellent teacher and it had been one of the studies which most appealed to her. The fact that the young fisherman was one of the Franco-Belgian colony here gave him an added glamour; for all her life Celia had longed to travel, to get away from Storm Castle and her uncongenial relatives. All her life she had known that another and more exciting world waited for her somewhere beyond the horizon.

She found herself walking beside Paul up the winding path flanked with sea-daisies and the tall pink foxgloves, to the Castle. He was enchanted because she was able to speak to him in fluent French. She asked him about himself and his escape from Dunkirk, and seemed interested in all he had to say. When he told her that his father had been an artist she said:

"Then you must love pictures. You must come up to the Castle and see what a fine collection we have in the gallery. We have a Cézanne there which belonged to my grandfather on my mother's side. He, too, was a painter."

"A Cézanne!" That made Paul's eyes open wide, for he had read much about the great painters of France and remembered his father taking him to the Louvre in Paris to see the Cézannes there. The fact that Celia's grandfather had been a painter too established a bond between them.

Celia was astonished at the knowledge with which the young fisherman spoke and at his obvious love of art. She was not slow to discover that Paul Manton was no ordinary rough and uneducated fisherman.

Paul was saying:

"*Mon Dieu,* I would love to come and see the paintings one day, *Mademoiselle.*"

She gave him a shy smile. She thought she had never seen anything more vivid than Paul's brown, ardent face and black curly hair.

He, too, smiled at her, with a touch of shyness.

"Every day I see you on the rocks alone," he said. "Always alone."

"I'm used to being a good deal by myself," she confided in him.

He glanced up at the Castle. They were drawing nearer the great place which seemed so magnificent from a distance, but at close quarters had a more formidable aspect. A high wall, as old and lichened as the walls of the Castle itself, enclosed the grounds. Nothing could be seen of the gardens until they reached the top of the cliff, and then through great iron gateways Paul glimpsed smoothly-kept lawns, flanked by beds of roses, formal clipped hedges and a few trees—for the most part stunted and swept backwards by the force of the winter gales. It struck Paul at that moment that Storm Castle might almost be a prison, and that this slender, fleet-footed girl with her cloud of silvery hair might be happier in a tiny homely cottage such as the Hoskins owned, instead of in this vast unfriendly place.

Celia seemed to read his thoughts, for with her gaze fixed on her ancestral home she said:

"Yes, isn't it enormous? Most of it is scarcely habitable. You would be surprised to see how many rooms and corridors are damp and shut up. We live in the right wing which faces the sea. There have been rumours that the Army or the Air Force mean to requisition it, but so far nothing has happened. I should like to turn it into a hospital, but my stepmother says it would not be suitable."

At the Castle gates she turned and held out her hand to Paul for the basket of fish.

"Can I not bring them further?" he asked.

Celia blushed a little and said:

"I . . . I would like you to come in, but I am not allowed to ask anybody here without my stepmother's permission."

Paul's brilliant black eyes opened wide. *Mon Dieu,* he thought. He conceived an uncontrollable hatred then and there for this unknown stepmother. He said:

"I understand."

And she looked at him and thought how much she would like to walk with him through the Castle grounds and show him her own special books and treasures which she kept in her turret bedroom: the bedroom that was her haven away from the family and Isobel's friends. It was the highest room in the right wing of the Castle, with octagonal walls and many little windows looking out to the sea. Paul followed her gaze and murmured:

"It is where you sleep, up there?"

"Yes," she nodded and smiled.

He pointed down to the thatched roof of the Hoskins' cottage six hundred feet below them and laughed.

"And my room is down there."

"If there were no black-out, I could send you a signal—from my window—like the lighthouse that used to flash from Land's End before the war."

"And I would answer," he said. "How wonderful that would be."

They laughed together, and for the first time in her life Celia Trevarwith experienced a sense of excitement, for she had found a friend. Someone who spoke a language which she understood.

Romance stood there incarnate in the form of the handsome, brown-skinned young Frenchman whose sensitive fingers were the fingers of a poet, a musician, a painter—anything but a fisherman.

He said:

"I would like to talk to you again sometime, *Mademoiselle.*"

"I would like it too," she said eagerly. "I'll come down to the harbour and watch you bring in the fish, and perhaps one day . . . I could get permission from my stepmother to show you the Cézanne."

Then she was gone. For the fraction of a moment her small fingers had touched his as she took the basket from him. He stood a moment watching the slender figure disappear into the Castle grounds. Then with a feeling of one who has come upon sudden enchantment, lifting him out of the dull routine of daily life, Paul Manton retraced his footsteps down the cliff-side to the little harbour.

3

Celia expected her stepmother and the party that she
was bringing down from London for the week-end by
the train which should get them to Helston at half-past
six. Old Thomas had gone with the car to bring them
back to the Castle. Within an hour from now they
would be here. Celia, having laid the table, filled the
place with flowers and helped Mrs. Trenown in the
kitchen, now finished her bath and dressed.

She put on a dark blue dinner-dress, touched her lips
with rouge and creamed and powdered her face as her
stepmother had recently taught her to do. She had a
vague idea that Isobel did not like her to look too attractive, yet had a reason for turning her from a schoolgirl into a sophisticated young woman. Fulke Withers
was that reason, maybe. It seemed to Celia senseless,
for if Fulke ever asked her to marry him she would
certainly say no.

She had been thinking about Paul Manton. If only
he were coming here tonight instead of Fulke!

She found herself wondering what Paul would think
of her like this.

Something—she did not know what—drew her towards the gateway that opened on to the cliff. A little
wind was blowing from the sea, but it was warm this
June night and even without a coat Celia was not cold.
She drew close to the edge of the cliff and peered down
at the thatched roof of the cottage in which Paul Manton lived.

For a long time she stood looking. She swung round,
startled, when she heard a voice say:

"Good evening."

She saw Paul, himself, standing there with his beret in his hand; still in his red fisherman's jersey, but with a silk scarf knotted around his throat. He looked clean and fresh. Celia gazed at him as she might have gazed had one of the immortal gods suddenly appeared out of the clouds before her.

"Oh, where have you come from?" she exclaimed.

He said:

"I often walk over the cliffs as far as Mullion when I have finished my work. Tonight I have been wandering around the Castle, *Mademoiselle.*"

"That wasn't very interesting for you," she laughed.

"But it was in the hope of seeing you," he said simply.

The girl's heartbeats quickened. In the sunset her face glowed, and Paul thought he had never seen anything more entrancing. *She* was more lovely than a dream tonight in her blue dress and with a ribbon in her hair.

He stammered suddenly, uncontrollably:

"You are beautiful in this dress, *Mademoiselle,* so very beautiful. *Si belle,*" he said in French, and Celia had never heard more poignant words. Only one other man had ever told her that she was beautiful. Fulke Withers! And it had made her hot and uncomfortable. But the young fisherman's praise thrilled her. She answered:

"Thank you very much."

Then they were silent, looking at each other. She with her hands clasped behind her back, and he fingering his beret nervously. They were held by each other's gaze as Romeo and Juliet must have been in the ages past—knowing nothing of each other, yet ready and willing, suddenly, to live and die for each other—and for love.

Paul broke the silence.

"The wind blows cool. You must not catch cold without a coat."

She thought that so delightful. Few people bothered about her. She said:

"I am not cold. It's a heavenly night."

The young man looked at her with his soul in his eyes and would like to have said:

"You, too, are heavenly."

Suddenly, Celia, filled with an almost childish excitement, had an idea.

"It is another three-quarters of an hour before my stepmother comes. I am going to take you into the Castle to see the Cézanne."

"That would be thrilling," said Paul.

She showed him all the pictures, including a painting of her mother—the mother she had never known. She talked to Paul as she had never talked to anybody in her life—conscious of absolute confidence in him. They exchanged ideas—learning more about each other, until they were no longer strangers but old friends. Time flew by—neither noticed it—both under a strange sweet spell, talking eagerly in Paul's language. At length Paul came to a standstill and said:

"Your Castle is very wonderful, *Mademoiselle*. But it has a haunted feeling. I should like something more gay—more suitable for you if it is not an impertinence for me to say so."

"I don't want gaiety very much, Paul. Only friendship and happiness."

"And love," he added softly. "You should have much, much love from everybody in the world."

The extravagance amused her, but she was enthralled by it.

She stammered:

"I don't want it . . . from *everybody* in the world."

He stood close to her. So close that he caught the fragrance of her fair hair. And suddenly he caught her hand and lifted it to his lips.

Celia caught her breath. Paul's kiss filled her with happiness. She was about to speak when suddenly she heard footsteps, and a hard, metallic woman's voice:

"Celia! What on *earth* does this mean?"

Paul dropped the young girl's hand. They both turned and saw who had broken in so rudely upon their idyll. Isobel Trevarwith, holding a small boy by the hand, stood before them. Paul saw a red-haired handsome woman in her thirties, smartly dressed in grey.

Celia's heart sank like a stone.

Mrs. Trevarwith's cold blue eyes swept from her stepdaughter to the young man wearing Breton trousers and red jersey. She did not know him, but recognized the fact that he belonged to the Franco-Belgian fishing colony in Ruthlyn. Most of them wore this attire.

"What does this mean, Celia?" she spoke again. "Why is this fellow here . . . kissing your hand in that absurd manner?"

Celia began to stutter an explanation, but could find none suitable.

Isobel summed up the affair shrewdly. She could see what had happened. Celia was interested in this young fisherman because he was good looking. Yes, she had to admit that he was *that*. And he of course found the girl attractive. But there was going to be nothing like that for Celia, who was coming into a fortune. Downstairs Fulke Withers waited. Fulke who was Isobel's friend and who, once he was married to Celia, *and* the money, might make life very much easier for Isobel and her son.

Anthony Trevarwith, red-headed and blue-eyed like his mother, tugged at her hand and said:

"Mummy, I want Celia to look at my new book."

Isobel Trevarwith addressed Paul:

"I don't know what your name is," she said curtly, "but I think I know where you belong. And since you have dared to behave in this familiar fashion with my stepdaughter, I shall make it my business to see that you leave Ruthlyn Cove at once and work somewhere else."

Paul stared. Celia was horrified.

"But you can't do that, Isobel—you *can't*."

"Kindly tell this young man to leave the Castle at once," said Isobel, "and then join me downstairs. Fulke is waiting to see you."

4

Paul and Celia looked into each other's eyes fearfully.

"*Mademoiselle,* I have done wrong. I should not have come here," he stammered.

"It wasn't wrong. I asked you."

"But *Madame* is very angry, yes?"

"Yes . . . but I'll put it right, I won't let her have you sent away from Ruthlyn Cove."

Paul's dark eyes opened wide with amazement. Anger stirred his blood.

"She could do that? She could have me sent away? Is it possible?"

Celia bit her lip.

"Anything is possible with my stepmother. She seems to control so many people . . . so many things."

"If she is not kind to you, *Mademoiselle,* then I hate her," said the young fisherman simply.

"How mad I have been," Celia told herself, "to bring Paul into the Castle and let Isobel find him here. Time must have flown by. I felt sure I would get him away again before they came."

She heard Paul's musical voice speaking in his own language.

"*Soyez tranquille.* Do not be afraid, *Mademoiselle.* I can take care of myself, and I am not afraid of *Madame* or anything she may do. I only hope I have not been the cause of trouble for you."

Celia thought of Fulke Withers waiting downstairs to see her. That was what Isobel had said. She felt crushed, suddenly, by this life which she had to lead, disciplined and completely dominated by Isobel.

"You must go at once. Good night, Paul, and thank you for coming."

"*Adieu, Mademoiselle,*" he said, "and thank you for showing me your pictures."

She walked with him along the gallery and stole a look at his brown, glowing face. She did not want him to go. She felt that he was the only friend whom she had in the world.

Paul turned his head and caught her wistful gaze. All his heart went out to her. With the quick emotion of his race he seized her hand and pressed it to his lips in a burning kiss.

"Good night . . . I will see you again . . . I must . . . adorable *Mademoiselle,*" he whispered.

She could only nod her head. She whispered back to him:

"Somehow, in the morning, perhaps, I'll try to get down to the cove when you bring in the nets. Look . . . here's a door. It leads down a spiral staircase into the pantry. Tell Elspeth to let you out."

Outside her bedroom Celia faced Isobel, and the woman had a few short, sharp things to say.

"Picking up with a common fisherman . . . you slut!"

Such venom made Celia feel rather sick.

"I've done nothing wrong. I've not behaved badly. And Paul's father was a painter in Paris. Paul has good blood in him. He is not common."

"I don't care—you are not to have anything more to do with him."

Celia said nothing. But her lips tightened, and Isobel Trevarwith, seeing the way that mouth closed, seethed with new dislike of her stepdaughter. Celia was docile enough in a way, but stubborn as the devil in others. Getting more difficult to manage as she grew older.

One could not make easy conquests of the Trevarwiths—any of them. Isobel had learned that when she had come up against her husband once or twice during their marriage, and she had learned it, in no uncertain fashion when Francis had refused to leave Anthony the money that once belonged to his first wife. It never failed to anger Isobel when she remembered that in three years' time this girl would hold the financial reins and be able to dictate to *her*. It was essential to Isobel that she should marry Celia off to Fulke.

She changed her tone suddenly, which was a habit with her. Having failed to dominate Celia by unkindness, she often swung to the other weapon. Celia could rarely withstand kindness.

"Now listen, my dear," she said. "You made me very angry just now when I found you with that boy, and I'm quite sure your father would have been horrified at the idea of your hobnobbing with such a person. It is quite natural for you to want boy friends at your age, but for heaven's sake choose one from your own class."

Celia's grave eyes looked into her stepmother's.

"Do you wish me to consider Mr. Withers as a boy friend?" she asked, and her young voice was freezing.

Isobel could have hit her.

"Well, certainly he is older than you, but he is only forty and very attached to you and . . ."

"I don't like him," broke in Celia, "and I wish you wouldn't make me see him alone."

"Now listen," said Isobel. "If you want that young fisherman to stay in the colony, you go and make yourself pleasant to Fulke, or out the fisherman goes. So I leave it to you."

She turned and walked away. Celia could see that Isobel meant what she said. It was a mean advantage to take and a mean bargain to strike. But if she could save Paul from being sent away from a place which he loved and where he was happy, she would do anything—even try to entertain Fulke. Besides, she could not bear the thought of Paul going—she *could not*.

She went downstairs to play her part with Fulke.

In the drawing-room, Withers stood by the tall windows of the embrasure which occupied almost the whole of one end of the room.

Celia advanced slowly toward him. Her heart sank at the mere sight of the familiar, powerfully-built figure, the square reddish face, the very white teeth which he showed continually. His thick, fair hair was peppered with grey. He had a fair moustache. He favoured the wearing of rather loud, checked suits and always looked, so Celia thought, like an over-fed, over-healthy animal. She hated his hearty laugh and his hearty manner. He was supposed to be a clever engineer, but in her opinion he lacked all the qualities that mattered.

Fulke came to her.

"Ah! *Dear* little Celia. What a sight for sore eyes. Worth going away in order to come back and see you again. There's a pretty speech for you and nobody prompted me. Ha! Ha! Ha!"

His great laugh and admiring eyes woke no response in Celia. But remembering her bargain with Isobel, she did her best to twist her lips into some kind of welcoming smile.

"I'm glad to see you back," she said.

"What have you been doing with yourself? Come and tell me. You're looking a bit downcast. Too much alone in this great place. Time you got out of it and had a home of your own."

He pulled her on to the seat. She tried to draw her fingers away, but he held on to them and she forced herself not to be openly antagonistic and drag them away. But she hated those red, coarse fingers and thought of Paul's sun-tanned, expressive hands.

"Storm Castle is my home," she said.

"But not your own. After all, your stepmother is mistress here. Wouldn't you like to be your own mistress, little Celia?"

She looked not at him but out of the window. She could not see beyond the stone walls, but she could picture the thatched cottage in the cove down there, where Paul would be eating his simple supper with the Hoskins. She said almost with tenderness:

"Yes, I would like a home of my own."

"How about Kyland House?"

She felt uncomfortable. Fulke Withers had spoken in this way so many times. She knew what he was leading up to. Kyland House was his home—a small place compared with the Castle, but big and handsome enough, standing inland about ten miles down the coast. It was famous for its grounds, and the farms and pastureland adjoining, all of which belonged to Withers. One saw the name "Withers" everywhere around these parts. Fulk's firm undertook most of the engineering jobs in south Cornwall, and before the war he had one of the finest racing-stables in the West Country.

But Celia did not want Kyland House for her home. Fortunately for her, at this particular moment she was saved from the necessity of having to say so by the entrance of Isobel, who had changed into a black dinner dress and wore an emerald clip which was one of Angela Trevarwith's jewels, and which really belonged to Celia. Not that the young girl had any particular taste for jewellery, or objected to Isobel's appropriation of her treasures.

"I'm famished and wanting a drink and my dinner," said Isobel. "Come on, you two. You can do your hand-holding afterwards."

Celia winced. Fulke guffawed and made a jesting reply.

He had never "fallen" for Isobel. She was far too hard and sophisticated for him. He liked inexperience and innocence, and Celia offered both, along with a handsome income. But he liked old Isobel. He had known her when she was a girl and she was ambitious, which he understood. He had always been the same. But he thought she treated the girl rather shoddily, and his wish to marry Celia and take her to Kyland House had in it a touch of sincerity. He would like to see Celia look happier.

Little Anthony came running into the room and made a beeline for his stepsister.

"I want you to read me my new book," he yelled. She picked him up and kissed his thick red curls and promised to read to him in the morning. Tyrant though he was, she had always been fond of the little boy.

But she did not enjoy her dinner tonight. She sat

still listening to Isobel's chatter. Isobel had a party tomorrow . . . two Naval officers coming over from Penzance for the night and a girl from Plymouth. There was a dance at the R.A.F. Mess near the aerodrome. She knew a Squadron Leader. They would all go over and dance.

Fulke looked across the table at Celia.

"We'll show 'em how to step it, shall we, Celia?"

She loved dancing—but not with him. She thought how wonderful it would be to dance with Paul. With her lashes veiling her eyes, she said:

"I think I ought to stay at home and look after Anthony."

Isobel snapped at her:

"Nonsense! You'll dance with Fulke."

"It will be lovely," said Celia obediently.

The rest of that evening was a martyrdom . . . trying to be nice to Fulke with Isobel's blue malicious eyes fixed upon her . . . Isobel encouraging Fulke . . . accepting for Celia an invitation from Fulke to take tea with him at Kyland House on Sunday.

Later that night, after Fulke had gone home, Celia was summoned to her usual task of brushing Isobel's flaming hair and massaging her face. Isobel liked Celia to do these tasks for her every night before she slept. The girl had exquisite and soothing fingers. During the proceeding, Celia timidly broached the subject of Paul. She felt that she could not go to bed until she had discovered what Isobel meant to do.

"You won't . . . get Paul sent away from his job, will you, Isobel?" she asked.

Isobel yawned.

"Who the devil is Paul?"

Celia coloured, and continued to brush Isobel's hair with rhythmic strokes.

"The . . . the young French fisherman. You . . . you were angry because I showed him Father's paintings."

Isobel laughed.

"Good heavens, are you still harping on that ridiculous fool who brings the fish? You'd better find some more work to do, my dear. You must have too much time to indulge in trashy romance if you are reduced to consorting with *that* class."

Celia inwardly burned with indignation, but she controlled herself.

"You won't send him away, will you, Isobel," she asked patiently. "He didn't do any wrong. It was my fault asking him in, and it wouldn't be fair . . ."

"Oh, don't worry, I haven't got time to bother myself about him. Just keep away from him and his sort. I hate the smell of fish."

Celia's cheeks were scarlet. How dared Isobel speak like that of Paul? But she was so thankful that her stepmother did not mean to vent her spite on him that she said no more. Before she left the untidy, over-scented bedroom the older woman gave her a sharp glance and said:

"There will be plenty for you to do tomorrow to help Elspeth get ready for the party, and if you have any time on your hands you can take Anthony for a walk. And mind you are pleasant to Fulke when he drives you over to Kyland on Sunday."

"Must I go?"

Isobel almost pushed her out of the room.

"Don't be a fool. Most girls round here would give their souls to be mistress of Kyland House."

Celia did not argue. Every instinct in her revolted. She felt almost like running away, down to Hoskins' cottage and saying to Paul:

"Take me away from it all. Let me live somewhere where I can see you . . . speak to you . . . lead the most humble life with you . . . anything so long as I don't have to go on seeing Fulke."

5

Celia was up soon after dawn that next morning. There was a faint haze over the sea. It was going to be another warm day.

Celia knew that Isobel would stay in bed for breakfast. Anthony generally had it with Celia at half-past eight.

Once the whole household was awake, Celia knew that she would have no chance of slipping out alone. So, with her thoughts full of Paul and the new friendship which was so sweet and exciting, she got up at half-past six, put on a blue jersey and a pair of old slacks, and slipped out of the Castle. She made her way down the winding path to the cove. At this early hour most of the fishermen were sorting their nets and preparing for the day's catch.

Paul Manton, amongst them, was sitting in his boat, baling out water. He looked up and saw that slender, swift-moving figure coming down the cliff, and in a trice was out of his boat, darting up the path to meet her before she reached the quay.

"Bon Jour!" he said gaily, *"Bon jour, chère petite Mademoiselle.* But what an early hour."

She knew, when she looked at him and spoke to him again, how much she had needed this moment. Last night with Fulke and Isobel had seemed sinister, and the future held nothing but misery. She felt too inexperienced to deal with the situation. She said impulsively:

"Oh, Paul, I had to see you."

He heard the frightened child in that cry and was deeply concerned.

"Is anything wrong, *Mademoiselle?*"

"Everything," she said, "except that my stepmother is not going to have you sent away. Oh, I am so thankful for that."

"I am thankful too," said Paul, "but I do not see that *Monsieur* Iverley, who runs our colony, would have the right to dismiss me."

"I know that, Paul, but Mr. Iverley is very friendly with my stepmother—she entertains him—she entertains a lot of people round here, and people are so awful. They do anything because we live in a castle and are supposed to be rich. It wouldn't do for my stepmother to say a word against you to Mr. Iverley."

"I am deeply touched," said Paul in his own language, "by your consideration for me."

She sighed.

"Oh, Paul . . . it may be difficult for us to be friends. I am so worried. There's this man you may have heard of—Mr. Withers. He is building the aerodrome at Kyland. My stepmother wants me to marry him. I'm almost frantic."

The confession tumbled out because she had nobody else in the world to whom she could make it—indeed no one to whom she wanted to talk except Paul. He was shocked by her words.

"You cannot be forced to marry anyone you do not love, *Mademoiselle.*"

"No, I know," she said in a low voice, "but he is always at the Castle and my stepmother will make life impossible for me if I don't do as she asks. I'll have to run away."

The young fisherman stared at her. Run away! Was this the pitch they had driven her to? Was she as unhappy as all that? His blood boiled at the memory of *Madame* up at the Castle. As for Monsieur Withers— yes, he had seen the big fair Englishman many times— he was a well-known local figure. A gross creature and impossible to imagine him as the husband of this exquisite young girl.

"You must not be forced into marriage," said Paul in a vehement voice. "Better to run away than that."

"But where could I run?" she said. "I have no money—at least I have, but my stepmother controls it, and I have never been allowed to make friends. I have no one —no one in the world."

In a flash came his reply:

"You have me . . . *Mon Dieu,* if I can be of any use, I will serve you, *Mademoiselle.*"

"I don't know what I'd do without you," she said. "You're the first real friend I have ever had."

"Oh, *Mademoiselle* . . . if only I were not just a poor fisherman exiled from my own country. If only it were peace and I could take you to my mother in Dunkirk . . ."

She shook her head in silent misery. Then suddenly she dropped down on the long grass and buried her face on the crook of her arm.

"I've never been so miserable, Paul . . . or so afraid."

Paul stood a moment staring down at her, horrified. He had enshrined her in his heart as a goddess to be adored. Yet this morning his goddess seemed just a forlorn child, in desperate need of help and love. And to see her in tears shook him to the core.

He looked quickly around. There was not a soul in sight. The mists were gradually dissolving and the golden sunlight breaking through on the deep blue sea. They were alone here on the side of the cliff; hidden for a moment from the eyes of the world. Paul dropped down on the grass and put an arm across Celia's shoulders. He himself was shaken . . . the longing to comfort her. He forgot the difference in their stations. They were just boy and girl, on equal terms, and it seemed the most natural thing in the world to the young Frenchman to draw her into his embrace. He whispered against her ear, passionately:

"You must not cry. I shall look after you. I shall not

66

let them force you into marriage, Celia . . . *adorée* . . .
mignon . . . *belle amie* . . . you must not cry."

And it was the most natural thing in the world for
her to turn to him and surrender to the exquisite comfort of his arms.

"Oh, Paul," she said, and put her tear-drenched
cheek against his brown warm face. And for a moment
they lay like that, close clasped, until suddenly, as
though by mutual consent, they turned their heads and
their lips joined in a kiss which bound them irrevocably and for always. The first kiss of real love that
Paul had ever given, the first she had ever received.
She cried:

"Oh, Paul, Paul, I love you."

He answered against her lips:

"*Je t'adore.* Soul of my soul."

So engrossed were they with each other that neither
of them saw nor heard the small boy with red hair who
had come running on rubber-soled shoes, silently, down
the side of the cliff. Anthony Trevarwith saw the two
figures in that passionate embrace and recognized his
stepsister. He did not understand, but he thought the
sight strange, and now when the man beside her lifted
his head he was revealed to Anthony as the black-
haired fisherman who had been in the picture gallery
with Celia and who had made Mummy so cross.

Anthony, with that malicious spirit bequeathed to
him by his mother, decided that Mummy would be
much more cross with Celia if she could see her now.
So, without disturbing the lovers, he turned and raced
up the pathway, determined to impart the exciting
news.

Unsuspecting of this treachery, Celia lay in Paul's
arms, knowing the perfect joy of loving and of being
loved at last.

Paul said:

"I cannot believe that you love me. I am not good
enough for you."

"That's absurd. You are just what I've always

wanted. I knew I'd fall in love one day, but I didn't think I'd be so lucky as to meet you so soon."

Gently he kissed a handful of her silvery hair, marvelling at its silken texture and its sheen.

"But, my angel," he said huskily, "I don't know what we are going to do. I want to run away with you, now, this very morning. But you are still of an age when we can be forbidden to marry, can we not? Is that not the law in your country?"

The light died a little from her eyes.

"Yes," she said forlornly.

"Mon Dieu!" he said, and knit his brows fiercely. "Then what can we do?"

6

Celia sat straight and still, the palms of her slender hands pressing the earth on either side of her. She looked down at the sea. Every moment now the heat mist was clearing and the water was changing from a milky opalescent to a brilliant blue . . . On Gull Rock the seagulls settled like a white cloud. A Beaufighter, flying very high, droned overhead, a reminder that the world was at war.

"What can we do?" Paul kept repeating, and finally Celia turned and looked at him.

"Nothing," she said. "We can neither of us do anything. I can see that. It's this awful question of my age."

"*Adorée* . . . I love you so much . . . I want to make you happy. You were made for laughter."

"My dearest Paul, you have made me divinely happy. I have never been so happy before in my life."

"I can do nothing but adore you."

"It's lovely to be adored, Paul. You don't know how lonely I've been . . . how I've longed for love like this."

He drew her back into his arms.

"I can't bear to think you have ever been lonely or miserable. Oh, Celia, why can I not take you down there to my little cottage . . . make you my wife . . . know that you would be there waiting for me when I bring in my nets? And yet . . ." he paused and shook his head . . . "That life would not be good enough for you. *I* am not good enough for you."

She leaned closer to him as though afraid of being torn from his embrace.

"Oh, darling Paul, that's the second time you've said

that. Please don't say it again. You are more than good enough for me and I would so gladly exchange my Castle for your cottage."

"To have you for my wife . . . *Mon Dieu!* . . . it would be heaven," he said huskily.

She trembled a little and smoothed the brown warm cheek of the young man. She was learning, swiftly and ecstatically, the meaning of love. She knew that never again would she be the old Celia who had run about these very cliffs, bare-foot, as a child, ignorant of such love as this. She knew now that she had been born for this hour—that she had grown up and become a woman for Paul. At the bare memory of Fulke Withers and the marriage that her stepmother wished her to make, the blood seemed to drain away from her heart.

"Oh, Paul," she exclaimed, "I can't marry Mr. Withers, I *can't.*"

His dark eyes flashed.

"You shall never marry any man but me, my dearest . . . my little Celia. Promise me that you will not."

"I won't. Whatever my stepmother does, she can't force me to marry Fulke."

"I would kill him," said Paul grandly.

Then Celia laughed. He thought how much he would like to hear her laugh often.

"Oh, Paul! It's so marvellous. You don't know what you mean to me."

"But I know what you mean to me, my sweet. One day we are going to be together, I swear it."

"One day," she echoed, and pressed her cheek against his.

For a moment they sat there close together staring down at the inviolate sea.

And after a long silence, both of them shaken, both afraid of the future, but not wishing to say so, they rose to their feet, and stood with hands locked, staring into each other's eyes.

"I must go home before they find me here," Celia said breathlessly.

"And I must go down to my boat."

A little feeling of panic enveloped Celia. She did not want him to leave her. The thought of going back to the Castle, to Isobel, to Fulke, made her heart sink.

"When shall I see you again, Paul?"

"Any time that you wish it, my darling . . ." he used the English endearment and she found it enchanting— "darleeng" he pronounced it.

"Oh, Paul," she said, "I'll slip away when I can. Promise me you'll think of some way that we can be together."

"I'll think," he said. "And know this, that whatever happens I shall love you always. Always it will be my life for yours . . . my heart for you . . . *tout pour toi.*"

"It's the same with me," she whispered.

He lifted her hand to his lips.

They found it hard to separate. But Celia knew that she must go or her absence from the Castle would be discovered and she would be questioned. Whatever happened now she must not let Isobel guess that she was in love with Paul Manton. She would have to resort to deceit now . . . to stolen meetings . . . to all kinds of little tricks and plans whereby she could meet Paul and have her happiness, even though it might be impossible for them to run away just now. But whatever Isobel said or did, Celia vowed that she would not marry Fulke and would not stop seeing Paul.

Quickly she ran up the steep tortuous path to the top of the cliff and in through the gates of the Castle.

In the big hall she met her small stepbrother who eyed her with a slightly baleful look which was hateful in one so small.

"I've told Mummy," he greeted her.

"Told Mummy what?"

"That I saw you with that fisherman," said Anthony gleefully. "Oh, it was funny!"

Celia stared at the small boy, her face one burning blush, her heart rocking. Anthony was shouting with laughter. She could have slapped him. She had never felt less affection for the small boy than in this moment when she realized that he had betrayed her. He had seen her with Paul down there on the cliff-side and had told his mother. It was mean and hateful, and yet he was so young. She must forgive him. He was too young to understand what he had done.

She walked straight past him, determined to meet and answer the questions that she felt sure would be hurled at her by Isobel. Love had brought her strength. She could tackle her stepmother or anybody else now. Her one fear was for Paul; in case he should be the one to get into serious trouble and be sent away from Ruthlyn Cove.

Elspeth's hunched little figure met her on the staircase. The old woman's wrinkled face softened as she saw the slim girl, and with a covert look around her she whispered:

"Better go see her. She'm in a bad mood. And asking to see you, Miss Celia."

Celia smiled and patted Elspeth's shoulder. She loved the old maid. She had soothed many a childish fear and dried many of Celia's tears; told her old Cornish folk-stories, played childish games with her when everyone else ignored the presence of the lonely child in the Castle.

"Thank you, Elspeth," she said and ran to her stepmother's room.

Isobel sat up in her big divan bed eating her breakfast, which consisted of tea and toast. She was generally liverish and bad-tempered in the mornings after her drinking parties at night. She wore a satin bed-jacket over a thin chiffon night-dress. The room was never in good order. The windows were shut. Celia's nose wrinkled with disgust. She always hated the heavy perfumes, the warmth of this room, and most of all she disliked the woman with her sharp pale face and flaming red hair, although she could see that there was in Isobel a vitality which drew a certain type of man to her.

"Good morning, Isobel," said Celia calmly, and waited for the onslaught.

To her surprise it did not come. Isobel lay back on

the pillows and eyed her stepdaughter through narrowed lids.

"Well, well!" she said in a purring voice. "So our little Celia has forgotten her education and good breeding and is to be found like any cheap slut necking with the boy-friend. *So* refined . . . *so* delightful. Anthony came back with his eyes popping out of his head, I assure you. *So* good for him."

The bitter malice of the older woman's voice bit at Celia as it was meant to do. Her colour rose high, but she did not flinch. She looked Isobel straight in the face and said:

"I hope Anthony has come to no harm through what he saw, Isobel. I admit that I was . . . with Paul. I won't attempt to deny it."

"You couldn't. The child saw you."

"I love Paul," said Celia.

Isobel laughed . . . pushed away her tray and shook with laughter.

"You little fool. Having an affair with a fisher-boy. Could you *believe* it? I'm sure if your father were alive he would turn you out of the Castle and tell you to go to your fisherman and good riddance."

"I don't care what my father would have done. I don't care if you turn me out. I'd like to go to Paul. He wants to marry me."

"Marry you? What do you think a fisherman earns down there in the cove? Hardly enough to keep himself, let along a wife. You are putting us all to shame. It's a screaming disgrace. The sooner you realize it and come to your senses the better. And with a man like Fulke waiting for you!"

"But I tell you I love Paul, Isobel. I don't love Fulke and I don't intend to marry him," said Celia.

Isobel Trevarwith could willingly have picked up the breakfast-tray and flung it at the girl. How she hated this obstinacy.

If Celia were really infatuated, she might be tempted to run away and follow the young Frenchman. It would be an endless bother dragging the girl home. And after all she was eighteen and there might be the devil of a lot of trouble getting her back at all. To drive Celia out of the Castle and into the arms of a penniless exiled Frenchman was not at all what Isobel wanted. She had made up her mind that Celia should marry Fulke, and that was that.

It was not that she entertained any hopes that Fulke could get control of his wife's money. In these days a husband could not touch his wife's income unless she assigned it to him, but once Celia was married to Fulke, no doubt he would know how to handle her and at least the money would "stay in the family." And if she, Isobel, played her cards cleverly enough, she might persuade Celia to help with the upkeep of the Castle and do things for Anthony. She was forced to realize that she was hard up and Celia was an heiress, and the day had passed when she could do too much bullying. Celia was a woman. Celia must be led rather than driven.

With a complete change of tune, Isobel held out a hand to the girl.

"You make me furious, but I think I understand. First Love, and all that nonsense. Dear me! Come here, stupid."

Slowly Celia advanced toward the bed. Isobel drew her down upon it.

"Stupid," she repeated. "I've been through it myself. But not for a common fisher-boy. I'm surprised that a daughter of Francis Trevarwith hasn't better taste."

"But, Isobel, Paul is self-educated—clever, he reads and thinks—he isn't common," protested Celia.

"Nevertheless, my lamb, you can't marry him, so just pull yourself together and realize it."

"Why can't I if I love him?"

"Oh, no, my dear. You don't love him. It's just a—a silly girl caught by a handsome face. Just make up your mind to be sensible and never to see him again."

Celia dragged her hand away from her stepmother's. She was not deceived by the apparent kindness or sympathy. She sensed the hostility, the cruelty behind Isobel's smile.

"I shall see him. I must."

"You force me to get this boy flung out of Ruthlyn." Celia flung a hot retort:

"If you do, I swear I'll run away—I'll follow him."

Isobel's fingers clawed at the bedclothes. The damned little fool, she thought furiously. She would have enjoyed hitting that defiant young face. But Celia must be led, not driven. It would be fatal to use all her weapons now. She said:

"Very well, I shall not go to Mr. Iverley. I shall ignore the whole affair. Quite honestly, it is beneath my contempt. I am your legal guardian and I shall never consent to such a marriage. Kindly remember what I say. And remember our bargain of yesterday. You make yourself pleasant to Fulke . . . or I'll lose my patience and your fisherman shall get the boot . . . whatever you say or do. Run along now. I want my bath."

Celia breathed again. Without a word, she turned and left the room.

She knew that she had only half won the battle with Isobel. But at least Paul would remain in Ruthlyn. That was all that she desired for the moment. To be near him, to see him. But one thing was obvious . . . so long as Isobel was her guardian, and *she* was only eighteen, she could never run away and marry Paul.

7

The dance at the R.A.F. Mess, near the aerodrome, some ten miles inland from Ruthlyn Cove, was nearing the end.

Celia had danced every number—most of them perforce with Fulke Withers.

She was waltzing now with one of the naval officers who were guests tonight at the Castle.

She wore a white dance dress made for her under Isobel's direction. Celia did not really like it. It was too sophisticated; severely cut, showing every line of her exquisite young figure, two narrow straps pressing into the firm sun-browned shoulders. Her fair hair was piled high on top of her head. Isobel had made up her face. Celia Trevarwith looked twenty or more tonight, and devastatingly beautiful. And she was not unaware that Isobel had created this effect entirely for Fulke Withers.

She dreaded the rest of the week-end. She could see that Isobel was going to give her little chance to slip away and meet Paul. She would be spied upon from now onwards.

The R.A.F. dance which she should, at her age, have thoroughly enjoyed, had been a martyrdom for her, and she was thankful when they played "God Save the King." But less thankful when Isobel suggested that Fulke should drive Celia back to the Castle in his car and that she, Isobel, would follow with the others.

During that drive along the cliff road Celia sat as far away as she could from Fulke. It promised to be a most unpleasant drive in every way because the beautiful day had ended in a bad storm. They had come out of the gay, brightly-lit dance-room to find a dark turbulent world. Outside the rain lashed down. Lightning zigzagged across the sky. Fulke grumbled as he drove.

"I hate these infernal storms on this coast. I wanted to have a nice walk with you in the moonlight," he said. "You've been looking like an angel out of heaven all evening. Do you know that?"

Celia made a noncommittal, cold reply.

She felt Fulke's warm, heavy hand on her knee, and drew sharply away, pulling the coat, which she wore over her white dress, more tightly around her.

Fulke breathed in her ear:

"You know I'm mad about you, Celia. You've been driving me mad all the evening, you lovely thing."

"Please," protested Celia, "don't."

Deliberately he switched off the engine and pulled her into his arms.

"To the devil with the storm. We're cosy enough in here. Celia, you've got to kiss me, you've *got* to."

"Please stop, and drive me home," she said.

But the man had lost his head. He dragged her against him and tore her dress.

"You've got to love me and marry me," he said thickly. "It's no use you fighting. I'm not going to let you get away."

"I hate you," she said. "Let me go. I don't love you and I won't marry you."

She felt his hand on her thigh and breasts. She hit at his face and then when he loosed his grip of her, laughing at her, she managed to open the car door and jump out. Her slippers squelched into muddy water. In a moment she was drenched by the rain which was coming down in sheets. She heard Fulke's voice:

"Celia! Little fool; come back!"

But she ran through the rain and the storm. She could not bear him to touch her. Fulke's hoarse voice was following her. A moment later she heard the car and knew that he would overtake her unless she got away from the road.

She knew every inch of this cliff. They were within a

few hundred yards of the Castle walls. To the right was a narrow pathway zig-zagging down to Ruthlyn Beach. When the tide was out one could walk from there over the rocks into the harbour.

A beam of light illuminated her figure. Fulke's car was upon her. Panting, she turned and cut across the cliff and in a moment was down the side of it, thankful to be in the darkness away from that revealing light. She was not afraid of the storm. Lightning and thunder had no terrors. But of Fulke Withers she was terrified.

Familiar though she was with the pathway, it was a difficult descent with high heels. The rain beat against her face and half-blinded her. Now and again the sea was lit up by a flash of lightning. Once she stumbled and fell. Then she decided to take off her shoes and ran on her stockinged feet.

How she ever reached the harbour she never afterwards knew, but fortune favoured her in so far that the tide was out and she was able to climb over the rocks and along the beach until she rounded Ruthlyn Point. She paused a moment, exhausted, and looked at the harbour and the Hoskins' cottage. Here all was quiet and peaceful. At two in the morning the fisher-folk were sound asleep. Celia half hesitated. Then she look upward and saw the Castle high above her. It looked sinister, lit up now and again by a flash of lightning. She shuddered and thought:

"I can't go back there. I won't."

She walked along the beach up to the quayside and knocked on the door of the Hoskins' thatched cottage.

It was Paul who opened the door. He had been lying, uneasily listening to the storm. When he heard the knock he slipped on a pair of trousers and went downstairs. He opened the door and dumbfounded, gazed at Celia, her wet, disordered hair, her torn stockings. She carried her slippers in her hand; her face was white. He lit the gas.

"Mon Dieu!" he exclaimed. *"C'est toi!"*

"Paul," she said, ". . . save me . . . save me from that man."

He drew her into the cottage. The humble little living-room was quiet and warm. Here Celia was safe from the storm, but Paul noticed now that her feet were bleeding. The hem of her white evening dress was torn.

"Oh, my angel, what has happened?" he asked her.

She gave him a wild look.

"All night I have had to dance with him, Paul."

"With whom?"

"Fulke Withers, and he drove me home. He tried to . . . rape me. I ran away, down the cliff, down to Ruthlyn Beach."

"And you have walked all the way round the Point like this," he asked horrified. "In this storm?"

"Yes," she said. "Paul, don't let him get me . . ."

And then she fainted.

He picked her up. He laid her on the couch and called up the stairs:

"Come quickly, Mrs. Hoskins, please!"

8

Edith Hoskins, a coat over her nightdress and a torch in her hand, came hurrying down the staircase. She stared incredulously from her young lodger to the girl in the bedraggled evening dress lying on her couch.

"Mercy on us, Paul, whatever is this?"

He explained, adding rapidly in broken English:

"They have frightened her, the poor angel. They are not kind to her. *Mon Dieu!* Maybe it is that they have killed her."

Mrs. Hoskins, only half-understanding the French boy, hastened to the couch. She knelt and lifted Celia's hands in hers. She was a sensible woman, good in an emergency. Vaguely she realized—had realized for a long time—that all was not well with little Miss Celia up in the Castle. And there wasn't one of them down in the cove who did not dislike the present Mrs. Trevarwith and her spoiled son. But Francis Trevarwith's first wife they had all loved and respected.

Two more people had come downstairs, roused from their sleep—Will Hoskins, himself, amazed by the sight of the young lady from the Castle; and Jean, the other young French boy who lodged here . . . a delicate lad of sixteen, unfit for active service, but clever with the nets.

"Jean had best go for Dr. Ingles," said Edith Hoskins. "And you, Will and Paul, help me carry Miss Celia up to our bedroom. Then get the fire going, Will, as I'll want hot bottles. She's drenched through and as cold as a stone, the poor lamb."

Hoskins scratched his tousled head and beard.

"You'm taking something on yourself, Edie lass," he

said in a doubtful voice. "Shouldn't we let Mrs. Trevarwith know the young lady's here?"

"She's not going back to the Castle," put in Paul quickly. "I will not have that she should die of their cruelty."

They all turned to him. His gaze fell before their searching glances and he flushed a little. Of course these people did not know what he and Celia felt about each other. His heart sank. What could he do?

Edith, whose feminine instinct led her to make a sharp guess as to the true state of affairs between Miss Celia and this handsome Frenchman, kept her thoughts to herself for the moment. Her main object was to get the poor young lady into a warm bed.

She scattered them all with decisive orders.

"You get on with carrying Miss Celia upstairs, Will, and don't worry about Mrs. Trevarwith. She'll know soon enough that Miss Celia has come down to us. And as she's come, I'm not turning her out. Jean, knock up Dr. Ingles. Put on your oilskins, lad, and take a torch."

Jean hurried to get his coat. The other two men carried Celia up to Edith's room. The woman came up and set to work to take off the girl's clothes. At the same time she bid her husband fetch up a drop of whisky from the cupboard. Gloomily Paul watched while the fisherman uncorked the bottle and poured out a generous portion. Once Dr. Ingles got here, of course, he would feel it his duty to telephone to the Castle and tell them up there where Miss Trevarwith was to be found. That meant that Celia's stepmother would come down and take her away. Paul could not bear the idea of her being dragged back to her captivity, but he felt utterly helpless. He thought of Celia lying up there. A sweet white bird that had striven for freedom and would soon be forced back behind the bars of her cage.

He filled the kettle with water as Mrs. Hoskins had asked, but every now and again went to the foot of the stairs and listened, longing to know that Celia had recovered consciousness again.

The storm still raged with intermittent violence. It was stifling now in the cottage and Paul longed to throw open the casements, but dared not because of the black-out. He felt that he could not breathe.

Mrs. Hoskins leaned over the banisters.

"Is that kettle on?"

"Yes, it is," called up her husband.

"How is she?" asked Paul.

"She's opened her eyes and knows me," said Mrs. Hoskins, "but she has a rare fit of shivering, and is in for an illness."

"Poor lil maid," said Will Hoskins, shaking his head. "So pretty and always with a smile for us. Surely she'm not going to die?"

Paul started as though he had been shot.

"Die!" he repeated. *"Mon Dieu!* There is no chance of that, is there?"

The older man looked at Paul with astonishment. The young Frenchman was behaving queerly, he thought, as though Miss Celia were a personal concern of his. He patted Paul on the shoulder. He was a stupid man, but kindly, though he understood nothing.

"Now, now, lad, I never meant to startle you. Dr. Ingles will put the lil maid right again, we needn't fear."

Edith called out again:

"Paul."

Eagerly he leapt up the staircase.

"She wants me . . . she is calling for me, yes?"

Edith Hoskins nodded, but laid a restraining hand on the young fisherman's arm.

"Yes—but go easy, lad. It's a kind of delirium. She hardly knows what she's saying."

"We love each other," he said. "It is that we are in love and I wish to protect her. . . ."

Edith Hoskins stared. Bewildered she went down to her husband to discuss this new turn of events. A love-affair between little Miss Trevarwith of Storm Castle and a penniless French fisher-boy! That shocked the Hoskins, and yet they liked Paul well enough, and as Will Hoskins said to his wife while he lit his pipe:

"The young take to the young, and up there in the Castle they are too old for Miss Celia. That Mr. Withers I can't abide."

It was no wonder, in Will's opinion, that Miss Celia would have none of him.

In Edith Hoskins' bedroom Paul Manton knelt beside the big double bed. One of Celia's hands was pressed against his lips. She lay there, looking so small and helpless, and, to him, lovely beyond words. She wore one of Edith's flannel night-gowns. Her hair floated like a silver cloud on the pillow. But the big eyes were glazed, wandering restlessly. The tapering fingers which Paul held were as hot now as they had been ice-cold.

"Paul!" she kept moaning the name. "Paul!"

He spoke to her in his own language, smoothing the hair back from her forehead.

"I am here, my darling, my sweet. Do not worry. Paul is here beside you."

"Paul!" she repeated the name piteously, and then added in a voice of terror: "Leave me alone. Let me go. Don't touch me, Fulke . . ."

"He shall not touch you," said Paul. "You are with me, safe, my heart's love. There, there. Lie still, my darling."

Babbling with fever, she moaned and tossed in the big old-fashioned bed. Paul was terrified. He was thankful when young Jean returned with Dr. Ingles, who lived at the top of the hill, at Penlyon.

The doctor, an old man who would have retired but for the pressure of war work, was astounded to find Miss Trevarwith lying here in the humble home of the Hoskins. None of them seemed to know why she had been out in the rain and how she had come here. He received only a garbled version from Mrs. Hoskins. But inevitably he decided to telephone to the Castle as soon as he got home. Isobel Trevarwith was a good patient of his, and this was all rather improper. The girl was delirious and called repeatedly for the young French boy who lodged here.

Briefly the doctor told Edith that Miss Trevarwith was very ill. She seemed to be suffering not only from exposure and exhaustion, but from shock. He gave her an injection to quieten her, left two tablets with Mrs. Hoskins, and orders that the patient was to be kept warm and not left alone for a moment. He would inform Mrs. Trevarwith where to find her step-daughter and a car could be sent for her in the morning.

Something impelled Edith Hoskins to say:

"Wouldn't it be better, Dr. Ingles, please, sir, if miss was to stay in bed here until she was better?"

"Maybe, maybe," said Dr. Ingles, "but Mrs. Trevarwith must decide."

Paul sat at Celia's side. Refusing to leave her for a single moment, he stayed there, vigilant, holding one of her feverish hands between his own.

9

Meanwhile, up at the castle, Isobel Trevarwith and Fulke Withers were having a few hot words. Isobel had returned from the R.A.F. Mess with her party to find Fulke alone, looking sick and rather ashamed of himself, waiting with the story that Celia had suddenly jumped out of his car and disappeared down the side of the cliff. He had followed and tried to find her, but by the time he got down the path in the darkness, he said, she had gone.

Isobel raged at him. He was every kind of a fool. What had he done to scare the girl? Well, he ought to have known that Celia was quite unused to "necking parties."

Fulke lost his temper and snapped back to the effect that it was not so much his fault as hers if Celia was difficult to manage. She had bullied the girl until she was a bundle of nerves. Isobel flamed into one of her violent tempers. Bullied the girl indeed. She had been far too kind and easy-going with her. Did Fulke realize that the little idiot fancied a common fisherman in the Franco-Belgian colony here, and that Anthony had seen them in each other's arms?

Then Fulke went white with jealous rage and accused Isobel of not looking after the girl properly. If she had been happier in her home, she wouldn't have wanted to strike up a friendship with a fisherman.

"You can say what you like, but you've put the tin hat on it now," Isobel screamed at him. "Where is Celia? Thrown herself into the sea! You fool! You'd better ring up the police, and organize a search-party straight away."

Fulke calmed down and went to the telephone. This was news . . . that Celia had a penchant for one of the French fisher-boys. Once they got the girl back safe and sound, he'd soon fix matters. He wasn't going to stand by and see the girl he wanted for his wife turn him down for a dago.

As he was about to call the police and make inquiries about the girl, the telephone-bell rang. Dr. Ingles to speak to Mrs. Trevarwith. A moment later Isobel turned to Fulke, her flushed, angry face relieved.

"Thank heavens for that! Celia is down in the Hoskins' cottage. Apparently she rushed to them. Ingles says she has got pneumonia or is getting it."

"Oh, lord," muttered Fulke. "What the devil did she go there for?"

"Because that is where her boy-friend lives," Isobel flung at him acidly.

He darted a furious look at her.

"I see. Well, I presume that you'll go down in the morning with the car and bring her home, unless you want to see her tied up to this frog."

Isobel smiled. It was not a very sweet smile, but she definitely felt better now that she knew that her stepdaughter was not about to be washed up a corpse on the beach. It wouldn't do for the people round here to think that she had treated the girl unkindly. Neither would it do, really, for her to quarrel with Fulke. She said:

"Certainly I will. And it is stupid for us to slang each other. You know perfectly well, Fulke, that I want Celia to marry you."

"Then you'd better set to work a bit more tactfully."

"And you, too, my dear Fulke. Celia is romantic. Don't be quite so hearty with her."

Dawn was breaking over Storm Castle before these two finished their arguments and got to bed. And it was dawn when Celia first recovered her senses sufficient to realize where she was and who it was who sat beside her holding her hand.

Paul had drawn back the curtains to let the fresh air into the stuffy little bedroom. After the storm it was dead calm now. Sea and shore were blanketed in a thick fog. Even the little harbour was wreathed in the mist. It was much cooler. But Celia's body burned and ached with fever. The light hurt her eyes and Paul hastened to draw the curtains across the casements again. Then he went back to her side and held a glass of lemon and water to her parched lips.

"Pauvre petite," he murmured.

"Paul," she whispered weakly. "It is so wonderful to be here with you."

"For me it is heaven, *adorée,* but I am afraid they will come down and take you away. Dr. Ingles has told Madame where you are."

A shudder went through Celia as she remembered last night . . . Fulke's hot hand on her thigh, his breath against her neck. Back to Isobel's vicious moods . . . back to *that.*

"Oh, no, no," she said under breath and began to cry. "Don't let them take me, Paul."

"How can I stop it? What in the name of the *bon Dieu* can I do?" he groaned.

She gazed at him through her tears. He looked tired. There was a dark stubble of beard on the firm young chin which aged him. She forgot her own troubles and felt suddenly sorry for him.

"Poor Paul," she murmured, and smiled through her tears.

"If I could only keep you with me, my precious angel."

She began to cough, and moaned as a sharp pain tore through her side.

Quickly Paul called for Edith. The woman was next door.

Edith hastened in, banished Paul from the room and took charge of the patient. Paul did not go back to bed. He washed and shaved and put on a fresh jersey and then went out to his boat to prepare for the day's fishing. He hated the fog, but the melancholy morning was in tune with his own wretchedness. From his boat, by the quayside, he looked with passionate resentment up at the grey Castle which frowned there above him from the cliffs. At the thought of Celia being forced back there by her stepmother, his very soul felt sick.

It was soon after eight-thirty, when the harbour was busy and alive, that Isobel Trevarwith's well-known car came down the winding road into the cove. Isobel, followed by Dr. Ingles and the district nurse, hastily summoned, presented themselves at the Hoskins' cottage.

Edith was upstairs with Celia. Will, Paul and Jean were eating their breakfast. It was their custom to go out to the boats very early after a cup of tea, and then come back and eat the meal that Edith cooked for them later in the morning.

All three fishermen rose as Mrs. Trevarwith entered the cottage. Will Hoskins greeted her with a respectful:

"Good morning, M'm."

The French boys stood by silently. Isobel, wearing a tweed skirt and a suède golf-jacket, with a scarf twined around her red head, ignored Will's greeting and shot a swift venomous look at Paul. He returned the look steadfastly with hatred in his heart, but did not flinch before her gaze. She said:

"Where is Miss Trevarwith?"

Edith Hoskins heard the sharp authoritative voice and came bustling down the stairs, neat and clean with a fresh white apron over her print gown.

"Good morning, M'm. This is a bad business, M'm. Poor Miss Celia has pneumonia, I fear."

Isobel looked at her coldly. She was suspicious that Edith Hoskins, who had been so long with Celia's mother, was in league with this upstart Frenchman who dared to associate himself with Celia. Isobel said:

"Miss Trevarwith is to be wrapped in blankets and carried out to my car at once."

Edith looked worried.

"Isn't it dangerous, M'm? Wouldn't it be better if I kept Miss Celia for a day or two . . . ?"

"That is for Dr. Ingles to decide," broke in Isobel sharply.

"Yes, M'm," said Edith, but her proud Cornish blood boiled. Very different from Miss Celia's mother, this red-haired shrew, with never a civil word for the fisher-folk. It was sad to think of that poor lamb upstairs being taken away, although no doubt she would have proper nursing and all the modern conveniences at the Castle.

Paul stood by like a figure of stone while Mrs. Hoskins and Nurse Trethewey, with the help of Will, carried Celia down the stairs. His heart beat madly with conflicting emotions as he caught sight of a lock of fair hair. Celia's face was hidden from him. The nurse had wrapped her well and truly in the blankets. Paul wanted to rush forward and snatch that beloved young form away from them. But he had no right.

His anguished eyes watched while Celia was carried into the car, doctor and nurse directing operations. Then Isobel came back into the cottage and said to Paul in a menacing voice:

"If I were you, young man, I'd pack my things. I think you'll find Mr. Iverley will be moving you from Ruthlyn Cove."

In the car, Celia, only half-aware of what was happening, moaned the name of the one and only person in the world whom she loved: "Paul . . . Paul!"

Nurse Trethewey and Dr. Ingles exchanged significant glances. Isobel came back, stepped into the car, slammed the door, and backed away from the Hoskins' cottage.

Inside the cottage a grim silence had fallen upon all. No one seemed to want to meet each other's eye. Then suddenly Paul flung himself into a chair and put his head down on his folded arms.

Mrs. Hoskins moved to his side.

"There, there, Paul, don't take on," she said in her

kindly way. "It's no use you feeling like that about Miss Celia."

Jean, young though he was, understood in his romantic French fashion, and broke into voluble French, trying to soothe and sustain his compatriot.

Paul raised an anguished face.

"I hate Mrs. Trevarwith. I hate all of them up there in the Castle. They make her suffer, my little Celia. They have taken her away. She will die. Without me, she will die."

"Now come," said Mrs. Hoskins. "Be sensible, Paul, I tried to get them to leave Miss Celia here, but you see they wouldn't. And no doubt she will get better attention up at the Castle. It's where she belongs, Paul. You must remember that. Don't take on. She's not going to die."

"They shouldn't have taken her out into the cold," said Paul frenziedly. "Oh, *mon Dieu!* That woman is a monster without a heart."

Will Hoskins, pipe in his mouth, shook his head.

"What did she mean, lad, when she said you'd better pack your things?"

Paul gave a bitter laugh.

"She will go to Mr. Iverley and have me removed from the colony. She will do that—this abominable woman."

"*Non, non,*" interposed Jean, who was devoted to Paul. "They shall not send you away."

"Mercy on us," said Edith Hoskins. "You do seem to have got yourself into a jam, lad."

Once again a gloomy silence descended upon the inmates of the little cottage.

Up in the Castle, Celia was put to bed in her own comfortable room, and Dr. Ingles left her in Nurse Trethewey's care while he drove into Truro to get another nurse and antibiotics.

Once Isobel got her stepdaughter back to the Castle, she behaved admirably. She did everything that could be done for the girl. Making suitable apologies to Diana Thorne and the two naval officers who were in her house-party, she arranged for their transport to the station. Celia had been taken seriously ill, so the party must be cancelled. Anthony was detailed to amuse himself and keep as quiet as possible so as not to disturb Celia. The whole Castle was now concerned with but one thought—to save Celia's life. By the time Fulke Withers drove over from Kyland House to make inquiries, and the doctor returned from Truro with a nurse, that young life hung on a thread.

Celia was critically ill . . . so ill that she did not know what was going on around her; whether she was in her own room or still down in the little cottage where she had taken refuge.

Dr. Ingles cancelled all other appointments and remained in the Castle.

All through that day Ruthlyn Cove was wrapped in fog. The boats stayed in harbour unable to get out. All activity was suspended. The gulls huddled on top of their island crying plaintively amongst themselves. It was as though Nature was in sympathy with the battle which was being fought at Storm Castle—a battle for Celia Trevarwith's life.

When darkness was falling, Isobel Trevarwith joined Fulke, who had been sitting in the library taking strong drinks to fortify himself. By now he was covered with remorse, feeling himself responsible for Celia's illness. It was his stupidity that had driven the girl out into the storm.

He looked in a scared way at Isobel as she came into the room. Even she was subdued and frightened.

"How is Celia?" he asked.

Isobel answered:

"Desperately ill; Dr. Ingles says she must have been in a bad state of health. She seems to have no resistance and she doesn't seem to want to live. And she keeps calling for this damned Frenchman."

"Calling for him!" repeated Fulke.

"Yes, in fact Dr. Ingles thinks we ought to bring him here. He thinks it might save her life."

Fulke flushed darkly.

"Rubbish!"

"That's what I say, but the doctor and nurse think differently. It's outrageous . . . an impossible position for us, but there you are. Maybe you'd better go down to the cove and fetch the wretched Paul."

10

"Fetch that French poodle up here? Damned if I will!" exclaimed Fulke Withers, and poured himself out another stiff whisky.

Isobel cast him a sardonic glance from her sharp eyes.

"Steady with the liquor, Fulke. It isn't all that easy to get these days. And don't be a fool. If the 'poodle,' as you call him, can save Celia's life, isn't that what counts with you? Once she's passed the crisis, you can get Iverley to chuck him out of the cove."

Fulke raged and argued for a space, then collapsed before the woman's argument. His brain was fuddled by the fumes of the whisky he had been consuming for hours. Isobel was right. To save Celia's life was what mattered most. He had made up his mind to get final possession of that frail gold and white beauty of hers, that aloofness which perpetually maddened him. She was the one girl he had ever wanted to marry; one of the few to resist his strong animal attraction. He had never wanted a woman more. And she lay up there, dying . . . because he had tried to force her to respond to him.

Let the young French fool from the fishing colony come up and see her if that was the only method of saving her life. He'd deal with him later!

Fulke put on his cap, took a torch and left the Castle. Within ten minutes he was at the door of the Hoskins' cottage. Edith, respectful and without betraying the antagonism both she and her husband had always felt toward Mr. Withers, greeted him and told him that Paul was up in his room, reading.

"Fetch him down," said Fulke rudely.

Paul came down. The young Frenchman's face was pale and weary, his eyes red-rimmed. When he saw the gentleman who wanted to marry Celia and who had driven her through the storm down here last night in her extremity of terror and disgust, Paul's taut body shook.

"You want me, *Monsieur?*"

"Yes, come up to the Castle with me. Now, this moment," said Fulke peremptorily.

"To the Castle!" repeated Paul, astonished, and Edith Hoskins, behind him, listening, held her breath.

"That's what I said."

"Et pourquoi, Monsieur?"

Fulke licked his lips. He had never come to anybody on a more distasteful errand. Half in fury, half in envy, he looked at this boy whom Celia was supposed to care for. This was a queer, rare specimen of the Franco-Belgian Colony, this tall, undeniably handsome boy with the sloe-black eyes and proud features. Fulke was filled with a frantic jealousy. But he controlled it. He was the biggest landowner in the district, in control of the biggest engineering job the Government had yet given to any firm of builders or engineers in South Cornwall. He had money and power, and he was *persona grata* at Storm Castle with the Trevarwiths. He had no need to fear a penniless poet in fisherman's clothing. He would soon get rid of Paul Manton. The issue of the moment was Celia . . . Celia's critical fight with death.

Fulke looked narrowly into Paul's dark eyes.

"Mrs. Trevarwith wishes you to come with me. Miss Trevarwith is very ill—in fact—dying. She has asked to see you."

He spoke the words with difficulty. Mrs. Hoskins instinctively put out a hand and placed it on Paul's shoulder.

"Mercy on us," she whispered, and began to cry.

Paul stood like a creature of stone. His brain refused

94

for an instant to take in the full significance of that word *"dying."* Celia could not be dying. Celia, whose slender hands had clung, helplessly, to his, upstairs in Mrs. Hoskins' bedroom last night, and who had cried his name in her delirium.

"Be quick, you . . ." began Fulke.

But the words were lost as Paul came to life, and with a swift movement brushed Mr. Withers unceremoniously aside and ran . . . ran like one demented away from the harbour, down the little quay.

Fulke shrugged his shoulders. The boor—not even to wait for him! He followed Paul.

Paul raced up that cliff path, heart and brain on fire with mad longing to reach his loved one.

He reached the gates of the Castle. They were open. Through the darkness he ran, the sweat pouring down his cheeks. He knocked wildly on the big studded door. The sound of the iron knocker echoed through the still night.

Then he was in the lighted hall, blinking a little. He stood before Isobel Trevarwith. Coldly she acknowledged him.

"So you've come. Very well. Elspeth will take you to Miss Trevarwith's room. The nurse and doctor will give you your instructions. But kindly remember that I have sent for you only because I have *had* to. Miss Trevarwith is delirious. She wants to see you. You might save her life. I don't know which way things will go, but I warn you that as soon as your work is done I shall expect you to go away and stay away for good. *Pour toujours,*" she added, with an atrocious accent. *"Comprenez?"*

The madness which had impelled Paul to run at double speed from the harbour to the Castle, died. He said, in a frozen voice:

"I understand, Madame, but we shall see later, from whom I take my final orders."

Isobel opened her lips to make a stinging retort, then closed them again.

"Go on up," she commanded.

He turned and leaped up the stairs two at a time. Then he saw the doctor who had attended Celia in the Hoskins' cottage . . . then a strange nurse in uniform. He found himself being taken by the arm and led to the bed on which Celia was lying. A Celia whom he hardly knew, so pinched, so waxen had her face become even in twenty-four hours. And it was his own name which he heard from those pale dry lips . . . *"Paul, Paul, Paul,"* she kept repeating.

Regardless of the disapproving gaze levelled upon him from all sides, he went down on his knees by the bedside, staring through the dim light of a shaded lamp at that beloved young face, smoothed the hair back from the wet forehead. He said, in French:

"Heart of my heart . . . my soul . . . my dearest dear . . . speak to me. I am here. Your Paul who adores you. Celia . . . Celia . . . *mon ange* . . . do not die. Live . . . live, my soul's treasure, live for me . . ."

She stirred and moaned. She answered him in his own language.

"I am so tired . . . let me sleep in peace. Paul, darling, let me die if I cannot be with you always."

"But you shall be with me always," he answered her, crazy with joy because she knew him and had spoken to him. . . . "You shall be, my adorable love. You cannot die. You cannot go from me now."

"So tired," she repeated in a whisper.

She felt his fingers touch her hair, her cheeks, her throat.

Isobel Trevarwith, in the background, exchanged scornful glances with the doctor and nurse and tapped her forehead significantly. She whispered:

"A bit mad, my stepdaughter, poor child . . . delirious still, obviously. But let her have her way . . . she'll come to her senses once she's better."

Celia did not hear her stepmother's voice. For the first time since she had been carried away from the Hoskins' cottage *she wanted to live* . . . A touch of colour stole into her face and she smiled. With a deep sigh she closed her eyes.

Paul, holding her close to him with utter devotion, knew even before the doctor told him that the crisis was past.

If Isobel had had her wish, she would have wrenched Celia there and then out of the young fisherman's arms and turned Paul out of the Castle. But Dr. Ingles forbade this. The whole affair was far from *"comme il faut,"* as he afterwards told his wife, who had known and loved Celia's mother . . . but he hadn't the heart to drag those two apart. His crusty old heart was touched by the sight of the lovers. And although Isobel was a rich patient, he had no liking for her or her horrid little Anthony.

"I advise you to let the boy stay a while," he said. "She'll sleep peacefully now but she mustn't wake and find him gone. Just give it until morning."

Isobel bowed to superior advice, but she was "fed up," she told Fulke downstairs, when she broke to him the news that Celia would live.

"The whole business is too fantastic. Celia and that fisher-boy! But in the morning out he goes, and down you go to Steven Iverley and have the boy transferred to another colony."

Fulke nodded. He was drunk and sleepy. He shambled off to bed, muttering what he would do to Paul Manton . . . tomorrow. Isobel went to her own room.

All night long, Celia slept in the circle of Paul's arm, her head against his heart. All night Paul sat in a cramped position, not wishing to move lest he disturb her. And to him those uncomfortable hours were the most beautiful he had ever known.

The nurse, touched despite herself by the sight of the fair-haired girl cradled in the arms of the dark, poetic-looking fisherman . . . drew back the curtains at half-past five. The turret room was flooded with gold light. Paul, his eyes red-rimmed with exhaustion, looked out and saw that it was going to be a perfect summer's day. He heard the surge of the sea breaking against the rocks below, and the screaming of the gulls. He knew that it was time for him to be down on the quay, at his nets. And he knew that this beloved girl in his arms was safe, for the time being.

The nurse came to the bedside and took her patient's pulse.

"Grand," she said. "Very different from yesterday. She'll do. You'd best go now. I want to give my patient something to drink."

Paul looked at the woman anxiously.

"You are sure she is . . . all right?"

"Quite."

Paul gently laid Celia back on her pillows. He bent and kissed her hair.

"Look well after her," he said to the nurse. "And please to tell her that if she needs me . . . I am ready—*toujours.*"

The nurse nodded and smiled. As far as she knew from gossip with the staff the young Frenchman wasn't likely to see much of little Miss Trevarwith in the future. But she hadn't the heart to tell him so.

11

Some days later, Isobel Trevarwith, holding her son by the hand, paid a visit to Celia. She advanced to the bedside with a friendly smile, and urged Anthony forward. The boy had a big bunch of roses in his hand.

"Well, well," said Isobel, "and how's our invalid today? Doctor said you were so much better, I thought you'd like to see little brother."

Celia, lying weakly propped against a pile of pillows, looked in silence a moment at her stepmother and brother. Anthony threw the roses rather rudely on the bed and immediately seized the bunch of grapes that lay in a dish on the bedside table.

"Want some," he said.

"Now, Anthony, behave," admonished his mother.

He started to whine, and when Isobel took the grapes away, set up an ugly howl. The noise made Celia's brows contract. She held out a hand.

"Anthony, you can have my grapes," she said. But the small boy howled afresh, and was finally dragged out of the bedroom by the nurse, who refused to allow such a disturbance in the sick-room.

Isobel was left alone with her stepdaughter. The girl's face looked transparent, but Isobel was no longer worried about her. Dr. Ingles had brought a specialist from Truro yesterday, and both physicians had agreed that Celia was out of danger. But she would need careful nursing for the next week or two.

Isobel said:

"I was wondering if you would let me bring poor Fulke in to see you for a few moments this evening. No

—don't say you won't, Celia dear. You young girls are so intolerant. The poor man has been dreadfully miserable ever since you dashed out of his car like a little lunatic. He didn't mean any harm. You know he is deeply in love with you."

Celia's face flushed crimson and she turned her face away.

"I'd rather not see him," she said in a low voice.

Isobel bit her lip and fought back her rising temper. She said sweetly:

"Well, well, I will humour you for a bit, but at the end of the week you *must* see Fulke. You mustn't be unkind and rude to my old friend, and you must allow me to know what is best for you, Celia dear, and get any foolish thoughts you may have about the young Frenchman right out of your funny little head."

The colour receded from Celia's face. She had learned from the nurse of that critical night when Paul had been sent for, and how he had stayed with her till morning and given her back the will to live. Now, with her returning physical strength, there waged within her a still more ardent spirit and wish to be with Paul. The thought of Fulke Withers was a nightmare. She gathered together her courage and questioned her stepmother about Paul.

There again, the older woman would have liked to have given the girl a piece of her mind and dealt with her in no kind fashion. But she was forced to remember the doctor's orders that Miss Trevarwith must not be unduly upset. So she put a sugar coating on the pill which Celia must needs swallow.

"Paul is no longer in Ruthlyn Cove. Mr. Iverley—er —thought he might like a change, and so he has been sent away."

Celia sat up, her cheeks bright carmine.

"Oh! Oh, my God!"

"Now, Celia dear, you *must* remember that I know what is best for you," began Isobel.

Celia flashed at her stepmother:

"*You've* had him sent away. And he loved the

cove and his home with the Hoskins. Poor Paul. And his only crime was loving me."

"My dear Celia . . ." Isobel broke off, for Celia, still in a weak state, had burst into tears. The nurse came hurrying into the room.

Celia flung herself face downwards on her pillows, choking with sobs.

Isobel shrugged her shoulders. She would wait a week or two, and when Celia was quite strong again she would soon see that all this nonsense was stopped.

On the stairs she met old Elspeth carrying a letter.

"What is that?" she demanded.

"A letter for Miss Celia."

"Miss Celia is not allowed correspondence . . ." began Isobel, and snatched the letter. Then, when she saw the writing, a small, fine, slanting hand and the postmark "Cadgwith," her eyes narrowed. So Paul Manton was writing to Celia. Isobel knew that Iverley had sent Manton to Cadgwith, which was about ten miles down the coast, the other side of Mullion. She tapped the little hunchback on the shoulder.

"Listen to me, Elspeth, don't you dare tell Miss Celia that this letter came, and in future give all her letters to me. Those are my orders, do you see? If you disobey them, you shall be dismissed."

Old Elspeth looked at her mistress from under lowered lids. It was a malevolent look which escaped Isobel, but the maid made a respectful answer. Isobel knew where Elspeth was vulnerable. The old servant had lived in the Castle ever since she was a young girl. The idea of being sent away was enough to send her into hysterics. She was deeply attached to the place and had no relations and no home to go to. Isobel was well aware that Elspeth would not risk losing her place.

Later, Elspeth took up Celia's tea-tray.

Celia lay against the pillows, looking exhausted. Her beautiful eyes were rimmed with crying. The moment she saw Elspeth she sat up again and some vitality returned to her.

"Elspeth," she said. "Elspeth, I want you. Come here."

The old woman set the tray down and came up to the bed.

"And how is my lil dear?" she asked, in her soft Cornish voice, and her beady eyes were tender behind the steel-rimmed glasses.

"Elspeth, tell me about Paul Manton. Tell me anything you've heard—where he is—anything," Celia said feverishly.

The little hunchback looked fearfully over her shoulder.

"No one can hear you," said Celia. "Nurse has gone down to tea."

Elspeth said:

"Cook and I have heard he'm away to Cadgwith, Miss Celia."

Celia repeated the name. Cadgwith she knew well. It was one of the loveliest fishing villages in the south of Cornwall. Often, in her father's lifetime, she had gone with him to spend the day there with friends. It was a beautiful place which Paul would like. But ten miles from Ruthlyn. It made Celia's heart sink to think that the only person in the world whom she loved was no longer down there in the cove . . .

The ready tears sprang to Celia's eyes again.

"Oh, Elspeth . . . you're the only person I can talk to. Dear Elspeth . . . help me. Can you find out his address?"

"I'll try, Miss Celia. I'll slip down in my off-time and speak to Mrs. Hoskins."

"Oh, bless you, Elspeth."

The old woman looked over her shoulder again, then whispered:

"Swear you won't tell Mrs. Trevarwith if I tell you something."

"You know I won't."

"He've written to you," whispered Elspeth. "I was bringing up the letter, but *she* took it away, and *she'm* given orders all the post is to be given to *her*."

"How dare she! Oh, I shall demand my letter. You say it was from him?"

"Yes, Miss Celia. It looked to me like a foreign writing and had the Cadgwith postal-mark."

"I shall insist on getting it," exclaimed Celia indignantly.

"No, no," said the old woman in a scared voice. "If you do she'll know I've been talking, and turn me out."

Celia, once more devitalized, sank back on her pillows. Elspeth was right. She couldn't ask for her letter. She couldn't risk having her mother's old maid turned out. Isobel was as cruel as the grave. She wouldn't hesitate to be revengeful.

Elspeth tried to soothe the girl. She would do her best to waylay the postman and smuggle the next letter up to Miss Celia, she said, and she would go down to Edith Hoskins tonight.

With that Celia was forced to be content. She lay restless and feverish, wishing that she had the strength to get up and escape from this prison and from Isobel.

When the nurse came back, Celia demanded pen and paper. She would write to Paul and she would get Elspeth to post it for her.

After tea Elspeth returned to the sick-room. She had more news for Miss Celia. Edith Hoskins, herself, had come up to the Castle just now and asked to see her, but the mistress had refused and said that Miss Celia was too ill to see anybody. So the woman had been forced to go away.

Celia could have wept again. Of all the people in the cove she most wanted to see, it was Mrs. Hoskins, who probably had news of Paul for her. Oh, how she loathed her stepmother! She would not tolerate this tyranny. She would run away the moment she was strong enough to get up and put on her clothes.

But Elspeth had an unexpected treat for her "lil dear." Mrs. Hoskins had managed to talk to Elspeth, had told her that she had been in touch with Paul. He had telephoned this morning from Cadgwith post office to the Three Bells, which was the inn down on the quayside. Mrs. Polpenny, who ran the Three Bells, was a cousin of Edith's and she had fetched Edith to the 'phone. Edith had talked with Paul. His main purpose was to ask Mrs. Hoskins to send all his love to Celia, and to say that somehow he would manage to meet her once she was up and about again.

At last a smile crossed Celia's face.

"Oh, Elspeth, how wonderful. And do you know his address? If so, I can give you a letter to post for me."

"Yes, Elspeth knew the address. Paul was lodging with some Cadgwith fishing-folk named Pencomb. A letter care of Mr. Pencomb, Redruth Cottage, Cadgwith, would find Paul.

Celia felt better already. She addressed an envelope and placed in it the long letter which she had written to Paul, thanking him for what he had done for her and expressing her sorrow and regret that he had been sent away from Ruthlyn because of her. But, she had said, she loved him now and always and would never belong to anybody else.

Elspeth put the letter in her apron pocket.

"Whatever you do, you won't let anyone see you post it, will you, Elspeth?" Celia asked feverishly.

Elspeth gave her every assurance.

Another forty-eight hours went by. Celia, knowing that it was necessary for her to do so, tried to keep calm and eat her food and gradually gain strength. Every day Isobel visited her and they both studiously avoided the name of Paul, but at the end of a further week—when Celia was allowed to dangle her legs over the bed for the first time and try her weight on the floor, Isobel insisted upon bringing Fulke Withers up to see her.

"You can't be rude and unkind to him any longer," Isobel declared. "You must pull yourself together, Celia, and make an effort in his direction."

Celia protested, but Isobel, confident that Celia need not now be humoured to the same extent, turned a deaf ear, and brought Fulke into the invalid's room just before dinner that night.

Celia received Fulke with a coldness which infuriated her stepmother, but which Fulke pretended not to notice.

He advanced to the bedside feeling decidedly foolish, and mumbled that he hoped she was better.

"Yes, thank you," said Celia, without a smile.

Fulke laid on the bed a huge bunch of red carnations.

"They were grown at Kyland," he said, "and the best blooms have been cut for you."

"Thank you," Celia repeated sullenly. She shivered at the very memory of his rude licentious hands on her that night of the storm.

Fulke sat down by the bed.

"Suppose I'd better not smoke in here," he mumbled.

"I think it would be better," said Celia, "if you went downstairs."

"Now, Celia," began Isobel sharply, with rising anger.

Fulke stood up, his face a dull red. For days he had been wanting to see her. But he remembered Isobel's warning that he should be as tactful as possible. Celia certainly needed handling. He said:

"That's quite all right. I won't worry you any more. Maybe I can come again in a day or two when you are feeling better. I'm sorry, Celia, about everything. I really am, my dear."

The sight of his big red hands nauseated her. Isobel could not resist bending over the bed and muttering spitefully:

"You've been thoroughly rude, and when you are up and about again, my lady, I'm going to make you change your tune."

The door closed upon them. Celia sighed and looked through her open casements. It was the end of a beautiful day. Celia felt a great longing to be well again, to go out and down to the sea . . . down the coast in the direction of Cadgwith.

So far there had been no more letters from Paul. She felt heartsick with longing.

It was when twilight was veiling the landscape that

Elspeth came running into the room, her wizened face scared.

"Oh, Miss Celia," she gasped.

"What is it?"

"Oh, Miss Celia, I got such a fright. It's Paul."

"Paul!" repeated Celia, her heart plunging. "Paul *here!*"

"He rode over from Cadgwith on a bicycle, Miss Celia. He came round to the back of the Castle and tried to get news of you, and Mr. Withers saw him. He had just been having drinks with the mistress. He raised his voice against Paul and said he had no business to come here, and Paul said he wished only for news of you. I don't know what was said, but I think Paul said something Mr. Withers didn't like, and Mr. Withers struck him."

Celia put her hand to her heart. "Struck him! Oh, Elspeth . . . you mean they've had a fight?"

Elspeth whimpered:

"The mistress would kill me for telling you, but Mr. Withers laid Mr. Paul out, and he'm lying there on the cliff outside the Castle."

For a moment Celia was dumb. Her big eyes stared out of her pale young face. Then she threw off the bed-clothes.

"I'm going to him," she said. "Help me dress, Elspeth. Help me before nurse comes back."

12

"Dear life," said old Elspeth, "you mustn't get out of your bed, Miss Celia."

But Celia was already on her feet. She threw on her dressing-gown. There was no strength in her limbs, but she stumbled across the room to the window and stared wildly out upon the Castle grounds. But she could see nothing. To the left lay the sea and the cliffs. It was out there that Paul was lying, Paul unconscious, hurt. Shivering, she turned back to Elspeth.

"Don't stand there . . . get me my coat. Quickly, Elspeth."

The old servant wished that she had never told her young mistress what had happened outside the Castle. If Miss Celia got a fresh go of pneumonia it would be her fault. Shaking her head, muttering to herself, the old woman handed Celia the coat for which she asked. The girl, summoning all her strength, put on a pair of slippers and tied a scarf over her hair.

"Now, Elspeth, help me . . . not down the main staircase, but down the back way. I'll miss both nurse and Mrs. Trevarwith like that."

"Oh, miss," said Elspeth, sniffing, "if I'm found doing this they'll turn me out. They'll make me leave the Castle, and you, Miss Celia."

"Then I'll go alone," said Celia, and before Elspeth could stop her she hurried out into the corridor.

Celia never afterwards knew how she managed to get down to the back door. Her legs felt non-existent. There was no need for her to go farther, for coming toward her she saw Paul with young Jean from the Hoskins' cottage. Later, when Celia heard the whole story, she learned that news had travelled like lightning down to the cove, that there had been a fight between Paul and Mr. Withers, and Jean, the French boy, had come racing up the cliff to aid his friend and compatriot.

Celia gave a wild look at Paul. He leaned on Jean's arm. There was a gash over his right eye and a swelling on one cheek. His black hair was dusty and matted. But when he saw the figure of the girl his eyes grew brilliant, as though he looked upon a vision.

"Oh, mon Dieu, c'est toi—my Celia," he said.

She threw herself into his arms.

"Paul, darling, darling Paul."

His arms went round her. They clung together. With passionate longing they embraced. His kisses rained upon her eyelids and her lips. In return she kissed every inch of his face and, with tender fingers, touched the bruise and the torn eyebrow.

"He's hurt you . . . that foul brute . . . he has hurt you, Paul. I hate him. I could kill him!" she cried.

"It is nothing," he said in his own language. "It was stupid of me to come here, perhaps, but I had to know how you were, little one."

"I'm quite all right again."

He held her a little away from him and caught a glimpse of the night-gown peeping from her coat.

"But, *mon Dieu!*" he exclaimed. "You are just out of bed. You are not yet well. You should not be standing here in a draught."

"I don't care," she said. "I won't be separated from you any more. I can't bear it."

"Mon amour," he said huskily. *"Ma douce cherie . . ."*

"Take me away, Paul."

The young man was agonized. He could not bear to see her like this. She was so thin, so pale, so changed from the golden girl who used to run down the cliffs to meet him. Yet what could he do? Mr. Withers had told him just now that he had no business to come here

. . . a penniless fisherman . . . daring to pay attention to Miss Trevarwith of the Castle. And there was some truth in those words. Love alone gave Paul the right to pay attention to Celia Trevarwith. But what could love do without means, without permission? . . . He was in a quandary.

He tried to comfort her, to find a solution to this problem. He only knew that somehow they had to be together—or die.

"Listen, my darling . . . my love," he said, "I will think of something . . . I will write to you. But I must leave you now. You are not yet well. You must go back to bed and get strong before we can carry out any plans. Be brave, my darling. Have faith in me. I shall come for you . . . I shall find a way out. You must believe me."

"I understand. I'll be patient, Paul. But it was so grim not getting any news of you."

"I have written to you every day."

"My stepmother has taken the letters."

"She is a wicked woman," said Paul.

"Miss Celia!" said a whispering voice behind them. "Miss Celia!"

Celia still in the circle of Paul's arms, turned and saw the fat figure of old Mrs. Trenown, the cook, in her blue gown and white apron, her hands smeared with flour.

"Miss Celia," repeated Mrs. Trenown. "You'd best come in, m'dear. The mistress is after you. Come, lil lamb. Don't stay here. We'll see to Paul. I'll do something for that eye of his, and drat Mr. Withers."

"Yes, go back to your room, for the sake of the *bon Dieu,* my darling," said Paul.

With a deep sigh she wrenched herself from his arms.

"Have faith," he added. "We will be together in time. Night and day I think of you. Good-bye for now, *bien aimée!*"

Somehow or other Celia managed to find her way back to her room. Once there her strength deserted her. The nurse was waiting for her, looking scared.

"Where on earth have you been . . . mad to get out of your bed in your state of health," the woman began.

Celia heard no more. There was a singing in her ears. The vision of Paul and the moment of rapture in his arms had passed. The world was black and hopeless again. She fainted.

Hot bottles were rushed to Celia, brandy forced between her lips, but she was not to suffer any dire consequences from that crazy interlude. She lay white and shivering, but her reactions to that stolen meeting with Paul were purely nervous. Her body was on the mend, and when the doctor arrived her temperature was normal, and he found nothing further to worry about.

By this time Isobel Trevarwith had heard of her stepdaughter's escape from her bedroom, and putting two and two together she guessed that Celia had managed a meeting with Paul. She stormed down to the kitchen and questioned both Mrs. Trenown and Elspeth. Neither had anything to say. Isobel could feel that there was an air of conspiracy about the place which infuriated her. But she could do nothing. She might bully Elspeth, but dared not risk losing the one and only cook who would undertake the huge kitchens of the Castle without a kitchen-maid.

Later that evening, Isobel came to Celia's bedside resentful.

"I know perfectly well you saw that Frenchman . . . very clever of you, my dear, but you won't be able to go on with that sort of thing. I shall see to that myself. You'll have to be treated as a mental case when you are up, and kept under strict supervision."

Celia's large eyes looked back at her stepmother with an expression which intimated that Celia was by no means beaten.

Isobel snapped:

"You are just making a fool of yourself. What do you suppose they think in the village of this fantastic affair between you and a low fisherman?"

Celia whispered:

"I don't care what anybody thinks."

"Well, you're under age, my dear, and I'm your guardian, so you're going to be made to care what *I* think," said Isobel sharply. "And if that young man comes round the Castle again I'll get the police to deal with him."

Celia raised herself on both elbows. Something approaching hatred was written on her small, wan face as she looked up at her stepmother.

"And I shall advise Paul to summons Fulke Withers for attempting to molest me and assault," she said. "He had no right to hit Paul . . . no right at all."

"And may I ask who gave you that information?"

Celia, quick to protect old Elspeth, said:

"I heard it. I heard it all from the window. I shall never speak to Fulke again. You need never ask me to."

Isobel went red with rage. She opened her lips as though to say something venomous, then closed them again. The nurse had told her just now that Celia was still very much of an invalid.

Isobel had begun to work herself up into the belief that Celia really was a mental case and must be carefully watched, and that it was her duty, since she stood now in the place of both father and mother to the girl, to protect her from her own insanity.

She turned and without a word walked out of the room. Celia heard a key being turned in the lock. But that was too much for the girl. She was not going to be treated like this . . . kept a prisoner by Isobel. She screamed:

"If you don't unlock that door, I shall throw myself out of the window."

Outside the door Isobel stood fuming, hesitating. But she knew Celia. The girl was not easily broken down. She might do what she said, stubborn little brute! With a vicious exclamation Isobel unlocked the door again and marched downstairs.

Celia fell back on the pillows, exhausted. The ready tears came to her eyes. This awful atmosphere of force and hatred within these walls. Of one thing she was certain, she must leave Storm Castle. Her father had shown no particular love or understanding for her, but he had always been just. She was quite sure that he would not want her to stay here and be so unhappy. Years ago Isobel had captivated him with her youth, her vivid looks and vitality. But she was a mean detestable character, and all that was worst in her had come out since Mr. Trevarwith's death.

Before she went to sleep that night, Celia hugged to herself the memory of Paul's arms, his caressing hands, his voice murmuring:

"Je t' adore, ma douce cherie."

When the nurse came to look at her just before retiring, she might well have expected to find her young patient feverish and restless after the excitements of the evening. But to her astonishment she saw that the girl was sound asleep with a look of happiness, and even peace, written on her face.

13

Despite the fact that outwardly Celia suffered no harm
from the upheaval and excitement of that meeting with
Paul, it actually put her back considerably, and it was
a full fortnight before the doctor would allow her to go
downstairs again.

By this time Celia was in a state of frantic impatience. Seeing nobody but the nurse and Elspeth, and
receiving occasional visits from her stepmother and
Anthony, did little to brighten life for her. She burned
with longing for the day when she could get in touch
with Paul.

Isobel, after having shown her anger and disapproval
on the day that Paul fought with Fulke Withers, had
lapsed back into apparent tolerance and was being her
sweetest to the girl. On the morning that Celia came
downstairs, Isobel herself took Celia's arm and led
her into the drawing-room, which she had filled with
flowers. Anthony, with rather a bashful and foolish
look on his face, stood there waiting for Celia with a
posy of sea-daisies which he had picked himself, Isobel
announced.

Celia had learned to be cynical and distrustful of
her stepmother. She was quite sure that all this pala-
ver meant only one thing . . . a prelude to the arrival of
Fulke Withers, who was bound to be thrust on her
again. But she was touched by the little boy's simple
posy. Naughty though he was, this was no doubt a
genuine gesture on his part.

"Thank you, Tony, it was sweet of you to pick these
lovely daisies for me," she said, kissing him.

Anthony grinned at her and said:

"You do look funny."

Celia laughed a little.

"I expect I look ghastly, but I'll soon get fit again if I can go out in the sun."

"Uncle Fulke is coming to tea," announced Anthony.

Isobel went scarlet with vexation. *L'enfant terrible!* She could never say anything in front of her son. She had meant that Fulke should surprise Celia. Now the silly girl would say she was tired and might insist on going back to bed before tea.

Isobel made haste to coax Celia, whose lips had compressed, and in whose large eyes the cynicism had deepened.

"Now, Celia, be nice," murmured Isobel, patting the girl's shoulder. "Poor old Fulke adores you and you are always so horrid to him."

"And what did he do to me and the person I love best in the world?" demanded Celia, reckless of what she said, now she was stronger and her feet were more firmly planted on the ground.

Isobel Trevarwith looked daggers at her step-daughter but said nothing. She was determined not to fall out with her. She led her to the wide-mullioned windows. She knew this was the girl's favourite place because from here she could look down at the sea.

"Now," said Isobel, in a purring voice, when the girl was settled, "Tony is going to sit by you and read his book quietly, aren't you, Tony darling?"

"Want Celie to read to me," said Anthony, and thrust his book into the girl's hands.

"Now don't worry sister," began Isobel, but Celia interrupted:

"I don't mind. I'd like to read to him."

Isobel suddenly noticed that her small son's hands were much begrimed, and bore him off for a wash. Celia lay back on the cushions for a moment, shut her eyes and let the warm sun beat on her face. She still felt weak, but her whole soul throbbed with yearning toward her young lover. Paul.

If only she could go down to the cove and find him there as of old, with his nets.

Elspeth chose that moment to steal into the room and, full of excitement, press a letter into the girl's hand.

" 'Tis from *him*. I waylaid Mr. Tremaine, the postman, to get it for you, Miss Celia. For mercy's sake, don't let the mistress see it, or she'll murder me."

Celia's heart throbbed at the sight of the fine, slanting handwriting.

"Oh, Elspeth, you blessed angel!"

Anthony returned to the room. Celia just had time to put the letter into the pocket of the cardigan that she was wearing. She was crazy with longing to read that letter. Anthony was a young tyrant demanding story after story to be read to him. It was not until lunchtime that Isobel called the little boy to his meal. Then at last, with a sigh, Celia opened her letter.

It was long . . . several sheets closely written in Paul's own language. The gist of it was to assure Celia afresh of his adoration and his undying wish to make her his wife, to give her happiness and peace for the rest of her life. It stated also that she had no cause to worry about him, since his face had completely healed and he was feeling fine; only he was half-mad with impatience to see her again. The moment she was well, he wanted her to try to get to Kyland Point, which lay half-way between Cadgwith and Ruthlyn. If she would send him a telegram to tell him which day she could walk along the cliff, he, too, would walk and they would meet . . . preferably at two o'clock one afternoon when Mr. Withers, whose house was not far from the Point, would be engaged on his job at the aerodrome. They must trust to luck that nobody else saw them—or, if they did, that they would not betray them.

He had made up his mind, he said, that he could not remain in the fishing colony. Now that he had *her* he must do more for her. He wished to win the world for her. He wished also to play an active part in the war. They would not take him in the infantry because of his limp, but he was sure he could get into the Free French Navy. It would be more fitting, he said, that Celia Trevarwith's future husband should be a sailor who might eventually win promotion and distinction. Then she could be proud of him.

Celia was thrilled by this letter. It was quite a literary effort and confirmed all her beliefs that Paul was no ordinary young man. He was more than her equal in every way. But Paul as a sailor. That shook her. She did not know whether she wanted him to join the Navy. She could not bear him to endanger his life, and yet he was right . . . life as a fisherman was a poor one for a young man of his calibre, and whatever he wanted, she must want.

Again and again she read the last lovely lines of this, her first love-letter . . . not the only one he had written, but the first she had received:

> *"Tu ressembles á une fleur des champs, si fraiche, si innocente.'*

She translated it softly aloud to herself, savouring the words.

"You are like a wild flower, so fresh, so innocent."

She read on, her heart beating with ecstasy:

> *"Tes yeux sont bleus comme la fleur de chicoré qui posse dans les pres de mon pays."*

She pressed the letter against her breast, and there were tears in those eyes which he had called "blue as the chicory flower that grew in his own country."

Was there ever such a lover? Nothing, nobody should separate her from him now.

She heard Isobel's steps outside the door and hastily concealed her love-letter again. Isobel commented on her high colour.

"I hope you are not feverish."

"No. I am very well thanks," said Celia.

And so exalted was she by the pleasure that Paul's

letter had brought her that she did not even demur when Isobel announced that Fulke would be calling and that "she hoped Celia would be pleasant to him."

"I'll be as pleasant as I can," was Celia's answer.

The older woman looked at her sharply, her suspicions aroused. What did this quiescence mean? She didn't trust her. Isobel didn't trust anybody in the Castle. She was quite aware that they all hated her and would be glad to help Celia behind her back.

She thought:

"There's only one thing for me to do—get Celia away from Cornwall. I'll take her up to London, where Paul Manton can't get at her. Fulke can always come up when he wants to."

Fulke arrived, and Celia duly received him with a cool friendliness which did not deceive the man. He could see that she had no use for him, and was well aware that his battle with Paul Manton had done no good to himself. He half wished that he hadn't knocked the fellow down and so turned Celia still more against him. But he had not been able to control his temper when the young Frenchman openly announced that he had come to see Celia because he loved her and she loved him.

He felt full of impotent anger as he sat talking to Celia this afternoon. She was too thin yet those great eyes and pallor gave her glamour. She looked older to-day than the schoolgirl who had first captivated him.

In the midst of a discussion about nothing in particular, he suddenly broke out:

"You hate me, don't you?"

Celia moved uncomfortably and turned her eyes to the setting sun.

"I don't hate anybody really."

"Yes. You do. You fancy yourself fond of this fisherman and you are furious because I knocked him down."

The colour sprang to Celia's cheeks.

"I'd rather not discuss it."

"But I must discuss it with you. Can't you see that you're driving me mad?" he asked thickly. And suddenly he came to the sofa where she was lying and clasping one of her hands began to cover it with frantic kisses.

She drew away from him in distaste.

Fulke made an attempt to take her in his arms.

"Celia, you can't be so mad as to love this fisherman. I give you everything. He has nothing to offer you. I want you to marry me. I swear I'll be good to you. Celia . . ."

She struggled against him.

"Let me go, Fulke."

Celia fought for a moment, her fear and repugnance returning.

Isobel came hurrying into the room.

Fulke said: "I tried to kiss the girl. She's not normal."

Isobel looked at her stepdaughter and shrugged her shoulders.

"She's enough to drive you scats. And now, fresh trouble. I've just been interviewing a billeting officer, and despite all our efforts they are taking over part of the Castle that we don't use, and billeting twenty-five Waafs here."

"What a business!" said Fulke.

Isobel sat down on the sofa and patted Celia's hands. Celia was crying bitterly.

"Don't be a fool, Celia."

"I think you will be better away from Cornwall—in London."

A feeling of despair came over Celia. If Isobel meant to take her away from Cornwall she couldn't meet Paul or see him.

Isobel added:

"Two Waaf officers are arriving tonight, darn it. I've grumbled and complained, but they say I haven't got a leg to stand on."

Celia thought:

"I *must* pull myself together. I will see one of these Waaf officers. Perhaps I'll find a friend. Perhaps they'll help me get to Paul. But I won't let Isobel take me away from Paul. *I won't.*"

PART THREE

1

Section-officer Jill Hayling of the W.A.A.F. had—with every reason—been feeling extremely depressed since her transfer from a very nice R.A.F. station on the East Coast down to the newly-built camp in Ruthlyn, South Cornwall.

Not only was it a long way from her home, which was in Scarborough, but she was in the tragic position of having been married only a week to a young pilot officer, who, two months ago, had been reported "missing" after a night-flight over Germany.

This evening, having finished her administrative work and seen that the twenty-five girls under her care had been fed and housed in their new quarters, Jill wandered outside the grounds of Storm Castle, her gaze fixed on the sea, which was now the colour of gun-metal in the gathering dusk.

Anxiously, and with many painful and poignant thoughts, Jill Hayling scanned the horizon and watched the first luminous star light the darkness of the sea. If only that star were an omen, she thought. If there were only one tiny ray of hope to lighten the darkness of her heart and soul. But since that news about Tim had come through two months ago, she had felt utterly hopeless. Tim was dead. Tim had been shot down over Germany. All their love and their hopes were to no purpose and she was alone . . . left to carry on with her job . . . never to forget . . . always to remember that she had loved him more than anybody in the world and that life could never be the same without him.

With a deep sigh she turned her gaze from the sea

and looked up at the dark shadow of the Castle. Somehow it looked unfriendly and harsh in this light and increased her sense of loneliness and depression. Yet she loved Cornwall. Her memories here were all the more painful because her brief ecstatic honeymoon with Tim had been spent nearly on this very coast—in Cadgwith—which had seemed to Jill and to Tim the loveliest little fishing village in the world.

She had heard about Ruthlyn Cove, but they had never walked as far. They had spent that glorious week in May entirely in Cadgwith, exploring that part of the coast, radiantly happy like two children. Could any other couple ever have been so happy? Oh, Tim, Tim, with the eyes that were as blue as the Cornish seas, the thick brown hair, the gay brown face. And that way he had always had of laughing and making a joke of everything. He had never allowed her to be sad for a single moment, even on that last night of their honeymoon, knowing that on the morrow they must part . . . she to go back to her unit, he to his. He had still laughed and joked, aware that his work was highly dangerous. So many of his pals in his own squadron had already lost their lives.

For a few days after the news had been broken to her by a sympathetic commanding officer, Jill had felt that nothing was worth while, and resented bitterly the fate which had overtaken her young husband. At twenty-four, full of life and zest, he had died. At twenty-two she was a widow. It didn't seem fair. But gradually she had realized that such sacrifices must be made if this war was to be won, and that Tim would wish her to stay in the W.A.A.F. and carry on in his place.

"Chin up, my sweet," he would have said. She had tried in the first agony of grief to remember those familiar words. Tried to accept the comfort that her relations and friends had given her when they told her that there was a chance Tim might still be alive and a prisoner in Germany.

In happier circumstances she would have loved this

new job in Ruthlyn Cove and appreicated being billeted in this strange old Castle. But, under these conditions, it was too near Cadgwith. The very sight of these cliffs hurt atrociously.

Neither she nor her friend, A.S.O. Pat Parker, had taken to the owner of the Castle. Mrs. Trevarwith seemed a sharp-tongued, disobliging sort of woman, and the old hunch-backed maid stealing around the place in carpet-slippers gave them the creeps. Besides, their wing of the Castle had not been lived in for so long that it was damp and comfortless. But this was only their second night here. Jill supposed they would get used to it.

Jill looked up at the Castle and noticed suddenly a ray of light coming from one of the turret windows. Some people were very careless about the black-out, and on the coast like this it would never do. Whether Mrs. Trevarwith liked it or not, she was going to complain.

She went indoors and started to look for the owner of the Castle, but could find nobody, so made her way up the staircase. This part of the Castle was rather fine. Jill admired the tapestries and ancestral portraits.

Reaching the door of the room for which she was bound, she knocked upon it. A voice said:

"Come in."

Jill opened the door and for a moment stood hesitating. She saw a young girl sitting up in bed, writing. She had the most beautiful eyes Jill had ever seen, wide and long-lashed in a small pinched face; fair hair floating to her shoulders. As Jill entered she noticed the girl hastily secreted the block on which she had been writing, under her blankets. She looked nervous.

Jill said:

"Oh, hello! . . . sorry to disturb you, but there is a light showing from one of your windows."

The girl in the bed said:

"Oh, please fix it for me. How stupid of Elspeth!"

Then as Jill walked to the turret, added:

"You must be one of the Waafs billeted here?"

125

"Yes, I'm Section-Officer Jill Hayling."

"I'm Celia Trevarwith. I'm frightfully glad you've come up. I'd like to talk to you if I may. Only tell me first, is there anyone around?"

"What do you mean?"

Celia put a hand to her throat. Every gesture, Jill thought, was nervous. What was she so frightened of?

"I mean . . . my stepmother . . . she isn't anywhere around?"

"I didn't meet anybody. I found my own way up here."

"Thank goodness. Please do sit down and talk to me. It's so marvellous to see someone of my own age."

Jill Hayling sat down and smiled as she drew a packet of cigarettes from her tunic pocket. She offered it to Celia, who shook her head.

"May I? Thanks. You are a lot younger than I am, aren't you?"

"I'm nineteen . . . or nearly . . ."

"Gracious, I thought you were less. I'm twenty-two."

"Oh, Miss Hayling . . ."

"Mrs. Hayling," corrected Jill, "but Jill's the name."

"Oh, Jill, how marvellous. Do you know I haven't spoken to anyone like you since I left school."

"But why? Do you live here? Haven't you got any friends?"

"No . . . none . . . except Elspeth, my old maid. Everybody else is against me. You don't know what it's like here and I'm terribly in love with someone . . . I want to get away to him. My stepmother is trying to make me go up to London at the end of this week. I want to run away, but they won't let me out of bed. I was ill again in the night yesterday, and the doctor and my stepmother spy on me. I know I'll never, never be able to meet Paul."

These words poured from Celia in a torrent. Jill listened in amazement, realizing that here was something very out of the ordinary. This young girl was in the last stages of hysteria. Thank goodness she had come up here.

Jill, who came of a big family, had always been the one at home to "mother" brothers and sisters younger than herself and hold out a helping hand to the "lame dog." She could not bear to see anybody so scared, or wretched. Being a sensible young woman, she let Celia talk on. In a quiet way she helped to get from her the whole story of Storm Castle, and her love-affair with Paul Manton.

The last phase of the tale roused the deepest sympathy in Jill. How well she knew what it was to love. The poor kid! Why shouldn't she be allowed to see her young Frenchman? The stepmother was a bitch. (She and Pat had already decided that.) And no wonder Celia was in such a state. It was like a film, romantic; it temporarily lifted Jill out of her own despondency.

When Celia finished talking, Jill said:

"Good lord! I've never heard anything like it. I absolutely agree with you, too. Don't let them force you to marry this Withers man, or make you go up to London. I tell you what. I'll help you. I've got forty-eight hours' stand-off the day after tomorrow. I've got a bicycle and my friend Pat has got one. I'll borrow hers for you, and if you are strong enough we'll cycle to meet your Paul."

The light returned to Celia's eyes.

"*Jill!* What a heavenly idea! I'm sure I'll be strong enough. I'll *make* myself. And I can give you an address and you can wire Paul to meet us at Kyland Point. But how are we going to get away from the Castle without my stepmother seeing us?"

"Don't you worry. I'll fix her. We'll just slip out. Where does Paul live?"

"Cadgwith."

Jill flushed. Celia saw the shadow that passed across her face . . . a very winsome face with large brown eyes and tip-tilted nose.

"Is anything wrong?"

Jill took a grip on herself and answered quietly:

"I spent my honeymoon at Cadgwith in May. My husband was a pilot-officer. He has been missing for the last eight weeks."

Celia leaned forward and took one of Jill's hands . . . such a strong, capable hand in comparison with her own.

"Oh, Jill! I'm so terribly sorry."

The tears burned Jill's eyelids. How often she had wondered how it was that she still had tears to shed . . . she had cried so much since Tim had been taken from her. In a choked voice she said:

"He was a grand person and we were so in love. He was stationed at the aerodrome down in Wiltshire where I worked when I first got my commission. My parents thought it was a bit foolish for us to marry because we had only known each other a few months, but we were positive it was the real thing. Mummy and Daddy were marvellous and they didn't stand in our way, and now I'm so thankful I had that one week with him. Just one week, Celia. Can you imagine what it means to me?"

"Oh, Jill, I can. I feel like that about Paul. But perhaps I'll never even have one week of happiness . . ." Celia's voice broke, but Jill pressed her hand tightly and said:

"Yes, you shall. I'll see that you do. I'm not going to let that stepmother of yours get her way and I don't care who finds out that I have helped you."

"It's terribly lucky you being billeted here, Jill. I've had such bad luck lately. But now I think it is changing. You're an angel, and somehow I feel you won't be alone for the rest of your life. Your Tim has not gone for good, Jill. He is a prisoner—I *know* he is. I know you'll hear from him one day."

Jill puffed hard at her cigarette.

"Oh, Celia, if only I could believe it!"

"Ssh!" said Celia suddenly. "I believe I hear my stepmother. If she finds you here she'll think we are scheming about something. I'll never get out of this Castle with you . . . never."

"You leave her to me," said Jill grimly. She put out her cigarette and stood up.

Isobel Trevarwith entered the room.

She looked with surprise and annoyance at the girl in the blue uniform.

"Aren't you in the wrong quarters?" she said rudely. "My stepdaughter is very ill and nobody ought to be in her room."

Jill's hands doubled at her sides. She was a high-spirited girl, but training and discipline had taught her to keep her temper. This woman was like a vixen with her painted face and red hair and that venomous mouth. Jill would have enjoyed a battle of words with her.

"I must apologize, Mrs. Trevarwith, if I came to your part of the Castle without invitation," she said coldly, "but there was a light showing from this window and it was my duty to point it out. Now there is an aerodrome on this coast there should be extra care. I'll say good night." She turned to the bed and managed to wink at Celia: "Good night, both of you . . ." Then she walked out of the room.

Isobel sniffed.

"What have you two been talking about? I suppose you've been confiding in that stupid Waaf and telling her how cruel everybody is to you."

Celia made no answer. Isobel added:

"Sulky as usual. You are the most unattractive girl. I can't think why Fulke worries about you."

"Neither can I," said Celia. "He is wasting his time."

"And you are wasting mine," snapped Isobel. "The doctor thinks as I do that you are mentally deranged. We are going up to London the day after tomorrow. I shall take you to a mental home."

Celia began to breathe hard and fast. She wanted to rebel openly . . . then thought better of it. But she was torn with anxiety. The day after tomorrow . . . the very day that Jill meant to borrow that bicycle for her.

"We shall go on the morning train and you'll have to

129

pull yourself together and be ready to drive into Helston at half-past eight," added Isobel. "And please don't discuss our affairs with any of these girls who are billeted here."

She walked out of the room, and immediately the nurse returned to settle her patient down for the night.

Celia thought:

"I must get a message to Jill. Elspeth will take one. I must tell her that if we are to get away we must do it before Isobel is up and about. I must get to Paul. I *must*."

2

Sunrise over Storm Castle. One of those marvellous milky mornings of midsummer when sea and sky seem to dissolve together in a glittering mist. Below the walls of the Castle, Ruthlyn Cove cottages were veiled in the ethereal mist. The silence was broken by the first faint pipe of awakening birds. The flutter of white wings on Gull Rock.

In two hours' time, thought Celia, her stepmother would be breakfasting. The nurse would come to dress her in preparation for this trip to London. Isobel had made it quite plain to Celia that the trip meant total separation from Paul and fresh humiliation for her at Isobel's hands, backed by a London specialist who might well be a "quack," ready, for a sum of money, to agree with Isobel's malicious suggestions that her stepdaughter was "touched."

But Celia was in a state of wildest excitement. At this early hour Celia knew that Jill would already be awake. Her friend, Pat Parker, was in the scheme, too. Officially this was Jill's "stand-off" for forty-eight hours, so she was not breaking any rules. But Pat was going to help keep guard and make sure that the way was clear. Celia felt stronger this morning. Yesterday she had been allowed up, but confined to her room. She knew that she could have got out if she had wanted, but it would only have caused a row with both Isobel and the nurse, so she had submitted to their tyranny. But Elspeth had brought her one or two notes from Jill. Jill had been in touch with Paul by telephone. Paul was to meet them at Kyland Point in three-quarters of an hour's time. In her present state, Celia would have to cycle slowly. It would take her all of that time to reach the Point.

When Celia was ready she looked at herself in the mirror and wished that her face were not quite so thin. But a great deal of that colour this morning was natural, and the radiance that smiled back at her from her own eyes was that of a woman in love . . . going to her lover. Life in the Castle was over.

Celia opened her door. All was quiet and dark in the corridor. Nobody would be about for another hour. With her pulses leaping, Celia crept down the wide staircase, bidding farewell to every familiar object as she went . . . smiling wryly at the portraits of her ancestors, regretful only to leave the one painting of her beautiful dead mother.

This had been her birthplace. But it seemed no longer a home to be desired or loved. It belonged, in fact, to Anthony. She wished him joy of it. A dark fate hung over its old grey walls.

Downstairs in the huge hall old Elspeth was waiting with hot coffee and buttered scones. And Jill was there too, spruce and pretty in her W.A.A.F. uniform; excitement in her own eyes. As she had told Pat last night, she was going to enjoy helping this poor kid to get away to her boy-friend.

" 'Morning, Celia," she said, as she greeted the girl and took the suitcase from her. "Now take it easy and don't overdo things. We're going to be quite O.K. The cycles are all ready. Pat pumped up the tyres for us last night."

"You've both been so good," said Celia.

Old Elspeth put a corner of her apron to her eyes.

"Tain't going to be the same here when you'm gone, my lil dear," she said mournfully.

Celia put her arms around the shrunken figure.

"Darling Elspeth! When Paul and I are married and all is well we'll send for you. You'll come and look after us, won't you?"

Elspeth wept openly.

"Oh, Miss Celia, that I will! But where be you going to? You'm not strong enough to do much."

"Cheer up, Elspeth," said Jill cheerfully. "I'll look after Miss Celia for you, and wherever she goes, she will be happier than she has been here."

Suddenly all three stood still, tense, listening. They had heard steps. Celia's face went white as milk.

"Oh, goodness! That's *her!*"

Elspeth put a hand against her lips.

"You'm right. 'Tis the mistress's footsteps . . . she've heard us."

Jill thought rapidly, then took control.

"Get back into the kitchen, Elspeth. Don't make a sound. Celia. Take the case and go behind that curtain. Don't move till I tell you it's all clear. I'll manage Mrs. Trevarwith."

Elspeth fled. Celia, her heart hammering against her ribs, stood motionless behind the heavy tapestry curtain which hung across the archway leading from the hall into the kitchen quarters. She felt suffocated with anxiety. To be found by Isobel now, and stopped from meeting Paul, would be too bitter a disappointment. However she might protest, Isobel could defeat her . . . could call the nurse down and forcibly prevent her from getting on to that bicycle.

She heard Jill's voice, casual, clear:

"Good morning, Mrs. Trevarwith."

Then Isobel's voice, not far from Celia, sharp and suspicious:

"What are you creeping about the place for at this unearthly hour? It isn't six o'clock. It is bad enough to have you girls billeted here, but surely you needn't disturb the whole household in this fashion."

Celia held her breath, but Jill's answer came unconcerned:

"I'm very sorry, Mrs. Trevarwith, but I've been on night duty and am just home. I thought I'd been quiet, but perhaps I am not as light on my feet as I imagined . . ." she giggled.

A moment's silence, then from Isobel:

"Who were you talking to? I thought I heard voices."

From Jill:

"Then you must have heard heavenly ones, Mrs. Trevarwith. And I don't talk to myself . . ." she giggled again.

Celia was young enough to smile at that. But how would Isobel take it? Isobel had no sense of humour. She snapped:

"I dislike impertinence, and if I see your commanding officer I shall report you."

Silence. Celia's smile faded. Again she heard Isobel's footsteps. *She was going back to her room.*

Two minutes later Jill pulled aside the curtain. Laughing, she knocked a hand against her ribs.

"Oh, my poor heart . . . I thought I'd pass out," she whispered, "but it's all right now. I've just heard her shut her door. There is water running. She's turned on the taps in her bathroom. I think we are safe to make our getaway."

"Oh, let's go quickly."

"Steady," said Jill. "Conserve your energies, my lamb. You will need them all on that perishing cycle. I wish I had my old run-about here and could drive you to your boy-friend."

"As long as I get to him I don't care *how* . . ." said Celia.

The two girls walked on tiptoe across the hall and the next moment were outside the Castle and in the courtyard where the bicycles were waiting. Celia lifted her face to the sun, felt the cool sweet air against her cheeks, and experienced a sudden sense of freedom . . . of glorious happiness.

As she mounted her own cycle Jill looked anxiously at Celia. Lord! she thought, what a beauty Celia Trevarwith was, to be sure. This was the first time Jill had seen her out of bed and dressed. How pretty she was!

"All right, honey?" she asked.

"Fine," said Celia.

The two girls cycled out of the courtyard, through the gates, and on to the road.

For ten minutes Celia and Jill pedalled without speaking to each other. It did not take much to make Celia breathless and give her a slight pain in her side. It was hateful to be so weak, she thought. She could remember the day when she could have cycled three times this distance without turning a hair. But she was not going to give in. There was too much at stake.

With every moment now the mists were vanishing. The sea was turning to an exquisite blue. Cliffs and fields were emerald green, streaked with the pink of sea-daisies and wilf fox-gloves. Celia knew the road well. For a way it was straight, but after a while they had to turn inland and go down a steep hill, through St. Anstye and up the other side. Here Jill, with a brief look at Celia's wet, white face, insisted on taking her cycle from her and pushing it up the hill. Jill began to feel a little anxious.

"I really don't know whether I ought to have let you do this."

But Celia wiped her face with a handkerchief and smiled.

"This is one of the most wonderful moments of my life. You needn't worry about me. I shall make it."

"What do you think will happen when they discover that you've gone?"

"Oh, there'll be a frightful scene. My stepmother will rouse the whole Castle, and telephone for the doctor—and Fulke Withers, who interferes in everything. I suppose they'll get out the car and start looking for me."

Jill glanced at her wrist-watch.

"Hmm. That's why we've got to get you to Paul before *they* can get there. He's going to have a car waiting, you know."

"A car! Paul?"

"Yes, I told him that you weren't fit. There's a garage at Cadgwith, and an awfully nice man, and he's obliging Paul."

"Then where is he going to take me?"

"For the moment to some cottage in the village. He

135

seems to have made friends, and they are going to look after you until he can arrange something else."

The two girls had reached the top of the hill now. Celia took over the bicycle again. Once more the road was straight, and at the end of it was Kyland Point. Celia strained to see ahead. The colour returned to her face.

"Oh, Jill . . . we are nearly there!"

Jill smiled. But there was a deep sadness behind that smile.

"Oh, Tim, Tim, why aren't you here too . . . why can't I find you somewhere, my darling?" she thought.

Celia summoned up all the remaining strength in her body to cover that last mile. When she reached Kyland Point and the Coastguards' Station which was to be the meeting-place she almost fell off her bicycle. Jill supported her.

"Good show, Celia. You've got here," she said. "Buck up, my lamb; it's all over."

Celia, panting, looked around her.

"Paul isn't here."

Jill looked at her watch."

"He ought to be. I said between six-thirty and a quarter to seven."

"But it is seven o'clock, Jill. It's *seven*. You don't think he has made a mistake about the time or the day?"

"I know he hasn't. I only spoke to him on the 'phone last night. Don't be a muggins. He'll turn up. Maybe the taxi wouldn't start."

In an agony of anticipation, Celia searched the road which led to Cadgwith. There was nothing to be seen on it except a milk lorry. Three Beaufighters, in perfect formation, passed high in the blue distance above them.

"If he's late, he may be *too* late," Celia said despairingly. "Isobel is sure to come this way. She'll know I've gone to Paul."

Jill lit a cigarette and flung the match on to the road. She had to admit she was worried and could not understand why Paul was so late. For an instant it struck

136

her most unpleasantly that young Manton might not be all that he seemed. . . . (Frenchmen were not all that reliable!) Perhaps at the last moment he would back out of his responsibilities. That would be *too* awful. Enough to kill the poor kid in her present state.

The moments ticked by. Celia clung on to Jill's arm, staring down at the Cadgwith road. She was thinking:

"You will come, Paul darling. I know you'll come unless there has been an accident, or something. Paul, Paul, you *must* come."

Then the sound of a car broke the silence of the countryside. Both girls heard it, but neither smiled. For it was a car coming in the *wrong direction,* down that road over which they had just cycled from Ruthlyn Cove. The same thought struck them simultaneously. Celia gave a bitter cry:

"Oh, Jill, Jill, this may well be Isobel and the nurse. They'll find me. They'll take me back. Jill, *what am I going to do?*"

3

On the road between Cadgwith and Kyland Point, Paul Manton stood by the roadside, smoking a cigarette, pacing up and down with the restlessness of a caged lion, whilst an elderly man tinkered with the engine of a dilapidated-looking car which had long since lost most of its paint.

Every now and again Paul stopped and spoke to the man in a voice of frantic anxiety:

"Is it that you cannot mend the car? Is it that I had better get a lift to Kyland? How long will you be?"

The owner and driver of this car, by name William Trelawney, looked up at the young Frenchman and drew an oily hand across a face already smeared, then wiped both face and hands with a piece of rag. He shook his head.

"Sorry, lad, but th' old bus, she'm doin' something queer and I can't seem to get her going."

Paul flung away his cigarette and hunched his shoulders with a typically French gesture of despair.

"Mon Dieu, what bad luck, and *she* will be waiting for me."

Trelawney bent over the engine again.

"Reckon I might get her right in a minute, lad. Don't take on."

Paul started his anxious pacing again, straining his gaze in the direction of Kyland, where he knew Celia and her new friend must be waiting, wondering what had happened. For days now he had been doing his work with no heart, chafing at the separation from Celia and their apparently hopeless outlook.

He had grown thin. His high cheekbones stood out sharply under the taut brown skin. He had reached the pitch where he could neither sleep nor enjoy his food. His passionate love for the young English girl from Storm Castle seemed to be consuming him like a slow and steady fire, ever increasing in its warmth. He thought incessantly of her as he had last seen her. He knew that she was ill and unhappy and he could not bear it. He must take her away whatever the consequences. His delight had known no bounds when the English lady in the W.A.A.F., Mrs. Hayling, had got into telephonic communication with him and told him she was going to help Celia get away from the Castle.

Paul, with his charm, his good looks, and that romantic air which somehow clung to him, had not taken long to make friends at Cadgwith. His present "boss," in charge of the fishing fleet, was a kindly man, and the Pencombs at Redruth Cottage, with whom Paul lodged, would do anything for him. Rose Pencomb had a widowed sister living in the village. Paul had told them all about Celia Trevarwith, and the women, touched by his story and the romantic love which so obviously existed between him and the young English girl, were resolved to help him. Paul had seen them last night, and it was arranged that Celia should lodge with Rachel Taylor until Paul could make further arrangements.

Once more Paul stopped pacing and addressed old Trelawney.

"Please excuse, but tell me is it that the car will soon be mended?" he asked in an agonized voice.

Trelawney did not speak, but suddenly a noise sent the colour back into Paul's cheeks. The engine was running again. Old Trelawney turned and smiled at the boy.

"She'm off lad. Jump in," he said.

Paul needed no second bidding. Once again they were jogging down the road as fast as the old car could carry them.

They reached Kyland Point. Outside the Coastguard's Station they saw a car. Paul had not expected that. Mrs. Hayling had said that she and Celia would come on bicycles. Then, as Trelawney pulled up with a jerk, Paul sprang out and found to his dismay that it was Isobel Trevarwith herself who stood by that car, and with her was a woman in nurse's uniform. Facing them was his Celia. . . . Paul gave her a quick impassioned look and saw that she was obviously in a state of extreme exhaustion and agitation. Supporting her was a Waaf—who must, of course, be Mrs. Hayling.

As Paul jumped out of his car all four turned in his direction. Celia gave a choked cry and ran to him. He caught her in his arms.

Isobel Trevarwith stepped forward.

"Enough of this," she said in her high, sharp voice. "Celia, you are to get back into my car with nurse and myself immediately. You've made us lose the London train as it is, you little fool."

Celia clung to Paul.

"I won't go. Paul, don't let them take me . . ." she said in a hysterical voice.

He could feel her trembling.

"Madame, I regret—you must do what you want but Celia shall not go back to Storm Castle. She is coming with me."

Jill Hayling, watching, liked the way he stood up to that cat of a woman. She liked the proud poise of his head, and most of all she liked the way he had looked at Celia. He obviously worshipped her. She could well understand a girl falling for him.

Isobel Trevarwith looked from one to the other of them, her body shaking with rage. Then she shouted at Paul:

"You've caused enough trouble already and you're going to be sorry for it," she said furiously; "Celia is under age and I am her guardian."

"But you can't force me to live in the Castle with you any longer," put in Celia.

"Nurse," said Isobel, "help Miss Trevarwith into the car."

The nurse moved forward. She was not sure that she liked taking part in this extraordinary affair. In all her career she had never come across anything quite like it. She was even sorry for her young patient, but the doctor had told her to take orders from Mrs. Trevarwith.

She moved forward, but Paul was too quick for her. Swiftly he lifted Celia up into his arms, carried her to old Trelawney's car and placed her in the back seat. Jill ran to them and threw in Celia's case.

"Bless you both and good luck," she said. "I'll keep in touch with you."

Isobel screamed at Jill:

"You little toad, I'll have you up for this. I'll have you thrown out of the Air Force."

Jill laughed.

"Sorry, Mrs. Trevarwith, but there is nothing in King's Regulations to stop me aiding and abetting an elopement."

Paul jumped into the car beside Celia and slammed the door.

"Quickly," he said to old Trelawney, "back to Cadgwith."

"I shall follow you," screamed Isobel.

Celia, feeling fresh strength stealing over her called out to her stepmother:

"I don't advise you to follow me. It will do no good. I shall never go back to the Castle!"

"We shall see about that," said Isobel. "I have the law on my side."

Old Trelawney put his foot on the accelerator. The car moved forward. Jill called out:

"*Au revoir, mes enfants.* Good luck."

Isobel stood there impotently raging. This was a pretty kettle of fish. What would Fulke say? And what would they do? Certainly the law was on her side, Celia could not marry Paul Manton without her permission; but could Celia, approaching the age of nineteen, be forced back to the Castle if she refused to go there of her own free will? At any rate it would all be most difficult. Of one thing Isobel was certain . . . it would not pay her in the long run to lose all control of Celia who was coming into the bulk of the money. She, Isobel, had too many debts and future responsibilities. What was the good of Anthony being master of Storm Castle unless there was enough money to keep it going?

Once her initial rage had passed, Isobel began to think that she had made a mistake in so completely alienating Celia. It was that damned temper of hers. It had always let her down.

She must go back and talk to Fulke. What in heaven's name would *he* say when he heard that Celia had run away with the boy?

On the way to Cadgwith, Celia relaxed. With Paul's arm around her and her head against his shoulder she could laugh again.

"Oh, Paul, it's so wonderful to be with you."

"I could kill them all for hurting you, but I am not going to let them do it again," he said.

"But we've been a bit crazy, Paul. My stepmother is right; the law is on her side."

Paul's eyes looked anxiously out towards the sea.

"That is the trouble," he said.

"I needn't go back and . . . I *won't* . . . it was a nightmare. I've felt like a prisoner for weeks."

"Now you are going to be well looked after and happy for as long as I can arrange it."

"Where are you taking me?"

He told her about Rachel Taylor and her cottage in the village.

"It won't be as luxurious as the Castle," said Paul apologetically.

"It will be heaven. But, Paul, there is the question of money. What are we going to do without it?"

"You have none?"

"I am rich, Paul, but unable to touch a penny until I am twenty-one. All I possess now is my bag . . . a pound or two . . . and I am lucky to have that. I saved it out of my allowance just before I met you."

"Never mind, I shall give you everything that I earn," he said gaily.

"As long as I can be with you, I don't mind. But what is this about you going into the Free French Navy?"

He smiled at her.

"Ah yes. If I can get into the Navy, that will make a difference. I will be able to do more for you than now on the pay of a fisherman."

"But you'd have to go away."

"You could come wherever I was stationed."

That made Celia think. She had eloped with this young man who adored her and whom she adored in return, but there were snags and pitfalls ahead which she hardly dared contemplate. She was not able to marry him. And if Isobel remained adamant . . . this present situation might last for years.

Paul saw her downcast expression and bent and kissed her.

"You are not to be sad *cherie* . . . you are to be happy now and worry about nothing. The future will take care of itself. Something will happen for us. You will see."

During the rest of that drive, Celia told Paul about Jill and the pilot-officer husband who was missing.

"The thought of you going into the Navy rather terrifies me when I think of Jill," Celia ended with a sigh.

"But it will mean that I am doing something for my country . . . for your country, *adorée*."

"I must try to get used to the idea," said Celia.

"I think I am tired of fishing," said Paul. "I think I should like now to be a sailor . . . to fight for France; for you . . ."

They came to Cadgwith and the top of the winding hill that led down to the lovely little bay. Celia, in the circle of Paul's arms, looked with intense pleasure at the remembered headlands forking on either side like green arms embracing the blue waters of the tiny harbour. This morning in the shimmering sunlight it all looked so beautiful. And Celia now experienced a new sense of freedom, a resolve to face life with Paul. She held on to his hand as Trelawney drove them to Rachel Taylor's cottage.

4

Many and varied are the moods of Mother Nature on the Cornish coast, which can be as treacherous as it is fair. The weather changes with remarkable rapidity and storms blow up with an alarming suddenness.

That day of Celia's escape from the Castle, which had begun in such golden tranquillity, ended in a violent storm.

It had been a happy enough day. She had fully expected a visit from Isobel and Fulke Withers, but nobody had come near her. It was extraordinarily peaceful here in Mrs. Taylor's cottage.

Mrs. Taylor was a typical Cornish woman who, in her youth, had worked hard and borne several children, all of whom, save one, had died in infancy. The remaining son was now sheep-farming in Australia. Since the death of her husband, Rachel had lived here alone on a mere pittance. She was a kindly, generous creature, and when her sister, Rose Pencomb, had brought the French boy here, and she had heard about young Miss Trevarwith from Ruthlyn Cove, she had been ready and willing to give her a room. She liked the company, for she was often lonely, and also it meant a little more grist to the mill. In the ordinary way she could not take in lodgers like many of the women in the village because she had not the amenities. But little Miss Trevarwith seemed delighted with everything and, as Rachel told her sister later, it made her heart ache to see the poor girl. She looked as though she badly needed mothering.

Celia, after the strain and stress of her illness and her

rows with Isobel, would have been only too delighted to stay here always, so long as she could see Paul. But she felt sure that such peace could not last. Isobel would never let matters rest like this. Lack of money was bound to be a source of trouble. Celia could not allow Paul to pay for her keep, and until she was really fit she could not work for her own living, which she fully intended to do.

Twice already today Paul had run in to see her. Old Rachel had retired upstairs and left them alone. Celia had known for the first time the joy of sitting with Paul in uninterrupted bliss, listening to all that he had to tell her, returning his kisses and caresses with an ever-growing confidence.

She watched old Rachel cooking sausages for supper and listened to the gathering violence of the storm.

"What an awful night . . . I wonder where Paul is," she said.

"He'm sure to be here soon, dear," said the Cornish woman. "Don't fuss yourself."

Celia shut her eyes. She was very tired, although she had had two hours' good sleep this afternoon. Somehow she did not feel that all was well. She knew that she had defied not only Isobel, but the law in running away like this, and she was afraid there would be repercussions, not only upon herself, but on Paul. She wished, too, that she could see Jill. She wondered what was going on in the Castle . . . what line of action Isobel would take next.

A heavy gust of wind sent the raindrops spattering against the casements, across which Rachel had drawn the curtains. An oil-lamp burned on the table. Celia shivered a little.

"What an awful night. Where is Paul?"

"He'm coming soon," soothed the old woman.

For a while longer Celia sat still listening to the thunder of the gale. Every now and again the little cottage seemed to shake on its foundations. This was a real sou'wester. If it went on all night the waves would be mountainous in the morning, and when the tide went out the beach would be strewn with drift-wood.

Sometimes there were wrecks off this coast. Ships were driven by the gale and buffeted to pieces on the treacherous sunken rocks which were hidden dangers under the emerald sea.

"Do you think the fishing fleet is in?" at length Celia asked anxiously.

" 'Tis usually in before dark," said the old woman.

Then came a sound familiar to all who live on this coast and which sent the blood rushing to Celia's cheeks and made old Rachel pause in the act of dishing up her supper.

A rocket . . . the signal for the lifeboat. There must be a shipwreck somewhere just off this shore.

Celia struggled on to her feet.

"We must find out where Paul is; we must, Rachel," she said breathlessly.

Before Rachel could answer, the door opened and Paul Manton hurried into the cottage. He had to use force to close the door again, so strongly was the gale blowing. Celia looked at him wide-eyed. He was hatless and his black curls were ruffled and wet with the rain. He wore oilskins from head to foot.

"Paul!" exclaimed Celia. "Oh, Paul, I thought perhaps you were still out at sea."

He gathered her into his arms.

"*Ma petite* Celia. I've just come to tell you that I am going out with the others. There is a wreck. Did you hear the rocket? *Eh bien,* we are going to try and get near them or there will be a terrible loss of life."

"Oh, Paul," she exclaimed.

"*Adorée,* you wouldn't have me sit down and wait while the others risked their lives, would you?"

"Yes, of course you must go."

"We are all lending a hand—all who are young and strong."

"You'm a real Cornishman," said old Rachel, beaming at him.

"I love you," whispered Celia, and winding her arms

147

about his neck, covered his brown, rain-wet face with kisses. "Go on, darling, and come safely back."

A last warm kiss, and he hurried out again.

The supper which Rachel had cooked stayed in the pan untasted. Celia could do nothing but drink the strong hot tea Rachel brought her, and strain her ear for sounds. But she could hear little beyond the wind and the rain and the surge of the sea beating tumultuously down there against the rocks. She thought of Paul going out into that boiling cauldron . . . helping to man the lifeboat, which even now would be churning its way to the wrecked ship.

She thought:

"There is no peace. If it isn't one thing, it's another. Oh, Paul, my darling, come back soon."

As the moments went by, her feeling of anxiety and restlessness increased. Old Rachel tried to soothe her. Told her tales of bygone days when her husband, Ben Taylor, had been captain of the lifeboat crew . . . at that time there had been no motor-boat . . . they had had to row every inch through the teeth of the storm.

"He always came back," Rachel announced proudly. "Your Paul will be all right, my lil dear; never fear."

Celia only half-listened to the story. Every time the storm thundered and shook the cottage, her heart failed her. What boat could live in that terrible sea? She had watched so many storms . . . seen with her own eyes the power of a wave that could, by its own violence, snap in two a heavy plank of timber.

Nothing that Rachel could say would induce her to go to bed, in spite of the fact that she was still so weak and that she had had such an exhausting day, mentally and physically. She must stay up and see Paul again, she said, before she could sleep that night.

"If only I were as fit as I used to be . . . if only I could put on oilskins and go down to the harbour and watch," she said despairingly to the old woman.

"You'm not well enough to think of such a thing," said Rachel.

Celia sighed.

"I know. But waiting is so horrible. Can't you get any news for me, Rachel?"

"There is nobody up here could tell what is happening. You must wait in patience, my dear."

Somebody knocked at the door. Celia herself sprang towards that door, her heart pounding.

"They're back. That will be Paul," she exclaimed, and with a radiant look in her eyes she opened the door. For a moment she could see nothing but a dark shape silhouetted against the night. The wind tore into the warm living-room, almost knocking her off her feet. And then she heard a remembered voice which drove every spark of radiance from her face.

"Well, and how's the little runaway? I've come through the dickens of a storm to see you."

Fulke Withers walked into the room and shut the door behind him. Celia's heart sank. With fear and distrust she looked at her stepmother's friend. Fulke wore a waterproof and a tweed cap. He took off the cap and ran an eye round the living-room. Old Rachel, not quite knowing what to do, started to go upstairs, but Celia stopped her.

"No . . . no . . . stay down here, Rachel."

Fulke smiled.

"Scared to be left alone with me?"

Celia did not reply. She went back to her place on the couch at right-angles to the fire. Fulke said:

"Not a very warm welcome, and I've driven through the storm to get to you."

"How did you know I was here?"

"My dear girl, you can't hide yourself in a place the size of Cadgwith. It didn't take me long to find out where you were staying. Is Manton here?"

"No, he is not. There has been a shipwreck and he has gone to help the others in the lifeboat," she said, with a touch of pride that was both childish and pathetic.

Fulke put his hands in his pockets and stood a moment regarding her, almost curiously.

149

"You fancy yourself really in love with this fellow, don't you?"

"I know that I am."

"And you think you'd like to live in a place like this for the rest of time—ekeing out an existence—you, Miss Trevarwith. Francis Trevarwith's daughter and an heiress——?"

"I was never happy as Francis Trevarwith's daughter. I hated the Castle. You know perfectly well I hated it. I am happier here."

"But you forget, my dear, that you are under age and that your guardians have control of you for another three years."

"Did my stepmother send you here?"

"She talked things over with me—I am an old friend of the family's. You have upset your stepmother very much. I want you to be sensible and let me take you back to the Castle."

Celia's heart began to beat faster. All the time she was thinking about Paul . . . frantic with anxiety about him . . . wondering what was happening out there at sea in the teeth of the gale. She did not feel strong enough to deal with Fulke Withers alone. She wished Paul would come back. And yet . . . she dreaded these two men meeting again when she remembered the consequences of their last discussion.

She said:

"You might as well save your breath, Fulke. Go home and tell my stepmother that I don't intend ever to go back to the Castle."

"You can't stay here."

"Why not?"

"Don't you see what you are laying yourself open to? What people will say and think? They will say that you and this Frenchman . . ."

Celia interrupted, a high colour in her cheeks.

"If they think anything wrong, it won't be true. Paul and I love each other, but we intend to live apart until we can be married."

Fulke gave a laugh that was half-angry, half-amused.

"You are such a child! You have no experience of life. It's not possible for you, Celia Trevarwith, to live like this with Manton as your boy-friend. I know you hate me. That is as it may be. But I have your interests at heart. I promised your stepmother that I would not stand by and see you carry on with this absurd folly."

Celia swallowed nervously.

"You can't do anything. You can't *make* me go back to the Castle."

His eyes narrowed as he looked down at the slender figure, the lovely delicate face which haunted all his thoughts and drove him so crazy with repressed desire.

"Confound the old woman," he thought furiously. "If she wasn't in the room I'd pick the girl up in my arms and kiss her until she begged for mercy."

Aloud he said:

"No—I suppose I can't make you go home, but you'll live to regret this nonsense, Celia. Manton won't be able to look after you. And what about cash? People can't exist on air, you know."

She tilted her head.

"I shall learn to look after myself and earn my own living."

Fulke took a step toward her.

"Celia—be sensible—I——"

"Oh, do go away," she broke in, and shrank back as though he had already touched her. "I don't want you here. I don't need your help or advice. Go back and tell Isobel that I am staying here and that one day I am going to marry Paul. If I have to wait until I come of age—then I shall do so. I shall never change my mind."

Fulke hesitated. If he hadn't been so angry and so conscious of his failure to win her, he would have felt a tremendous admiration for this girl. She was small and frail and young, and yet there seemed to glow in her a veritable fire of determination. She had spirit . . . he could see that. And she was capable of great love. Why couldn't that love have been for him instead of the Frenchman?

Celia's voice interrupted his thoughts:

"Please go away and leave me alone."

He shrugged his shoulders, cast a resentful look at old Rachel, then picked up his cap and opened the door. His mission had failed. There was nothing to do for the moment but retire, rather ignominiously, to tell Isobel of his failure.

As he opened the door, Celia held a hand out nervously to old Rachel, who came to her side and whispered a word or two of encouragement. As the door opened and closed again after Fulke Withers, the rain and wind tore into the little living-room. They could hear the thunder of the waves on the rocks below. It was a violent, cruel night. Celia forgot Fulke Withers and all that he had said. She could think of nothing but Paul—her Paul in the lifeboat that was churning its way through those dark, turbulent waters.

"Oh, Rachel," she said with a sob. "Rachel, what is happening down there? Have they reached the ship? Are they turning back? We must find out. We must, or I shall go crazy."

5

Old Rachel shook her head dubiously while she rattled the poker through the grating of the little range and made the red sparks shoot up the chimney.

The gentleman who'd come after Miss Celia and behaved in what Rachel considered a most ungentlemanly manner had upset her not a little. She could not quite grasp what was going on. She was both puzzled and distressed. But she had promised her sister, and the young French fisherman, that she would look after this young lady, so she was going to do so to the best of her ability. But how was she to comfort the girl? How was she to teach her the lesson of patience, which the wives of all fishermen on this treacherous coast must learn?

"Rachel, what is happening down there?" Celia asked again, with a little moan.

"Don't take on, my love," said the old woman. "Eat your supper and wait till the lifeboat comes back."

But Celia, restless and miserable, could not eat, and could not go back to her place on the couch. Up and down the tiny living-room she walked, with her fingers feverishly clasped behind her back and her face drained of colour. Every now and again she stopped and listened intently as though for the sound of footsteps, but there was nothing to be heard save the strange wild cacophony of the storm. At intervals there would be a dead silence—as though Nature held her breath in preparation for another frenzied cry—then it would come, beginning with a low murmur, working up to a mad crash and thunder of waves and wind. Celia, who had lived all her life with these storms and never before been afraid, knew what it was tonight to experience absolute fear for Paul. It was the waiting that destroyed her. Waiting in here with old Rachel, where it was warm and safe. She wanted to be down there with *him,* rocking on that foaming sea, facing the same dangers that he faced. If only she could have been beside him, or even stood on the shore there with the other women who watched and waited! Tonight she hated her own frailty, her inability to be of any use either to Paul or anyone else.

Fulke Withers' visit had disturbed and worried her. But with his going there had passed even the memory of him. He was of no account in her life. Her stepmother, little Anthony, none of them at Storm Castle, were of any account. Celia Trevarwith had reached the ultimate conclusion in the depths of her being that she had been born into this world for Paul Manton alone. It was only Paul who mattered, now and for always.

During these tense moments of waiting for him, the love that had started as a tender girlish devotion developed into the strong searing passion of a woman. Celia understood now that the feelings of a woman were deep and secret and indestructible . . . that love meant pain and longing and, in good time, ecstasy and fulfilment. But for her, Celia, and for Paul, there might be no fulfilment. Their love was like this wild storm, against which they must battle and strive until they could reach their harbour. She only knew one sure fact: she was his and he was hers, and nothing would ever separate them—nothing but death.

In this hour she remembered her friend Jill. The little Waaf, who laughed so bravely and carried the lamp of her courage so high, had loved her young husband . . . and had lost him. Death had done that to her. Death could take away the man you loved, no matter how much you needed him, or how much he wanted to come back to you. Jill was outwardly brave. But inwardly she was broken, suffering. With all her heart, tonight, Celia pitied Jill. She pitied all women who loved. Young though she was, she was learning that life could be hard and cruel for lovers. And death could be crueller still.

She went to the little door of the cottage and put her hand on the knob in a passion of longing to open that door and go out into the storm and find Paul. In her distraught mind she prayed not only for him, but for Tim Hayling. A voiceless prayer that said: "Be merciful, oh God . . . bring Tim back to Jill. Bring Paul back to me. Oh, God, be merciful!"

Old Rachel looked at the girl's back and saw how she trembled and suffered. She went up to her and touched her on the shoulder.

"You'm making yourself worse by thinking too much, my lil dear. Come back to the fire and get warm," she begged her.

"Rachel, why can't you find out what has happened to the lifeboat?" Celia asked, turning her anguished face to the old woman.

Rachel sighed.

" 'Tis a bad night to go out, my dear, but seeing the state you're in I'll try to find Charlie Pencomb, my brother-in-law. He will know what is going on."

Celia's face cleared miraculously.

"Oh, Rachel, you darling—yes, find out for me, please. Or am I terribly selfish to ask you to go out?"

Old Rachel smiled knowingly.

"Young critters in love be always selfish, my dear. I know how you feel. When I was young, every time my man went out in that boat I was sorely afeared, but when you get older you learn patience and you take what comes."

Celia shook back her fair curls and said in a passionate voice:

"Then I never want to grow old. I never want to feel any differently. Oh, Rachel, you old darling, go and find out if the lifeboat is back again."

She helped the old woman put on her coat and tie a shawl over her white head. Rachel opened the door. The rain smote her wrinkled face and the wind curled

155

about Celia like a cold serpent. She tried to see into the night, but there was an impenetrable veil of darkness and torrential rain. The door closed behind Rachel. The girl sat down on the couch in front of the fire, steeped in her agony of love and anxiety, gaining her sharp new experience of love and the agony that goes hand in hand with it.

How long she sat there alone, brooding, she did not know, but suddenly there came a sound at the door, a kind of scuffling. Swiftly, Celia was up and on her feet and opened the door. A man with dripping oilskins stood there swaying. She saw, with one rapt look, that it was Paul. Behind him was Rachel, who said:

"The boat is in, and here's the lad himself, half-dead with cold and the buffeting he got. Quickly, let us in, my dear, and look to your lad, for he needs you."

Celia put out both her hands and Paul grasped them. She saw his face, wet and smeared, with blood on one cheek. His knuckles were torn. He was white and exhausted, hardly able to stand on his feet. He gasped her name:

"Celia, *mon amour—ma douce cherie,* I've come back to you."

Like a drunken man he swayed, trying to smile and to tell her that all was well with him, but she could see he had no strength left. His very limbs were frozen with the cold and the effort he had made down there in that wild sea.

Old Rachel, ever practical, started to drag off the young man's oilskins. She chattered as she did so, telling Celia how she had met her brother-in-law, and he had told her that the boys had made a fine show of it and had brought back most of the crew from the shipwrecked trawler. She had foundered on the rocks and it had been tough work getting alongside. They all spoke well of Paul down there, because he had taken an added risk going back to save the life of a young sailor who had been injured and slow to leave the ship. Paul himself had been almost dashed to pieces on the rocks in the effort. That accounted, he said, for his cuts and bruises.

He stood there swaying and smiling, pushing the black wet hair back from his bruised face.

"It was nothing," he muttered. "I am fine. It was nothing."

Celia, her heart swelling with pride, helped Rachel take off his soaked clothes. She looked at him with adoration. She, herself, felt suddenly strong and well, anxious to be of service to Paul—jealous even of old Rachel touching him. She wanted to be the one and only woman in the world to touch or help him.

At length he stood there clad only in his corduroy trousers, without a shirt, his body white, like marble, and as cold. Celia's warm young hands touched his icy shoulders shyly and with tenderness. She said:

"Oh, my darling, you are frozen through and through. Oh, my darling Paul, how marvellous you are!"

And she thought, in the pride of her soul, that he was as beautiful as a statue of a young god. There was something particularly young and defenceless about him like this, the brown line of sunburn accentuating the whiteness of his skin.

Old Rachel hobbled upstairs. She was going to fetch a flannel shirt that had belonged to her own man, and which, after all these years, she still kept in a bottom drawer.

In the warm firelit sitting-room, Paul and Celia looked into each other's eyes. Then she flung herself into his arms and he held her madly. Her lips covered with kisses the coldness of his shoulder, but he would not let her hide her face like that, and lifted it, and kissed her mouth. His kisses were burning. But his lips seemed as cold and salty as the sea itself.

"I would have died if you hadn't come back," Celia said breathlessly, brokenly, and her head swam with the ecstasy of his embrace.

"Je t'adore," he said in his own language. "You bring me back to life. You are so much part of me now, my

sweet little love. This night I feel you are completely mine."

"Completely," she echoed.

His face looked desperately tired and she would not let him stand there. She drew him to the couch and later, wrapped in the old grey flannel shirt and with a rug over him, he lay there growing warm and comfortable. He was infinitely happy. He had come back from the sea to his Celia . . . his angel of dear delight. She sat curled on the floor beside him with his hand locked in hers, her fair, lovely head leaning against his arm. Rachel had gone to bed. Later Paul must go back to Redruth Cottage, but not yet. He could not bear to part from Celia yet, nor she from him.

He refused to speak of his ordeal in the storm tonight. He wished to talk only of Celia—of their love and their future.

She told him about Fulke Withers' visit and of all he had said. Paul, smoking a cigarette that Celia had lighted for him, looked at her anxiously. She was well tonight, he thought. Happiness cloaked her in radiance. Her eyes were like stars. But he was still anxious for her.

"I don't know what we are going to do, *adorée*," he said. "I hate Fulke Withers, but he is right when he says one cannot live on air. You have been brought up in a Castle and have always had everything you needed. I have nothing to offer and . . ."

"Don't waste time saying those things, Paul," she broke in. "I was brought up in a Castle, but I had nothing . . . *nothing* that counted. I never knew love or tenderness. You are the first to give such things to me."

He put his lips against one of her small hands and groaned.

"I can't bear that you should have suffered so, *ma pauvre petite*. All your life you should have had worship."

"I wouldn't want anybody to worship me except you," she said with a little laugh. "And what does the past matter anyhow? It is the present . . . the future . . . that count."

"It is your future that I am worried about. I cannot marry you because you are not yet twenty-one. I cannot support you because I earn only enough to keep myself. How, then, have I the right to keep you here, away from your family?"

"Paul darling, I don't count Isobel and Anthony 'my family' any more. They hate me. The Castle is no longer my home. I have only you in the world. I am going to stay here and get a job in the village. There must be something I can do."

He threw away his cigarette and drew her close to him with a protective movement.

"I would give my life to you, you know that, heart of my heart."

"I know that and I am happier tonight than I have ever been in my life before. Think, Paul, if this were our little cottage . . . if we were married . . . if . . ."

Her voice broke. She hid her face against his shoulder. He covered her head with quick impassioned kisses.

"Mon Dieu! if it were only so. What utter happiness! I would pick you up in my arms now and carry you upstairs. You would be loved as no woman has been loved by man before. But you are still so young . . . I don't know what to do for the best. I am young, too, but older than you and more experienced. I am afraid for you . . . for both of us."

Celia kept her face hidden. Her heart was racing. This love which had made a woman of her tonight was still new and in many ways incomprehensible. But she understood what was passing through the mind of her young lover. She appreciated their difficulties, but was not defeated by them. She whispered:

"Don't be afraid for me, Paul. I will look after myself. We will help as well as love each other. One day we will be allowed to marry. Until then . . ."

"Until then," he broke in, "I swear by *le bon Dieu* that I will never hurt you and that I will be to you what

I would want a man to be to the little sister whom I left in France."

Celia looked up at him, her lashes wet with tears. He sat upright and put both arms around her. She smoothed back his black curls. They were rough and dry again. She could feel, too, that his whole body glowed; the strength and the magnificent vitality of his youth had returned to him. Tonight she knew that she was not wrong in believing that Paul Manton was a superior being, different from other men. . . . He was a poor fisherman . . . but he had a fine idealistic spirit . . . a greatness of soul which would not let him injure her or their love, nor offer her the counterfeit for love such as a man like Fulke Withers would offer.

"Don't be afraid for me, Paul," she repeated. "I know how you feel. I feel the same. I shall never belong to anyone else but you, and whatever happens we will both wait for that day."

He caught her warm sweet face between his hands and kissed her on the mouth.

"*Ma femme,*" he said after that long kiss, "I think of you already as my wife, whom one day I shall take back to France to find my own people. My mother will love you. I pray only that she will be allowed to live until she looks upon your face."

6

The night wore on. Outside old Rachel's cottage the
storm lessened in violence. The howl of the wind died
down to a sob. It grew warm in the little sitting-room
where the firelight still burned rosily, and the oil lamp
flickered on the table. Paul and Celia went on talking
. . . talking.

It was a night that Celia would never forget. The
night when Paul had come back to her from the sea,
frozen and exhausted, and she had known the wild
thrill and happiness of seeing him return to warmth
and life in her arms. The night when he had called her
his little wife and spoken of the day when they would
live together. The night on which, with all the flaming
idealism of his youth, he had hoisted the banner of his
honour and of hers, vowing never to lower it.

Was this sort of idealism out of date? Was it stupid,
a waste of time and emotion? Celia had come little into
contact with modern life herself, apart from her school-
days and the vacations spent on this lonely coast. But
she had listened to others' talk. She had seen Isobel and
her woman friends playing fast and loose with men,
sneering at morality, encouraging the go-aheads, the
lax, the set that believes in "eat, drink and be
merry, for tomorrow we die."

But Celia had never wanted to be like her stepmother. She had always had a higher standard. And now into
her life had come Paul, whose ideals were one with
hers. She was immensely happy and satisfied because of
this fact. It seemed to make everything more perfect.

She could not let him go. He did not wish to go, even

though it was now long past midnight. The passionate emotion, the gravely-taken vows, the seriously discussed future, had given place to a lighter phase. It was such fun to be here together alone. Celia made fresh tea. They drank it, and laughed and pretended that this cottage was their home.

"*Madame Manton,*" Paul called her, and that amused her enormously because it sounded so pompous and grand.

Then he teased her and told her she would always be young and gay, his *petite* gazelle, running up and down the cliff on her sandalled feet, with her hair blowing in the wind as he had first seen her. She could never become "*Madame*" anybody . . . a serious, married woman.

But she would, she assured him, and perhaps in ten or twenty years' time she would become fat and dignified and grow a moustache on her upper lip and bully him and their ten children, and he would wish that he was a young free fisherman again, flirting with the pretty girls in France.

Paul's dark eyes opened wide and he shrugged his shoulders with mock horror.

"What a picture . . . ten children! *Nom de Dieu,* how will I support them? And for you to be fat and with a moustache . . . *mais non,* not if you are to be my wife, Mademoiselle Celia. Never shall I make you *Madame Manton* if that is to be the case."

So, weak with laughing, she flung herself into his arms, promising she would never be fat or old and would stay, always, his slender gazelle. And they would have not ten children, but five, who would each be as exquisite as a dream. Poets, painters, musicians perhaps, but never sailors who might drown at sea, or soldiers to die in a war, or airmen to crash through space.

And then of course Celia fell to thinking of the terrible war that was going on in the world at this moment. So far, Paul's reserved occupation had kept him away from it. But he was trying to get into the Navy. She knew it. She was proud, and she was afraid also, remembering Jill. Quickly she steered her thoughts away from that channel and asked Paul to tell her about Dunkirk and his mother and the little sister of whom he had just spoken.

So Paul, who had a genius for drawing a vivid picture with the words he used, sat there smoking, stroking Celia's ash-gold head, telling her about his boyhood.

Poverty had been the keynote of those early days. He remembered Anna-Marie, his mother, who had been born and brought up in a fishing village near Ostende, as a strong but graceful woman with the sloe-black eyes and curls which he had inherited, and a wide, wonderful smile. She had passionately loved his father, Philippe, and lived only for him. Paul's earliest memories were of a sublime happiness which cast a glamour over the poverty-stricken little family. The glamour of father and mother who were lovers as well as husband and wife.

Anna-Marie, baking her bread, washing her linen, cooking the fish that she bought in the market every morning, lavishing her love and care on her three children—Paul who was the eldest, André a year younger and little Yvonne, who was three years younger still. A small family as families go in France, but quite enough for Paul's father, who was a painter and not a highly successful one. Oil paints and canvases were dear. Times were hard. A bachelor might paint and starve in the Latin quarter of Paris and fend for himself, but if he was a married man and he did not sell his pictures, the family must starve with him.

Yet Paul could never remember being really hungry. His mother was wonderful and managed somehow to feed her children. In her spare time she made exquisite lace which they sold. Paul had inherited the fine sensitive fingers of his father, who had been well-bred and cultured. But he revered the memory of Anna-Marie's red, coarse little hands which had been so clever, whether lace-making, managing fish-nets or baking the crisp loaves of bread on which he had fed all his life, washed down in early days by copious draughts of milk and later by the red, sweet *vin-du-pays*.

Paul inherited his father's artistic fancies, but Philippe would not allow him to indulge in them. Philippe admitted that a man must do practical work in order to live. His own life had been impractical and his little family never knew whether he would make money for them or have to borrow a sou. That was not good. Paul must learn to work. So Paul took to the sea and his mother's early trade.

André was a delicate child. He had had lung trouble from birth. Paul, who was strong and vital, had not found a companion in the delicate ailing youth, but in little Yvonne, his sister, who was a fine, beautiful girl, blue-eyed like her father and with Paul's dark curls and her mother's attractive smile. Paul adored Yvonne, and when she grew older and the young men of Dunkirk started to look at her twice, Paul kept a jealous eye upon her, determined that she should marry only the best.

Celia listened enchanted, her vivid imagination allowing her to picture in detail Paul's whole history. She could see that white-washed cottage on the beach where the Manton family had lived. The sand-dunes, the sunlit water of the sea stretching before it, and Paul playing with his small sister on that brown beach, or going into the country to hunt for *fraises de bois* and bringing back a bowl of them to eat with their supper. Philippe, the artist, sitting at his easel, when none of the children dared disturb him, or later drawing funny sketches to make them laugh. Philippe Manton, who was ever charming to Paul's mother. Paul said he never had seen his father angry or unpleasant. He was, to the end, the lover who had first captivated the beautiful Anna-Marie, and painted her in her striped petticoats and shawl with a basket of fish on her shoulder . . . the one fine piece of work he had ever seen hung in the salons of Paris.

The painter died when the boys were in their teens. After that, it had been Paul who had helped to support the little family. Then came the war . . . all the horrors of the German occupation, preceded by that terrible, wonderful epic of Dunkirk, when the little boats and the big boats had faced incredible dangers to take that weary, heroic army across to England.

Paul had been rejected for the Army because of his bad foot, a defect from birth. So he was still earning his living as a fisherman when the English and the French retreated from the grey German hordes which beset them that memorable day. And of that day Paul could speak only with a stricken face, holding fast to Celia's hands. For he had seen the little cottage, in which he had lived and known so much happiness, go up in flames. His mother he had already sent into comparative safety with Yvonne to their paternal aunt in Rouen. It was fortunate indeed that Paul had had the foresight to do this, but it had been a bitter day when the little family had broken up. And he had been afraid for them. Poor Anna-Marie and little Yvonne, with the tears streaming down their faces . . . and no André . . . for André had died only two days before . . . and they had scarcely buried him when the news had come of the German victory. Paul had made them leave Dunkirk while the flowers were still fresh on the poor boy's grave.

"But they are safe now in Rouen," Paul finished his story. "I know that, because my aunt sent a letter to me through friends in Lisbon. It is a year ago since I heard, but my aunt told me that my mother was well, and Yvonne was working there in a hospital."

"Oh, darling, you will see them again," Celia comforted him. "I shall go with you to France and love them as you do."

Paul sighed heavily.

"I could perhaps have stayed with them, but, *ma cherie,* when I saw those French soldiers going over to England, I had to join them. I had to help take one of the little boats across and rescue the wounded, who were being machine-gunned there on the beach where, as a child, I had played with Yvonne. I thought, too, that I would be more useful here. And here I am. But so far I have done nothing. To catch fish is of poor use for my country or yours. I am going to see a man to-morrow . . . a man in the French Navy who is staying in Cadgwith. I *must* get war work—be able to feel that I am really helping to set my country free. *La France Libre.* That is what I look forward to . . . and my marriage with you."

Celia pressed his hand against her cheek and then kissed it with sweet humility.

"Everything you have told me has made me love you more. And whatever you choose to do will be right. But, oh, Paul, Paul, I can't bear to think that you will leave me and that I haven't even the right to follow you as your wife."

He stood up and pulled her into his arms and kissed her with passionate tenderness.

"Don't worry, *plus adorable des femmes.* Whatever happens I will come back to you."

Celia found his oilskins and handed them to him.

"You must go now, Paul darling," she whispered. "It is so late. But you will let me know what this Naval officer says to you as soon as you've seen him, won't you?"

He gave her the promise and kissed her again. When she let him out of the cottage, it was into tranquillity after the storm. The moon pierced through the straggling clouds and silvered the still-mountainous sea. The wind had dropped, and over Cadgwith there was a deep silence. Celia watched Paul walk away from her and then shut the door and crept up to the tiny room next to Rachel's. She was so tired she could hardly stand, yet she was happy. She had grown closer to Paul tonight. In no way now did he seem a stranger. It was as though she had known him all her life . . . her Paul, and Anna-Marie, his mother, and the dark-eyed laughing Yvonne, who was working now in a hospital in Rouen and would be waiting for her brother to return to France at the end of the war. To return there with him seemed now to Celia the one thing in the world she wanted most.

She slept soundly, and without waking as she had done since her illness, nervy and unhappy. She had never felt so content and so free. In the morning she awoke refreshed, feeling stronger than she had felt for long weeks. She insisted on helping Rachel with the breakfast. She sang as she made the coffee and old Rachel smiled at her and said:

"You'm merry as a lark today, my lil dear."

Celia laughed and answered:

"I'm going to see Paul later on this afternoon."

Through the casements the sun was shining. The day was warm and cloudless, and the only reminder of last night's terrible storm was the driftwood on the beach and the little trawler out on the far point, lying half-submerged in the water, victim of the relentless elements.

It was one week later that Celia sat in Rachel's tiny garden, peeling potatoes, and could hardly believe that she had been ill for so long. She felt marvellously alive today. Whatever Paul decided to do, she intended to retain her freedom and this happiness. She would never go back to the Castle and to her stepmother's tyranny.

At lunch-time, half-way through the humble meal which she shared with old Rachel, somebody knocked on the door of the cottage and delivered a note for Miss Trevarwith.

As Celia read it, some of her radiance faded and the old anxious expression returned to her eyes.

The letter was from Isobel. It contained no reference to Celia's conduct in running away from home, but told her in plain words that it was necessary that she should return to the Castle at once because little Anthony had been taken seriously ill—so ill that they had not had time to move him from home and had sent for a surgeon who had operated on the small boy then and there. According to the doctors it was imperative that Anthony should not be allowed to cry or distress himself unduly for the first few days because of the stitches.

He asked continually for "Celie," as he called his half-sister. Neither Isobel nor the nurse seemed to satisfy him. The letter finished:

"However you choose to act in the future, I feel sure you will not refuse to come and do what you can for your little brother. I will send the car for you if you will let me know by telephone that you will come."

Celia read this letter aloud to Rachel.

Then, getting up, the girl walked to the cottage window and looked down at the beautiful beach and the milky sea. She wondered where Paul was and when she would see him. She said:

"It's difficult, Rachel. I never meant to go back, but I can hardly refuse a request like this. Anthony is my half-brother and I used to love him when he was very small, before he was old enough to become his mother's spy."

The old woman could not advise her. Miss Celia must do what she thought best.

Celia said:

"I'll go down to the post office and telephone my stepmother. Then I'll find Paul. He will tell me what to do and perhaps he will have news for me. Perhaps he will have found out what he is going to do."

7

Isobel Trevarwith had had a bad morning.

Young Anthony, spoiled and over-indulged, did not make a good patient. It was lucky for Isobel that the nurse who had been looking after Celia was still free and had returned to the Castle when Anthony had been taken ill, at noon yesterday. The small boy had run a high temperature and complained of severe internal pains. Dr. Ingles had reached the conclusion by the end of that day that the trouble was appendix. And, in his opinion, it was a case that needed immediate attention.

Hard, selfish, uncharitable though she was, Isobel Trevarwith had one soft spot—her love for her son. In panic she had telephoned to Penzance for a specialist. The Big Man had come out late at night in answer to that urgent summons and his verdict coincided with that of the local physician. What was more, he had decided to operate there and then. There was no time to get the little boy to hospital. His temperature was soaring and it would have been dangerous to take him out at night. By the time an ambulance got to Ruthlyn it might be too late. So the operation was performed in the Castle in Isobel's big bathroom, which had been turned into a theatre, and with Ingles giving the anaesthetic.

The operation proved both necessary and satisfactory. It was a case of burst appendix and threatened peritonitis. The main trouble was to keep the small boy quiet, once he came out of the anaesthetic. He was a bad subject for drugs, and the surgeon did not want him to be given them, which meant that his mother or the nurse, or anybody else available, must stay at the child's bedside and watch and amuse him without a break.

This morning Anthony's temperature had dropped and it was obvious that he would live. But he got it into his head that he wanted his half-sister. Pretty "Celie" who had always been so kind and who used to tell him such wonderful stories. He called for her continually. Then Isobel sent the message to Celia and, incidentally, it seemed to her a fair way of getting the girl to return to her home.

What a morning it had been! Not only Anthony's illness but trouble with the servants. Following upon Celia's escape with Jill Hayling, Isobel had returned to the Castle in a blind rage and dismissed old Elspeth, whom she accused of conspiracy. In tears and with bitter resentment in her heart, the little hunch-backed servant had packed and departed from the home she had known for so many years. But Isobel was to regret that action, for Mrs. Trenown, the cook, immediately untied her apron and followed Elspeth. She, too, had served the Trevarwiths for many years and loved Storm Castle, but she was not going to stay in a place where the mistress was unjust and ruthless. In her blunt Cornish fashion she told Isobel to her face that she had done a cruel and unnecessary thing, turning out the old cripple.

Isobel implored Mrs. Trenown to stay because of Anthony's illness, but Mrs. Trenown no longer cared for her mistress or the sudden trouble that had befallen the family. The servants had loved Celia. Isobel they had never liked. Celia had gone and Mrs. Trenown had no real wish to remain. So Isobel found herself having to cope with the cooking in the big kitchen which now was deserted. She could find no one from the cove to come and help her. Those who would have willingly helped Celia's mother in the past did not stir a hand to assist the present Mrs. Trevarwith. Her treatment of Miss Celia, alone, apart from her high-handed attitude towards her staff, had made her the most unpopular woman in Ruthlyn.

Isobel raged and moaned to no effect. The nurse was busy with Anthony. This main wing of the great Castle, which was in use, had to be cleaned. Meals must be prepared. Isobel, for the first time since her marriage to Francis Trevarwith, found no time in which to think of herself. She was forced to work, and it was work which she cordially disliked. She tussled with a range which she did not understand, filled the kitchen with smoke, ruined the fish which was to be their lunch, and ended up in a flood of tears.

And then Celia telephoned from Cadgwith.

It was a totally changed and chastened stepmother who spoke to the girl when she answered that call.

"Oh, Celia, please come home, if only for a few days to help me out," she whimpered. "Everything is awful. Mrs. Trenown and Elspeth have gone and my darling little Tony is desperately ill. He keeps calling for you. Please come, Celia. I was going to drive over myself to fetch you, but I can't get away. Take a taxi and I'll pay for it."

Celia's reply was cold. She sympathized about Anthony, but she was not going to show any particular sympathy for Isobel. She could guess why Elspeth and Mrs. Trenown had gone.

"You must come, Celia," came Isobel's anxious voice. "I know you think I have been very hard to you, but don't bear malice. After all, it was for your own good. I know your father wouldn't have liked you to go off with that . . ."

"I don't think we'll discuss my affairs," broke in Celia.

"Very well," said Isobel in an unusually humble voice. "But I am sure you won't refuse to come to Anthony. You are better yourself, aren't you?"

"Yes, thank you."

"Then please come, Celia."

A moment's pause, then Celia said:

"I'll come, but on condition that I don't have to see Fulke Withers."

Isobel swallowed and continued on the humble note. "Very well, I won't ask you to."

At half-past two that afternoon, Celia Trevarwith returned to her old home which she had not expected to see again so soon. As always now, Storm Castle seemed to her to cast a sinister shadow, standing there on the rugged cliff. It was full of unhappy memories. She shrank from passing through the gate into those grey, sombre walls. But she had felt that she could not refuse her stepmother's request. Anthony really needed her.

Just before leaving Cadgwith she had seen Paul. An excited, enthusiastic Paul, who had had his interview with a certain Naval Personage, with unexpectedly happy results. Happy for Paul, although Celia had felt a throb of anxiety when she heard his news.

For Paul it was to be a specialized job which required good seamanship . . . a secret mission . . . secret and dangerous.

He was to keep to the sea which he knew and loved so well, and from now onward he would be no ordinary fisherman, but a sailor, part of the crew of an organization known to few in the country. A little band of seafaring men who, in motor-boats of various types and sizes, travel nightly from the English coast to the Channel Islands and France and there pick up escaping prisoners both British and French.

It was a job after Paul's own heart, and with shining eyes he had explained to Celia as much as he could of the work he was to do. But there was little he could tell her, for he was under an oath of secrecy. Nothing must be said that could drift to enemy ears. The Germans knew that men were escaping, but from where, or how, they did not know. Celia could not be told from what harbour Paul would sail or where exactly he would land, but he might be away for two or three days at a time and always it would be a hazardous adventure . . . one that called for courage, for skill in seamanship and for the spirit which flamed so ardently in Paul Manton. The flaming spirit of desire to help Great Britain liberate his beloved France.

Celia had listened with mingled feelings. Her intense longing to keep him always near her conflicted with her pride in the part which he was now to play in the war.

"So we shall be separated," she had said, with a break in her voice.

And Paul, holding her close, had answered:

"Nothing can ever really separate us, heart of my heart. Wherever I go, you will go with me in spirit. You will help me to find and rescue those men from alien shores. What I do will be for France—and for you. There will be days of rest. *Monsieur le Capitaine,* whom I interviewed, has told me that I will have time off to come and see *ma petite femme.* Where I shall live, meanwhile, I may not say. Mostly, I think, it will be at sea."

So Paul was now in the Navy. Celia's heart was full to overflowing with love and pride in him. Part of the Navy and yet not in uniform. Still in his fisherman's jersey and oilskins, and in one of the little boats. The kind of boat that had done such mighty things at Dunkirk. It was to be a great job, performed in silence and secrecy, without publicity, but with a glory which Celia was sure would one day be rewarded.

He had not wanted her to go to the Castle in answer to Isobel's summons.

"They had treated you abominably, *ma douce cherie,*" he had said. "Why should you go back now?"

She had reminded him that Anthony was only a baby still, and a blood-relation. She would never feel right in her conscience if she did not do what she could for him. So Paul had given his consent. But he worried. For, after all, they had taken such trouble to get her away from the place which had become a prison to her. It seemed silly to go back there within a week. But Celia had reassured him. During that week she had had time to improve enormously in health and spirits. She would no longer be unable to move or look after herself. She could "cope" with her stepmother this time, she felt sure.

"I've grown up," she told Paul with a smile. "I feel a different person. And if Anthony is not really ill and it is just a trick, I shall come straight back to Cadgwith, darling."

Celia found, however, that this was no case of trickery. Anthony *was* very ill and Isobel in a state in which Celia had never seen her before. Much subdued, genuinely over-tired and overwrought. Celia hardly recognized her smart, over-painted stepmother in the woman who met her in the great hall. Isobel in dirty slacks and shirt, hair tousled, nails cracked and without their varnish, face white and tired-looking. She carried a duster and a pail. When she saw the slim figure of her stepdaughter she dropped the pail and immediately burst into tears.

"Oh, Celia, thank goodness you've come!"

Celia had never felt more surprised or embarrassed. She stared at Isobel.

"Why, Isobel——" she began.

Isobel fumbled for a handkerchief and hiccoughed with sobs. She was sure her son was going to die, she said. The Castle was haunted . . . had a "hoodoo" on it. All the servants had left . . . rats deserting the sinking ship . . . she, Francis Trevarwith's widow, was having to do all the work . . . and if she didn't do it, the nurse would go too and that would finish Anthony.

Celia listened to the torrent of words that poured from her stepmother's lips. There was much she would have liked to have said, but she kept silent. She knew it was no question of either Mrs. Trenown or Elspeth being "rats." It was Isobel herself who had driven them away; and Isobel's own reputation that accounted for the fact that none of the local women would come to help her.

Celia would have liked, too, to have pointed out to Isobel that there was a war on, and many women were doing their own work. Isobel had been spoiled and over-indulged ever since she became Mrs. Trevarwith.

"Aren't you sorry for me?" Isobel ended with a whimper.

Celia was not sorry for her. Celia was human enough to remember the tyranny and ruthlessness with which her stepmother had always treated her in the past, but she said:

"I'll do all I can to help. How is Anthony this morning?"

"Oh, it's terrible to see him," moaned Isobel. "We daren't let him move or cry and nurse is at her wit's end. We tried to get another to help her and can't. He keeps calling for you. Go to him, Celia. And you will stay, won't you?"

Celia untied the scarf from her hair and took off the short linen jacket which she was wearing. It was a warm summer's morning, but it was always cool here in the Castle. She thought of Paul and of Cadgwith and of the marvellous happiness of the simple life she had been leading with old Rachel. She sighed and said:

"I'll do what I can for Anthony for a day or two, but I intend going back to Cadgwith, Isobel."

The older woman gave her a sullen look. Worried and miserable though she was and anxious to enlist her stepdaughter's services, she hated to feel that she was being "downed" by this girl to whom she always felt such antipathy. Damn her superiority, she thought, and the cool independent spirit which always burned so brightly in that frail body. She had wanted to break Celia and had failed. Celia had escaped her. This morning she felt more than ever that, guardian and trustee though she might be to this girl, Celia was utterly remote from her . . . yes, henceforth quite inaccessible. She had gone to this man she loved. Fulke Withers would never get her now. Burying her resentment and giving way to curiosity, Isobel questioned Celia.

"What have you been doing in Cadgwith? Who are you staying with? How do you intend to live? You know you caused a scandal with everyone, leaving home like that."

"I'm sorry if I caused a scandal, but that is your

175

fault more than mine, Isobel," said the girl in a low voice. "You drove me to it. You wouldn't treat me properly and you know it. But I had no one to back me up until Paul came and Jill Hayling."

The old temper blazed dangerously close to the surface in Isobel, but she curbed it. She needed Celia, not only to help with Anthony, but for other reasons. Her financial problems were increasing and there was a pile of unpaid bills on her desk. She could not get at Celia's money without Celia's help. If big cheques were to be drawn there must be some accounting for them. Celia could say that she needed money for herself, and at the same time she could quite easily help with the upkeep of the place. Until now Isobel had fondly imagined that she would have entire control of Celia's money, but lately the lawyers and Fulke Withers had disillusioned her on that point. Equally was she aware now that she would never get the girl safely tied up to Fulke. So she must adopt other measures. And making herself more pleasant to Celia was one of them. She listened while Celia answered her questions, then shrugged her shoulders. If the girl wanted to live in a three-roomed cottage with a stupid old woman and waste herself on a common fisherman, then she must do it, but of course she was crazy. And no doubt in time she would change her mind. Isobel came to the conclusion there and then that if she made life more tolerable for Celia at Storm Castle and showed more sympathy over her love-affair, she might get the girl to remain. Celia might even eventually recognize the fact that Paul Manton was not a suitable husband.

"Oh well," Isobel said at length, "I suppose I have made a mistake in trying to control you. You'll have to go your own way now. I won't dictate any more, but I hope you realize that whatever I have done has been from the best motives. I stand in the place of your mother and I've got to try and protect you."

Celia smiled a trifle wryly.

"All right, Isobel, I'll remember that." Then with a

quick look around, she added: "Are the Waafs still here?"

"No," said Isobel shortly. "Thank goodness they have been posted elsewhere."

Celia's heart sank. She had so hoped to find Jill here. But she had had a card from her in the middle of the week warning her that there were rumours that they might be posted to a camp farther inland at any moment, so presumably that was what had happened.

She turned and walked with Isobel up the wide staircase to Anthony's bedroom.

8

At end of that afternoon Celia had wrought consider-
able changes in the household and it was a change
which Isobel had to admit was for the better. Celia was,
as she had always been, marvellously patient and sweet
with her small stepbrother. She relieved the over-tired
nurse of some of her responsibilities and amused Anthony by the hour, making up stories for him, cutting
out pictures, keeping him quiet. During that afternoon
she went down to the cove to see the Hoskins and appeal for domestic help for the Castle.

She achieved what Isobel Trevarwith could never
have done: the support of at least one or two of the old
friends who had loved and served her and her mother.
Edith, herself, volunteered to go up and cook the mid-
day meal, and the faithful Elspeth was traced and
found. She was lodging in the village with a friend.
Poor Elspeth was fretting for her familiar surroundings.
Nothing would have induced her to go back to Isobel,
but the knowledge that Miss Celia was once more at
home, and wanted her, soon made her change her attitude. So by nightfall Elspeth had been reinstated and
Isobel at night had only to heat up the excellent dishes
which Edith Hoskins had cooked. Isobel had never been
more relieved. But she resented, bitterly, her stepdaughter's popularity and her own lack of it.

Mrs. Hoskins and Elspeth were both overjoyed to see
Miss Celia again, and particularly, as Edith Hoskins
remarked, because she was looking so much like her
old self. The week's rest in the sunshine at Cadgwith
had given her a new tan, and a look of strength and

contentment which she had never worn before. The old servants were delighted because she had made up her mind to defy her stepmother's authority and stated openly that she was going to marry her Paul. But when they asked if she meant to remain at Storm Castle, her reply was in the negative.

"I must go back to Cadgwith as soon as I think Anthony is better. Paul may have to go away from me very soon and I must see him as much as I can."

The first day of her return to her old home seemed one of the longest on record to Celia. She missed the tiny cottage and old Rachel, and most of all she missed Paul, who all this last week had come daily to see her. But it was obvious to her that her presence was really needed in the Castle at the moment and she could not regret coming. Dr. Ingles, just before dinner, had looked in to see the patient, and said that Anthony's pulse was stronger and that he was already a better colour after a quiet day without tears or fuss. All Anthony's earlier devotion to "Celie" had returned. He was good and obedient when she was with him and took his medicine and treatment at her hand without whining.

"You're looking better too, young lady," Dr. Ingles remarked to Celia. "Seems to me that week's change at Cadgwith has done you a power of good."

"It has," said Celia, with shining eyes.

But she was homesick for Cadgwith and Paul. The Castle seemed empty and unattractive to her in every way. It no longer gave her the slightest suggestion of "home." Home could only be where Paul was. And she was not misled by Isobel's flattery or new show of friendliness. She knew that the woman would never like her, any more than she liked Isobel at heart. She wished that dear Jill had not been moved. One of the things she had most looked forward to was seeing Jill again.

Isobel did not seem to know the address of the camp to which Jill had moved, but presumably she, Celia, would hear before long. She knew that Jill would not forget her. Indeed, Jill had expressed the hope, when

179

she wrote, that if she got forty-eight hours' leave she might spend it in Cadgwith with Celia.

Celia slept that night in her old bedroom in the turret. How strange it seemed and how different her feelings were tonight, she reflected. The Celia who used to sleep up here had been a timid young girl with nothing in her life to look forward to. But the Celia who came back here was a resolute young woman ready to defy the whole world for the man she loved. She could never be bullied or frightened again by anybody. That was what Paul's love had done for her. She slept that night with the thought of him deep in her heart, flooding her whole being with ecstasy and thankfulness.

That next afternoon, by arrangement, Paul telephoned to Celia. Isobel answered the call and knew at once that it was the Frenchman. But whereas a week ago she would have jerked down the receiver and refused to let him speak to Celia, now she grudgingly handed the instrument to the girl. It had been such heaven to be able to stay in bed for breakfast again and feel relieved of some of her anxiety about her son. She dared not antagonize Celia. She knew well that the girl was solely responsible for improved conditions at the Castle.

"Here you are," she said. "It's your boy-friend."

Celia, with fast-beating heart, answered the call.

"Hello, Paul, my darling."

"My dar*leeng,*" he said in English. "How are you?"

"Well. Perfectly all right."

"And the little stepbrother?"

"Better today, but he has been very ill and I feel I ought to stay here for a few more days."

An instant's silence, and then came Paul's voice on a slightly changed note.

"Then we will not be able to see each other. I have just had my orders. I leave Cadgwith late tonight."

Celia caught her lower lip between her teeth and the colour ebbed from her face. Paul going so soon! She said:

"Oh, Paul, *Paul!*"

"I must see you," he said.

"And I must see you . . ." Celia turned and looked over her shoulder at her stepmother, who was standing there. Isobel was watching and listening. She saw the girl's change of expression.

"Anything wrong?"

"Yes, Paul is going away. I must get back to Cadgwith at once."

"Nonsense," said Isobel sharply. "You can't leave Anthony now. It would be inhuman of you."

"Hello! Hello!" came Paul's anxious voice.

"Hold on a moment, darling. . . ." Celia then put her hand over the instrument and turned back to her stepmother.

"Isobel, he's going and I may never see him again. It wouldn't be human for me to stay here and not see him. I *must* go. I'll come back. You and nurse must manage till I come."

The violent temper which was always so close to the surface in Isobel surged up, and she controlled it only by a tremendous effort, still fearing to antagonize her stepdaughter. She said:

"You mustn't go, Celia. For Tony's sake you mustn't, please!"

Celia felt cornered. She turned back to the telephone.

"Paul . . . Paul, are you there?"

"Yes, yes, I am here. What is it, *cherie?*"

"My stepmother feels that I oughtn't to leave. Oh, Paul, I don't know what to do."

"So! You are once more a prisoner. I knew it. I knew I ought never to have let you leave Rachel."

"No, it isn't that. I could get away if I wanted to," said Celia desperately. "But Anthony is very ill. It's my duty to stay."

Another instant's silence, then from Paul:

"*Mon Dieu!* But what can we do? We have so much to talk about . . . to arrange, in case it is a long time before I see you again."

A frantic feeling seized the girl. Duty to her little stepbrother paled into insignificance beside her overwhelming love for this man who . . . if the worst came to the worst . . . she *might never see again*. Once again she told Paul to wait and turned back to Isobel.

"I must go to Paul," she cried. "You've got to understand. I'll come back later today, Isobel, but I *must* go now."

Then Isobel lost her temper, her nerves already badly frayed.

She screamed at Celia in the old ugly way, calling her every name under the sun, accusing her of wishing to be the death of Anthony in order to satisfy her own selfish wishes. She was behaving like a kitchenmaid, she said, with her common fisher-boy.

"If you go, you go, and I have finished with you," she ended savagely. "You'll never see any of us again. I swear it. You won't get a penny of your money either. I'll fix it with the lawyers. I'll have you certified. I'll see you starve before I raise a hand to help you. I . . ." she broke off and began to cry with sheer rage . . . furious with Celia . . . furious, also, with herself for losing her temper when she had made up her mind to get Celia on her side.

"Celia . . . Celia . . . *cherie* . . . hello! What is going on?" came Paul's voice over the telephone.

The girl, sick at heart, answered him.

"I'll explain later. Wait for me at Rachel's. I'm coming, now, at once, somehow. Yes, I'll manage. *A bientôt*. Paul, my darling."

She put down the receiver and turned to her stepmother, who was sitting on the edge of a chair crying.

"Oh, Isobel," she said. "Must we go on like this? I didn't want this to happen. I wanted to do my best for Anthony, but surely you must see that if Paul is going away it is urgent that I should see him and settle up our affairs."

Isobel did not look up. She took on a new note.

"All right. Go, and be the death of Anthony," she moaned.

"Can't you sit with him for a while? Just for a few hours" . . . began Celia.

Then a shaft of the mellow light of the setting sun fell across the stone floor of the hall as the big oaken door slowly opened. The shadow of a man stood there on the threshold, silhouetted against the brightness. With a sinking heart Celia recognized Fulke Withers—the last person on earth she wanted to see. He came in, removing his hat, and fingering his tie and collar rather nervously. He looked harmless and stupid, but she hated him.

Isobel also looked up, saw her old friend and began to cry again noisily.

"For heaven's sake, Fulke Withers, why must *you* add to all the trouble? I thought I told you not to come while Celia was here?"

He regarded her coldly.

"I'm not used to taking orders from you, Isobel."

Celia gave a hunted look, first at the man, then at her stepmother.

"I'm sorry, but I can't wait . . . I must go. I'll find a car . . . a bicycle . . . anything."

"So you're going away, are you?" asked Fulke.

He stared at her slim figure with the old brooding, thwarted desire in his eyes. Why the devil couldn't he get this girl out of his thoughts? When he had last seen her at Cadgwith, the night of the storm, he had made up his mind to give up all hopes of getting Celia Trevarwith for a wife. But when he had heard that she was returning to the Castle to nurse young Anthony, that hope had revived. Now that he saw her again he was aware that no other woman counted with him. (He had tried this last week—he had been taking out a very attractive young woman whom he knew was his for the asking. But she had seemed to him stupid and too easily mastered.) Celia's remoteness was one of her great attractions, and the undeniable beauty of those large green-blue eyes—the blue-green of the Atlantic; as deep and as unfathomable. That sweet, passionate mouth. Her new tan was glorious in contrast to the extreme fairness of her hair, he thought.

He said:

"So you are going back to Cadgwith now, at once?"

"Yes, I've got to go. Isobel doesn't want me to leave Anthony, but I must—for today anyhow. Paul has got a new job and he is going away. I must see him and say good-bye. I must get to Cadgwith *somehow,* and at once."

Fulke's brain worked rapidly. So Manton had a new job and was going away. That was good news. Then a fresh thought struck him.

He asked her:

"How do you intend to get there?"

"I don't know," said Celia helplessly, "that's the trouble. It's expensive to hire a car and I haven't a bicycle. I must walk."

"Don't be a little fool," said Fulke. "You can't walk to Cadgwith. It will be dark soon."

"But I must see Paul."

"Very well. I'll take you. I've got my car outside."

Both the women stared at him. Isobel gave a harsh laugh.

"So you'll take her, will you? That's damned funny. Why not offer to be witness at the marriage?"

Fulke ignored Isobel and kept his eyes upon Celia.

"If you'll trust me, Celia, I'll drive you to Cadgwith. I mean it. I'd like to show you that I'm sorry for all that's happened. I don't see why you shouldn't say good-bye to your friend. After all, you've made it pretty clear that you are crazy about him, and it's not much good trying to stop you. Will you come with me?"

Celia hesitated. Her dislike of Fulke battled with her intense longing to get to Paul. Then in a flash she made up her mind.

"Yes, thank you . . . thank you very much. I'll come. Wait while I go up and get my coat."

She ran up the stairs. Fulke watched the swift grace of her bitterly.

Isobel shrugged her shoulders.

"You must be out of your mind? Why are *you* helping on this affair?"

He lit a cgarette and smiled wryly.

"Use your brains, my dear Isobel. There are at times many different reasons why a car doesn't get to its destination. . . . For instance, why shouldn't I divert the course and end up at night with a breakdown in a nice lonely spot. By the time someone came our way it might even be too late for Celia to see her Paul. He might have gone, mightn't he? And she might have to spend quite a few hours alone with me . . . mightn't she?"

Isobel drew a long breath.

"Oh! I see. *That's* how the land lies! Good old Fulke!"

9

Fulke Withers sat down and waited for Celia. He looked as he felt—ill-at-ease, bitter, knowing himself to be every kind of a cad, yet driven to this senseless torturing of the girl he wanted so madly for the very reason that his madness had no other outlet.

Isobel eyed him a trifle dubiously.

"All the same . . . I don't quite know where this is going to lead you, and it is only antagonizing that little fool of a girl still further."

Fulke raised eyes that were a trifle bloodshot. The hand carrying the cigarette to his lips trembled. He had been drinking more than was good for him lately. His powerfully-built body sagged a little. He was growing flabby. The sight of him astonished Isobel. She had always thought Fulke a hard nut to crack, keener about horses than about women. She could not understand what it was in her stepdaughter that could turn a man of Fulke's temperament into *this*. But she never had seen Celia's attraction. From the well-remembered night of her home-coming here to this Castle as a bride, when Celia had openly declared war, young and unformed though she was, Isobel had disliked her. She still thought of her as a maddeningly irritating child. What Fulke, or any fullblooded man, would get out of marriage with her, Lord alone knew. But that was Fulke's funeral. And if he could stop Celia from meeting Paul Manton, so much the better. After all, it *would* be a disaster if Celia and her inheritance went to the penniless Frenchman.

"Oh, well," Fulke was saying, "at least I can make

it hard for Celia to keep her date with this fellow. She says he is going away. Let him go . . . without seeing her."

Isobel's sharp ears detected Celia's light step on the stairs. She put a warning finger to her lips. Celia came hurrying into the room, her camel's-hair coat over her linen dress and her head tied up with a scarf.

"I'm ready," she said.

Isobel twisted her lips and eyed her stepdaughter coldly.

"I think it is very selfish of you, leaving Anthony like this, but as long as Fulke brings you back I don't mind."

"I'll come back," said Celia quietly.

Fulke rose and stubbed the end of his cigarette in an ash-tray.

"Come along then."

Outside, the warm summer's day was darkening. The faint lilac hue of twilight hung across the landscape and turned the sea to a mist of purple. Where the waves lapped against the rocks the foam creamed and sprayed. The western sky was ablaze with the crimson of the sun's last rays.

Celia settled herself in the car beside Fulke and gave a deep sigh. It was so lovely here at this hour. Peaceful and quiet except for the plaintive cry of the gulls as they wheeled and circled over the cliffs. If only it were Paul beside her instead of Fulke Withers, she thought. If only she and Paul were driving away together to some lonely spot where no one could follow or disturb them. Why must he be taken from her now when she loved and needed him so much? All her life she had been alone. Paul's coming had made all the difference to her. When he left her she would be more than ever lonely. He had said he would come back, would be able to see her at intervals. But she was afraid for him. She could not feel brave tonight. She hated this war; all its insensate cruelty. She felt like putting her face in her hands and crying as though her heart would break.

Instead, she tried to make polite conversation with Fulke.

"It's kind of you to take me to Cadgwith," she said in a set little voice.

"That's O.K.," said Fulke briefly, and put his foot on the accelerator. The car shot forward at high speed and made Celia catch her breath a little. She wanted to get to Paul quickly, but not at a dangerous rate, and Fulke appeared to be driving like a madman this evening.

Celia hid her nervousness by talking again.

"You still seem to be able to get plenty of petrol, don't you?" she asked.

"I get a supplementary allowance," was his reply. "I have to use the car for going around my works for a dozen reasons."

"Doesn't it use up more petrol when you drive so fast?"

He gave a hard laugh and stole a swift glance at her troubled face.

"On the contrary. Why? Are you scared?"

"The hedges are very high and there are a lot of bends on this road," she reminded him.

He laughed again and Celia's heart began to hammer as they rounded a bend on the wrong side of the road. Fulke must be crazy.

"There is no need for such hurry," she said.

Fulke did not answer. And suddenly, to Celia's surprise, he turned off the main road and accelerated along a by-road which, to her knowledge, led to the village of Kyland. And now for the first time a feeling of mistrust shot through her. She looked with startled eyes at the man.

"Fulke! Fulke!" she said, "this isn't the way to Cadgwith."

"It's my way," he said between set teeth.

The colour left her cheeks.

"Fulke, it's not the way to Cadgwith," she repeated. "You know I've got to get there. Paul is leaving to-night."

"Stop talking about Paul," said Fulke savagely. "I'm sick of the fellow's name."

Celia opened her mouth to protest, but closed it again and gave a little gasp as Fulke swerved to avoid a horse and cart, then careered on down the narrow roadway. Every moment now the light was fading. In the distance Celia could see a steeple which marked Kyland church. They were a couple of miles off the direct route to Cadgwith, and Celia realized at last, with a sense of utter dismay, how she had been tricked. This vile cheat of a man had never meant to take her to Paul. She might have known it. And yet she had not thought even him capable of this.

She half-rose in her seat.

"Stop, Fulke. Stop the car. Let me out!" she began to scream at him.

With his left hand he pushed her violently down.

"You'll kill us both if you don't sit still. This is my car and you are going just where I want to take you, so to hell . . ."

"Fulke!" she screamed again.

He took no notice of her. He was driving at eighty miles an hour now. The car was a Lagonda and could do it, but he was risking the fact that they might meet an oncoming car. This road was too narrow to allow two vehicles to pass each other at high speed.

Celia sat like one transfixed, and with a growing sensation of helplessness and horror. It flashed into her mind that Fulke was not quite sane—or drunk. Possibly that. She had heard her stepmother say that Fulke had lately taken to hard drinking. It was supposed to be because he was so madly in love with her. But that did not rouse an ounce of pity in her. He was vile to behave like this. If he cared for her at all he would never have done this to her. It was not that she was afraid of him, personally. She had "grown up" quite a bit since that night of the dance when he had made love to her in the car and scared her out of her wits. She thought she could deal with *that* side of him. But she was afraid that she might miss seeing Paul—mortally afraid. He would wonder where she was. He might even come in search of her, and then they would lose each other hopelessly. She would never be able to wish him God-speed or feel his farewell kiss on her mouth.

She looked with despair at Fulke.

"Please, please stop and let me out," she said in a frenzied voice. "It means everything to me. Fulke, if you are fond of me at all, let me out, or for heaven's sake let's turn back. Take me to Cadgwith."

"You're coming to Kyland with me," said Fulke thickly.

And then they met that other car . . . a big American saloon which bore the markings of the R.A.F. and in which there were two officers in uniform. It was too late for either car to pull aside. Fulke, the fumes of alcohol and madness clearing from his brain, jammed on all the brakes. The driver of the other car did the same. But not before the front wheels of both vehicles had looked and jammed, the two bonnets telescoping. A hideous sound of scraping metal and crashing glass rent the still air. Celia felt the violent impact, and from a distance heard the thin screaming of her own voice and Fulke's hoarse cry. Then she lost consciousness.

When she recovered, she found herself lying on a bank by the road. A young man in Air Force uniform was supporting her with one arm, and holding a flask to her lips.

"Come on, drink this," she heard a brisk voice saying. "It will do you good."

Celia choked and spluttered as the raw whisky trickled down her throat. Then she sat upright and pushed a wave of hair back from her face.

"Oh!" she moaned. "What has happened?"

"I'll tell you what's happened," said the young officer grimly. "Your pal was driving like a ruddy lunatic and might have killed us all if both our cars hadn't had such good brakes. As it is they are heaped up, and your boy friend has got a broken arm and a gash across his cheek which I don't hesitate to say he richly deserves. He must have been tight."

Celia swallowed hard. She gave a quick look around her. Twilight was deepening to the shadows of evening. Only vaguely could she see the two cars grotesquely twisted and locked together. Fulke was sitting in the ditch nursing one arm while an R.A.F. corporal tried to staunch the flow of blood from his cheek.

The young officer helped Celia on to her feet.

"Damned lucky you aren't hurt," he said. "Not a scratch. I think you just fainted from shock."

Celia nodded. She was still suffering from shock and she felt sick, but the thought of Paul was imminent in her mind.

"Listen," she said. "I don't know who you are, but I've got to get to Cadgwith. I've got to get there at once. It is terribly important."

"I'm Flight-Lieutenant Pierce," he said. "And you?"

"I'm Celia Trevarwith. My home is in Ruthlyn Cove, but I've got to get to Cadgwith."

"But you weren't going to Cadgwith!" said Simon Pierce, staring at the girl. "You were heading for Kyland."

"I know. I can't explain now. But do please help me get to Cadgwith. My . . . my fiancé expects me and he's due to leave in a few hours' time . . . he's going to sea . . . I must see him before he goes."

The Flight-Lieutenant stared again. Through the dusk he could see the beauty of this girl's slim form, her delicate face and fair, curling hair. Simon was very susceptible to feminine beauty. Good Lord! He'd been at the aerodrome here for months, bored stiff, and this was an event . . . crashing into a Lagonda driven by a crazy civilian and finding a damsel in distress, and that damsel a lovely blonde with the longest eyelashes he had ever seen. At the same time the word "fiancé" rather took the gilt off the gingerbread. Flight-Lieutenant Simon Pierce took off his cap and ran his fingers through his thick curly hair.

"Hm! Well, if you've got to get to Cadgwith, then it

must be done. Lucky for us we've got another R.A.F. car coming along any minute. And luckier still that . . ." he indicated the two shattered vehicles on the road . . . "wasn't bang in the middle. We must have both steered toward the hedge. There is room to get by. Not allowed to take civilians in our cars as a rule, but there are special circumstances. Can't leave you here on the road to face the night, can we? What shall we do with your boy friend? Take him to Cadgwith too?"

Celia gave a shuddering look at Fulke.

"No. He lives at Kyland House, and he is *not* my boy friend."

"Sorry. Kyland House, eh? But doesn't that belong to the fellow who is doing all the work at the aerodrome for us?"

"Yes—this is Mr. Withers."

Simon eyed the huddled man on the roadside with withering contempt.

"Then he ought to know better than to drive his bally car at such a speed. Ah! Here's our relief."

Celia looked eagerly at the R.A.F. car which was now coming along the road. Her heart began to beat more normally. The feeling of sickness passed. It had been a most unpleasant episode. Terrifying to say the least of it . . . but so long as she got to Paul tonight she did not care.

She took a step toward Fulke Withers and spoke to him.

"I hear your arm is broken. I'm sorry," she said in an icy little voice, "but it is entirely your own fault. You might have killed us both and injured these men. Besides, what you did to me tonight was a beastly rotten trick. I'll never forgive it or forget it. I've finished with you absolutely, Fulke Withers, and I'll never speak to you as long as I live."

He raised a face which looked grey in the fading light, nursing his injured cheek with his uninjured hand.

"Well, you've won. What does it matter anyhow?" he muttered.

"I think you must be out of your mind," said Celia. "Even if you had stopped me from seeing Paul tonight, you couldn't have kept me from him altogether. Nothing can. I'm going to marry him in spite of you and Isobel."

Fulke, however, had nothing further to say. He was sober now and vastly sorry for himself; fed up with the whole affair, and more than a little penitent that he had behaved in such a fashion. Bitterly he watched Celia being helped into the car which had just pulled up.

"Drive this lady to Cadgwith, Rex old boy," Simon Pierce said to the man at the wheel. "I'll wait here until you came back, then you can take me back to the Mess and we'll deposit this blasted lunatic at Kyland House. He ought to be locked up. I'll see that there is a case against him, I can tell you."

He slammed the car door, and Celia sank back in her seat with a little choking sob of thankfulness. She was going to Paul at last. With any luck she would get to him in time and there would be no more trouble with Fulke Withers. That was ended once and for all, she felt sure.

10

For the last two hours Paul Manton had been pacing up and down the tiny living-room of old Rachel's cottage. He had smoked every cigarette in his possession. Now he had no more. Every few minutes he opened the door and looked anxiously out into the dusk, only to return to Rachel with an expressive and very French shrug of his shoulders.

"No sign of her. *Mon Dieu!* Where can she be? She said she would come right away."

Old Rachel, standing over the fire on which she was cooking a rabbit stew, shook her head.

"She'll turn up, lad. Easy on!"

"But you do not understand. It is that I must leave here in an hour's time!" said Paul frantically.

It was nearly seven. At eight o'clock he must meet the two English Naval officers who were driving him to the secret harbour from which he was to start operations tonight. The thrill of going on this job—of having been chosen for it because he was French and knew his native coast—would have been terrific if only his adored Celia had been here to bid him *adieu*. But he felt sure that something had happened to her. Only one hour left. It would be difficult to go away without knowing why she had not come. In another moment he would telephone to the Castle, even at the risk of upsetting her stepmother, and that he did not wish to do in case it reacted on poor little Celia.

And then he heard a car pull up outside the cottage and his heart gave a great leap. He flung open the door and saw an R.A.F. vehicle and a young man in uniform helping Celia out.

"Celia!" Paul exclaimed. *"Bon Dieu,* are you all right?"

She ran to him and was caught and held close to his heart.

"Oh, Paul *darling,* I was so terrified you would be gone."

"But where have you been? What has kept you, *cherie?"*

"I'll tell you everything in a minute," she said breathlessly. "Just a moment."

She turned and held out her hand to the R.A.F. officer.

"Thank you. Thank you a thousand times for bringing me here," she said.

The officer murmured good night, gave a quick, curious glance at Paul, then saluted and returned to his car. Paul drew Celia into the cottage and closed the door.

"Now," she said, "I can explain . . ."

But first she embraced old Rachel, who beamed at the girl, delighted to see her back. Then she threw herself into Paul's arms again, half-laughing, and half-crying.

"You can't dream what I've been through. I was nearly killed. Fulke Withers was out of his mind . . . oh, it is so marvellous to be back here in this darling little cottage. I've hated the Castle. I've longed to get back!"

She proceeded to tell Paul and the old woman exactly what had happened tonight. As Paul listened, his brown young face hardened and his eyes narrowed to slits.

"Mon Dieu . . . that *swine* . . . I would like to kill him. It might have been the end of you . . . you might have been terribly hurt, *ma pauvre petite.* What a catastrophe!"

Celia smiled and pressed her cheek against his.

"But I am not hurt. I'm all right. And now that I've got to you, I'm in heaven again."

"My beloved, precious little darling," said Paul passionately, and covered her face and head with kisses. *"Mon Dieu,* if there is a scratch on your lovely little face, I will do a murder."

She laughed at his extravagance and clung to him, her heart at peace again as she surrendered to his caressing hands, his fervent kisses.

"I'm all right . . . absolutely . . . honestly you needn't worry, Paul. But it's a miracle that I've got to you . . . it was a near shave."

Old Rachel looked at the girl and said:

"Mercy on us, you'm going through it, my poor lil dear."

"But I'm so happy now, Rachel," said the girl, and her rose-flushed cheeks, her shining eyes proved the truth of her words. She sat on the little sofa, with Paul's arms around her. They drank in each other's gaze thirstily, as though they had been separated for years. He made her tell him everything that had happened to her since she went to Storm Castle two days ago.

"You are not to go back there again," he said. "I will not have it. You are to stay here in the cottage with our good friend."

"I must go back until Anthony is quite well," said Celia. "I promised my stepmother and I shall keep my word. I shall go back in the morning on the first bus. He really is pathetic, Paul. He has been desperately ill and since his operation he seems to love me again as he used to do when he was a tiny boy."

Paul looked at her anxiously.

"But this terrible man, Mr. Withers . . . he is not safe with you. You cannot be laid open to his madness."

"I don't think he will bother me again, Paul. It was my own fault for trusting him. I should never have let him take me out in his car, but it never struck me that anybody could behave so vilely. I told him tonight that I will never speak to him again as long as I live, and I mean it."

Paul sighed.

"Well! It must be as you wish, *mon coeur*. But I shall feel happier when you are back here again."

"At the end of the week I'll come back," said Celia. "And now tell me, my darling Paul . . . when do you go?"

He looked at the grandfather clock which was so much too big and clumsy for the little room, but which had belonged to Rachel's father and his father before that. (Nothing would have induced her to get rid of it.)

"I have three-quarters of an hour, *mon amour,* and after that . . ."

She put his hand against her cheek and looked at him with all her soul in her eyes.

"Oh, Paul—after that! . . ."

His features softened to the smile which was for her alone, and which made his young face look inexpressibly tender and charming.

"After that, maybe an exciting journey, *ma petite,* and then I shall come back to you, and we will be happy again—like this."

She shut her eyes and sighed deeply, pressing her cheek against the rough sleeve of his fisherman's jersey.

"I shall always be here, waiting for you . . . always, darling."

"Ma petite femme!" he whispered.

She gave a little laugh.

"Your *petite femme* must buck up and look for a job in the village. In lots of the big houses they will be glad of domestic help. I must be able to pay Rachel for having me here."

"I have already given her something for the next week or two," said Paul rapidly in French. "I am to get much more money now that I work for the Navy. I can afford to keep you just as though you were, indeed, my wife."

"No, I can't allow that."

He laughed and kissed her hands each in turn.

"It is the duty of a good wife to obey her husband."

"But, oh, Paul my darling, we aren't married yet."

"In mind we are married and I think of you as *ma*

197

petite femme. I must be allowed to help you. It gives me the most exquisite pleasure to do so. Please do not argue, *ma douce cherie.*"

She sighed and looked at him rather sadly.

"I wouldn't for the world waste these precious moments by arguing. And look—you must eat your supper—it is ready, Rachel's lovely rabbit-stew."

"I will eat only if you will."

Her eyes filled with tears. Such utter love, Paul's complete absorption in her seemed the most wonderful thing in the world after the long years of repression, of solitude, at Storm Castle.

In that moment she thought of her father and of the last words he had ever spoken to her on this earth:

"I wish I had been kinder to you, my poor little Celia . . ."

But he had died before he could show her any kindness, and she had gone on suffering at the hands of Isobel . . . eating her heart out. Now Paul was making up for everything. She wished that she could tell her father about Paul. Most of all she wished she could tell her mother.

The three of them ate their humble supper together, washed down by cups of Rachel's strong, good tea. All through the meal Paul and Celia held hands, scarcely taking their eyes from each other. Every time Paul laid down his fork Celia urged him to go on eating.

"You don't know what lies in front of you. You must eat well, my darling," she would say.

Then he would kiss the small hand that replaced the fork in his, and carry on with his meal, his dark intense eyes still watching her, his heart on fire with love and longing.

Finally old Rachel murmured an excuse and went upstairs so that they might have a few moments alone together.

Then the supper was pushed aside. The boy and the girl sat together on the sofa again, their arms about each other, their lips locked in one long kiss after the other.

Never as long as Celia lived was she to forget this hour of happiness with him . . . those slow, deep kisses that woke all the ardent womanhood in her and to which she responded with all the fervour of her being.

"Ma femme .. . mon coeur . . . soul of my soul," he murmured between those kisses.

Her eyes were wet with wild tears. She locked her arms about his neck and drew his dark, handsome head down to her breast.

"Mon amour . . . you must come back to me soon. I love you so much!" she whispered.

Against her lips he answered:

"I shall come back."

She wanted to believe him. She wanted to feel that they could never be separated either in this world or the next. But when she thought of Jill Hayling a little cold feeling of fear shivered through the warmth of her heart. He might not come back. Thousands of young men engaged on secret operations on the land, the sea and in the air bade farewell to the women they loved and did not return. She tried not to let that fear spoil this moment. In silence she returned Paul's kisses, glad that it had not been with her as with so many other girls who fell in and out of love easily. Paul was the first with her and would be the last. For him, too, she knew that in spite of his volatile Latin temperament and the great charm that he had for women, it was the same. She, Celia, was his first, his only love.

When the time came for him to put on his cap and coat and leave her, she was quite calm. She knew that this sort of thing might happen a great many more times in the future, as it did for all the other women in a world at war. There would be supreme moments together, then a parting and all the anxiety of waiting. But she wanted Paul to think of his *"petite femme"* as a creature of courage. The tears could come afterwards when he had gone.

One last fervent embrace, then Paul put her gently from him.

"Au revoir, my very dearest heart . . . or, as they say

in your country, 'so long.' It must never be good-bye for us."

"So long, darling," she said softly, smiling.

He gave a last impassioned look at the slender grace of her . . . cheeks still rich red from so much kissing . . . eyes luminous and beautiful, mirroring the passion from his own . . . fair curls tumbled about her neck, touched with deep gold from the firelight. And he thought:

"What man would not want to die for her as well as for his country, if need be? She is typical of all that is good and sweet in womanhood."

Then he was gone, and for Celia the tears came, wild and furious. She lay face downwards on the sofa. Old Rachel tried to comfort her.

"You'm going to be brave, my lil dear. He'll come back. 'Tis a cruel war and 'tis women who must go through cruel suffering when their men get taken away to fight."

"Oh, Rachel, it would be better if I could fight too. If I could be like other girls I have seen in uniform, or even in factories. If only my stepmother would let me join up . . . but she won't. If I did, she could stop me. Oh, I wish I were twenty. No! I wish I were twenty-one so that I could marry Paul."

Rachel patted the fair head and murmured:

"Now, now, you'm to be patient, my lil dear. I'll look after you. Old Rachel will look after you, meantime."

Celia kissed and hugged the old woman.

"You've been an angel to us both. I'll never forget it, Rachel."

And now that Paul had gone she wished that she need not go back to her old home, and that she could stay here with the old woman who liked Paul and who appreciated their feelings. But she had given Isobel her promise to return to the Castle, and the thought of the little boy calling for her when he was still so weak and ill induced her to keep that promise.

She was utterly exhausted in body and mind when she went to bed that night.

First thing in the morning she was up, and caught the first bus to Ruthlyn Cove.

The fine weather had broken. It had been raining during the night. A thick mist hung over sea and land. Celia felt cold and depressed. Where was Paul now? Was he at sea in that fog? She shivered at the thought. But better not to let her imagination play fast and loose with her now. She was in low spirits when she reached the Castle and walked up the familiar drive.

Elspeth was sweeping the hall. The little hunchback greeted the girl affectionately.

"Good morning, Miss Celia. 'Tis good to see your sweet face. The mistress, she'm asking for you. She said as soon as you come you was to go up to her room."

Celia, hands thrust in the pockets of her coat, walked upstairs smiling wryly. Already Paul and the wonderful moments in Rachel's cottage seemed like a fevered, passionate dream. Now she had slipped back to the old tyranny . . . the old sinister coldness and hostility of Storm Castle weighed her down.

11

Celia found her stepmother in one of her worst moods.
The room was in its usual state of disorder. Isobel was
in bed writing letters. Her red hair was flattened down
by a net, and there was grease on her face. She looked,
thought Celia, positively ugly, and she was beginning
to age. The thin, down-turned mouth, the whole expression, showed such bitter discontent.

"So you are back!" Isobel flung at her stepdaughter.
"And about time too. Nurse says Anthony is in a nice
state because you weren't here when he woke up."

"I'm sorry," said Celia, taking off her coat. "I'd have
been back before if Fulke Withers had behaved himself, but . . ."

"I don't care what Fulke did. I don't care about anything except that my home has been taken from me.
Why, Celia Trevarwith, if your father knew, I wonder
what he'd have to say . . ."

Celia stared.

"What's happened, Isobel?"

The older woman screwed a half-written letter into a
ball and flung it viciously on to the floor. The grey light
of the foggy morning, filtering through the narrow windows, gave her an unattractive greenish pallor. Certainly, thought Celia, Isobel looked sick and sorry for
herself. Her eyes were rimmed as though she had been
crying.

"What has happened?" Celia repeated.

"Only that they've requisitioned Storm Castle," said
Isobel, with a short, rasping laugh, "which means that

the Trevarwiths have to turn out as soon as Anthony is well enough to be moved."

Celia raised her brows. It was queer, but the idea of the Trevarwiths being turned out of the Castle hardly moved her at all. At one time she had loved it deeply, because it had been the only home she had ever known and it had been full of her mother's memories. But there had been so much unhappiness here, too . . . so much clashing of wills with Isobel, of disappointment, of frustration. She did not care what happened to it now. She only wanted to get back to Rachel's cottage and the hope of a life of peace and happiness in the future with her beloved Paul.

Isobel's voice rasped on, full of impotent rage.

"An Air Force billeting officer called here last night. The Castle is just what they want for billeting eight hundred R.A.F. officer cadets who are going to train at the new aerodrome."

Celia gasped a little.

"Good gracious!"

Isobel flung another piece of paper on to the floor.

"That's putting it mildly. Think of packing up and getting out! The home your father brought me to seven years ago and said would be mine and Anthony's. . . . Damn this war! Damn everything!"

Celia eyed her stepmother with cool disdain. She felt in that moment that Paul's love, and her escape from the old life to the new one that he had made possible for her, had also made her completely impervious to anything that this woman did or said. Only a few moments ago she would have felt nervous and anxious in Isobel's presence, willing to obey, forced to serve. What a little idiot she had been! Why had she let such a woman dominate her so completely? She despised Isobel. To-day more than ever she resented the fact that Isobel had been chosen by her thoroughly misguided father to take her mother's place.

"Well, Isobel," she said, "you may hate this war, and so does everybody, but it is for a purpose, and we are all supposed to do what we can toward it. So far, if you'll forgive me for saying so, you've done nothing, and you've stopped me from doing anything. But I know if Father had been alive—he would have done what he could, even at his age."

Isobel glared at the girl.

"I don't want any impudence from you. And don't tell me your father would have handed Storm Castle over to the R.A.F. without a protest."

Celia walked to the window and looked beyond the grey walls of the Castle. The faint hazy outline of Land's End was visible now. The fog was lifting. She said:

"I'm glad they are going to take the place over. I'm glad the Castle is going to be of use to the country, even if *we* are not. I've always thought it a dreadful waste —this huge place—half of it going to rack and ruin. I like to think of the R.A.F. cleaning it up and turning it into a barracks. They are brave and wonderful, all those boys. We should be honoured to have them here."

"Oh, you're scats, and always were," Isobel flung at her.

Celia turned and walked back to the bed.

"Why don't you let me go into one of the Services? Why don't you give me permission? I hate doing nothing and just because I am so young . . ."

"Oh, shut up," broke in Isobel rudely. "Let's concentrate on what's got to be done here. I'm not worrying about you. I'm worrying about having to pack up and leave Ruthlyn Cove. As soon as Anthony is well, they say. Well, I'll make the doctor spin *that* out, I can tell you."

"Why won't you let me join up?" persisted Celia.

Isobel deliberately ignored this question. She had her own private reasons for not allowing her stepdaughter to put on a uniform and be posted to some place where she couldn't keep an eye on her. Whatever their differences were, Celia was still the heiress to Angela Trevarwith's fortune, and Isobel was one of her guardians. It wouldn't do to let Celia slip too far out of reach. She said cunningly:

"No, my dear, and let me tell you this is *not* the time for us to quarrel and separate. When I leave the Castle I shall want you to come with me and give a hand with your little brother. *That* should be your war work. They won't let me have a governess, and he is too young to go to school."

A slight colour mounted Celia's cheeks.

"I'm sorry, Isobel, but I don't intend to live with you any more. I'm going to live with old Mrs. Taylor at Cadgwith and find work there."

"Don't be a little fool. Where will that get you?"

"I don't know, but at least I can live in peace, and Paul will come back there and see me whenever he can."

Isobel digested this in silence for a moment. She had never felt more thwarted or more secretly afraid for herself. Future prospects were not looking too well, and in some way or other, despite her authority, this girl over whom she had tyrannized for so long, seemed to be getting the upper hand.

Holding a handkerchief to her eyes, she began to whine:

"Your father would think it dreadful of you to walk out on me at a time like this—and on poor little Tony."

"I'm quite willing to stay this week, until he is stronger."

"And what about helping me get out of the Castle? They are going to store all our things for us, but we've got to take all our personal possessions. There is an inventory to be made . . . you know perfectly well there are thousands of things to be seen to. You are the daughter of the house and it is your duty to stay and help me."

Celia considered this. Her heart sank a little. She began to see the peace of Rachel's cottage slipping away from her. Perhaps it *was* her duty to help Isobel evacuate the Castle.

A trifle grudgingly she said:

"Well, if you think I ought to help you, I will, but as soon as it is all over I shall go back to Cadgwith."

Isobel gave her a sour look.

"Then I shall come to Cadgwith too. You must find rooms for me and Anthony. I'm not going to have it said that my stepdaughter is living apart from me. A nice lot of gossip it will cause."

"I thought you wanted to live in London," said Celia, and her heart sank still more at the prospect of Isobel pursuing her to Cadgwith. She had never had any liking for her stepmother. Today she had still less. She would rather live alone with Rachel and wait for the precious moments of reunion with Paul. She could not quite understand, either, why Isobel should want to cling to her like this. It did not for a moment enter her head that the whole thing was a question of finance and that her stepmother, having run up huge bills, was heavily in debt.

"You'd like Anthony and me to be somewhere near you, wouldn't you, Celia?" whimpered Isobel. "I know your father would have liked it."

Then Celia, with red cheeks and blazing eyes, broke out:

"Oh, no, he wouldn't have cared. He never cared about me all those years when I was a little girl. He neglected me. He hated me because my mother died when I was born. It wasn't until he was dying that he realized how cruel he had been to me, and then it was too late. And you hated me too. You did everything you could to break my spirit. Even when I was a little thing you burned my favourite doll. You were heartless to me, and when Anthony was born and I wanted to love him, you even taught *him* to treat me badly. Then when I found Paul . . . someone I could love . . . someone who loved me . . . you did everything you could to hurt Paul. Why should I care about you now? Why should I want you to live anywhere near me?"

Her voice broke. She burst into tears and ran from the room. All the injustices, the sorrows of the long years seemed to have welled up and poured like a torrent into that room. It left the red-haired woman in the bed gasping, white-faced, afraid. For now she saw

206

that this sweet and gentle creature whom she had tried to break was strong in her new love and faith, and that it was likely that she, Isobel Trevarwith, would, in her turn, be broken.

She lay there, struggling against a fit of hysterics, regretting her past behaviour to Celia, not because of what it had done to Celia, but because of what it had done to *herself*.

Celia dried her eyes and walked into her stepbrother's bedroom, where the nurse was trying to induce the small boy to eat a boiled egg. Anthony was snivelling and defiant. His small face seemed to have shrunk and his blue eyes grown large since his operation. All the tenderness and sympathy in Celia's nature was aroused by the sight of him. She forgot that he was Isobel's son and remembered only that he was a Trevarwith and her own kith and kin. That feeling was intensified when she saw the look of genuine welcome that brightened the little boy's face as he greeted her.

"Celie! Celie!" he screamed her name, holding out both arms.

The nurse shrugged her shoulders and gave Celia a sour look.

"You can take over and welcome. I'm fed up with the little devil."

Celia sat on the bed and put an arm around Anthony.

"Now, darling, you are going to eat a big breakfast just to show Celia what a good boy you are, then I'll tell you a lovely new story."

"Will you stay with me now?" he demanded. "If I eat my egg will you stay?"

"Yes."

"How long will you stay?"

"Till you're better."

"I'm glad because I hate that nurse. I hate everyone except you."

"Oh, Anthony, don't hate . . . it's terrible to hate," said Celia. "You must learn to love people and be kind and generous. Never, *never* make anybody unhappy."

The small boy eyed her without understanding.

"Mummy said she hated the war and those men who are going to turn us all out of the Castle. It's *my* Castle. They can't take it, *can* they, Celie?"

"Only for the duration of the war, darling. You must be glad and proud to let the R.A.F. have your Castle. They are going to live here while they learn to fly. You know they are fighting to keep little boys like you safe and sound, so you must give them everything you can."

"But isn't it *my* Castle any more?"

"It will be again one day, Anthony. And one day you'll be married and bring your wife here and you must make her very happy. There must be no more hatred and misery in Storm Castle. You must chase away all the ghosts and make everybody who comes into it feel happy too."

"Why are you crying?" he asked, as he looked up from his breakfast and saw a tear rolling down Celia's cheek.

"I don't know," she whispered, "I just feel sad this morning about everything."

"Tell me that story," he said impatiently.

She walked to the window and looked down at the sea. The morning did not seem quite so grey or desolate now. There was a rift of blue in the sky . . . a jagged line of emerald and sapphire where the sunlight pierced the water far out to sea.

She thought of Paul and of how empty life would be for her without him. He was everything to her now . . . the whole of her life.

In a husky voice she began to tell Anthony a story:

"Once upon a time there was a brave and handsome prince who, disguised as a simple fisherman, went out to sea in a little boat to rescue his friends who had been captured and made prisoners by wicked men . . ."

PART FOUR

1

One close thundery morning about a fortnight later Celia Trevarwith stepped off the bus at Cadgwith and walked into Rachel's cottage, carrying a suitcase in her hand.

The old woman, who was standing over her little copper, washing, smoothed the soapsuds from her hand and greeted the girl with delight.

"Why, Miss Celia, my lil maid, I thought you was never coming back!" she exclaimed.

Celia put the suitcase down, kissed the old woman and looked sadly round the tiny living-room.

"You don't know how much I have wanted to come back, Rachel dear. I love this little place. Somehow I feel it is Paul's home . . . and mine."

The old woman's dark, short-sighted eyes peered at her curiously.

"You'm a queer one, my dear. Fancy preferring old Rachel's cottage to your fine Castle."

"You're not always happy because you live in a castle. Rachel. Plenty of human beings are far happier in tiny rooms like this one. I know I am. I hate Storm Castle these days. And yet now it's rather tragic—to see it all breaking up. You know we are being turned out. The R.A.F. have requisitioned it."

"I did hear tell of it in the village, my dear."

"That's why I haven't been back. I've been helping my stepmother sort things and pack up. But, of course, the real reason why I've come back is because . . . because . . ."

Her voice broke off. She bit hard on her lip as

though to check her emotions. The old woman saw the girl's large beautiful eyes brim with tears. Then Celia finished:

"Because there has been no news of Paul."

Rachel hurried to put a kettle on the fire. She must make a cup of tea for Miss Celia. In Rachel's estimation, tea helped to cure most human ills. As she performed this simple task she murmured:

"No news, 'tis good news, they say."

"I hope so," said Celia in a low voice.

She stood a moment looking through the tiny casement at the village, the winding hill that led down to the little brown beach on which a few small boats were moored . . . and beyond to the jagged rocks of the headland. It was dead calm today. The waves broke persistently against the shore, making a soft hissing sound through the still August morning. The sky was stormy, banked with heavy clouds far out to sea. Celia thought of that storm on the night when Paul had gone out in the lifeboat . . . of her agony of fear for him . . . those nerve-racking hours of waiting.

She had learned, during those hours in his arms when he came back, what it means to a woman to love. Now she was having to go through all the pain of loving and waiting again.

When Paul had said good-bye to her two weeks ago he had told her that he expected to be back in a few days, or at least to get a message to her. What had happened to him? She knew so little about his job. But she did know that he had gone over to the enemy's coast . . . to his own country which was in the hands of the enemy. Perhaps he had not come back. Perhaps he was still in France—perhaps he was a prisoner, or . . . *perhaps he was dead.*

But she had resolved not to allow herself to dwell on that awful possibility. She must model herself on Jill Hayling, whose courage had not failed her even though it was more than a chance now that her husband was dead. Love was useless without courage or hope. She must cling on to the belief that Paul was busy somewhere, carrying out the work entrusted to him, and that he would come back to her as soon as he could.

But the waiting was hard, and still more so, the uncertainty. The fortnight at the Castle had dragged intolerably, although she had plenty to do. She and Isobel and Elspeth and Edith, who had come up to help, were hard at it every day turning out this cupboard and that, finding still more cupboards and trunks full of things which must be sorted and stored.

The hospital nurse had gone. Anthony had made an amazing recovery. He was a strong little boy, and once over the operation he had gone straight ahead. The doctor said that Celia had done the trick. She seemed to have remarkable control over him. And, indeed, Celia found her little stepbrother easy to handle and docile these days. He was up and out again, and although not allowed to do anything strenuous, would certainly be well enough to travel early next week. So early next week the Trevarwith family must leave Storm Castle and the R.A.F. would take over.

"I'm going to bring all my own things here, Rachel, if you don't mind," Celia told the old woman. "There is a suitcase with some of my books and treasures. And there is a trunkful of clothes and another full of my mother's things that I must get stored somewhere in the village. I don't want to clutter up your cottage."

"You'm welcome to any space there is, my dear," said the woman.

She poured out a cup of tea for the girl, who drank it, her gaze still fixed sadly and thoughtfully on the stormy sky. Certainly there would be a storm before tonight. If only she could be sure Paul was on land somewhere, safe and sound. If only she could stop thinking of all the young vital men like Paul who lay under the grey treacherous waves, and would never live or laugh or love again. She knew that she would feel better once she got back here again. Storm Castle, in its present state of disorder and eruption, seemed more than ever gloomy and depressing. Isobel whined unceasingly and still threatened to follow Celia. The girl had completely lost all her old childish terror of her stepmother. And although Anthony had endeared himself to her a little more since his illness, Celia would not really mind very much saying good-bye to either of them. Not a day went by without a dispute of some sort between Isobel and herself. Isobel seemed to want to get on the right side of her and yet hated to be thwarted or defied. Everything in the Castle that was of value Isobel claimed for herself and her son. Celia was only too willing to let her have most things, but she would not surrender anything that had been her mother's. Most of the pictures were to be stored in a room in the Castle by arrangement with the billeting officer. The Cézanne had been sent to London to the National Gallery. Upon this Celia had insisted. She would not allow Isobel to put it up for sale as she wanted. It was a great work, and her mother, who had owned it, would have wished the Nation to benefit by its beauty.

Reluctantly Celia had allowed the prized painting of her mother to go into store with the others. But the trunkful of clothes . . . the lovely silks, satins and velvets . . . many of the young Angela Trevarwith's gowns which had been made for her trousseau, and which Elspeth had taken out of Mr. Trevarwith's sight at the time of her death, Celia was bringing with her. She had wept over them and smiled, too, at the queer fashions. She and her mother must have had the same slender figure, because Celia had tried on one of the evening dresses and it had fitted her perfectly. She was going to wear it for Paul when he came back . . . *when he came back.*

Shivering a little, Celia turned away from the sea.

"I mustn't stay very long. I must catch the next bus to Ruthlyn, Rachel, but I'll be back here for good next week. If Paul turns up, you'll tell him to telephone the Castle at once, won't you?"

Rachel promised. She wished Miss Celia looked a little happier. Her general health was better these days, but she was painfully thin, the old woman thought.

Those high cheekbones of hers stood out more than ever. Poor, pretty creature, eating her heart out for her lad!

"Mercy on us—what it is to be a woman," Rachel sighed, as she kissed the girl good-bye.

But there was an unexpected pleasure waiting for Celia when she got back to Storm Castle. A familiar feminine figure in W.A.A.F. uniform—Jill Hayling, herself, standing in the doorway waving to her as Celia walked up the drive.

The two girls rushed into each other's arms.

"Oh, Jill, what a heavenly surprise!" cried Celia. "Where have you come from? How are you?"

"I'm fine," said Jill. "I've been on a course. That's why I didn't get in touch with you, Celia darling. But I've been posted back to the camp here, and as this is my stand-off I'm going to spend it with you. I've just seen your stepmother. I say! She seems to have changed her tune. What's been going on here? Why on earth did *you* ever come back after all the trouble we took to get you away?"

Celia bore Jill off to her own bedroom, sat her down, gave her a cigarette and did a lot of explaining.

Jill perched on Celia's bed, listening, unbuttoned her tunic, ran her fingers through her mop of dark curly hair and grinned at the younger girl.

"My word, you do go in for drama in a big way. Never met anybody like you. Abductions. Motor-car smashes. Appendicitis. What next?"

Celia, in the act of combing her long fair hair, turned and shrugged her shoulders.

"You may well ask. I've just got to wait for Paul to come back, and even when he does, there isn't much to look forward to if we can't get married. Oh, Jill, somehow or other I've got to persuade Isobel to give me permission."

"Well, it seems to me that Mrs. Trevarwith is a little more pliable these days. She spoke quite nicely to me when I turned up here—as though we had never had that dust-up, and said what a help little Celia had been

215

to her and to Anthony. Look here, my lamb, aren't you an heiress and isn't she your guardian?"

"Yes, but what of it?"

Jill gave her delightful grin.

"I'm a cynic, my sweet. I immediately suspect your stepmamma of wanting to get on the right side of you because she is needing some money. Well, you may be the one to supply it."

Celia stared blankly.

"I just never thought of that."

"You wouldn't! You're an infant in the affairs of the world."

"But not in the affairs of love," said Celia. "I'm so much in love with Paul that I don't know what to do."

Jill nodded.

"I know what you are feeling. I know every inch of the way, and it isn't easy."

"*You* still have no news, poor Jill . . ."

"No more, and yet I still won't let myself believe that I shall never see Tim again."

The two girls stood side by side for a moment, hand in hand, looking out of the narrow turret windows at the gulls which were circling restlessly round the island. Every moment it seemed to be growing darker.

"There is going to be a thunder-storm," said Celia.

"Yes, there is going to be a thunder-storm," repeated Jill.

Arm-in-arm they walked downstairs to lunch.

During lunch Isobel looked at her stepdaughter and said in a meek voice:

"Fulke 'phoned me up this morning from Kyland. He is still laid up with that bad arm and wants me to go and see him. I told him we were leaving here, and he said that Anthony and I could have a room at Kyland House if we wanted it . . . and you, too, of course, Celia."

Celia flashed her an indignant look.

"You know I wouldn't set foot in that house."

"I was afraid you wouldn't," said Isobel, in the same

meek tone, "but it might be a good thing for Tony and me while we straighten our affairs."

"I wish you didn't have to go there . . . I hate to think of any of our family accepting favours from that man," said Celia, her cheeks hot with the memory of her last encounter with Fulke.

"Needs must . . . beggars can't be choosers, can they, Jill?" said Isobel in a sweet voice, addressing the young W.A.A.F. officer.

Jill looked from Isobel to Celia, then put her tongue in her cheek.

"You'll have to borrow from our little heiress, Miss Celia Trevarwith," she said jestingly.

Celia said hastily:

"I don't come into my money until I am twenty-one. If I had it, Isobel could certainly borrow from me."

"Thank you, dear," said Isobel.

Finishing her lunch, the woman lapsed into silence. Her sharp brain was working. She was thinking:

"I wonder, if Celia were married, what the position would be . . . whether she would be allowed to use some of her money. I must go up to town and see the lawyers and find out. For of course if that were the case I might be persuaded to let her marry her boy-friend. *It might pay me to do so.*"

Lunch had ended, and they were all walking into the hall when Isobel suddenly remembered something and hastily addressed Jill.

"Sorry, I forgot to tell you, but while you were up-stairs with Celia they 'phoned from the camp and said would you ring them."

"Good lord!" exclaimed Jill. "I must do so at once."

But at that precise moment the big studded front door was pushed open and a girl in W.A.A.F. uniform appeared in the doorway.

"Hello," said Jill, "here's one of my girls."

The W.A.A.F., who was a corporal, saluted Jill and held out a letter.

"We 'phoned you, ma'am, and then Flight-Officer

Parker suggested I might come over on my bike and bring you this, as she said it was important."

"Is there an answer?"

"No, ma'am."

The girl saluted and retired. Jill shut the front door and walked back to Celia, who was trying to persuade her small stepbrother to go upstairs and rest for a while.

"I don't know what this is all about," said Jill, frowning. "It's Pat Parker's handwriting."

"Orders from H.Q.," suggested Celia.

"No. It wouldn't be delivered like this. This is Pat's private note-paper. I know it."

"Well, I'm going to take Tony up to rest," said Celia, "then we'll have a long chat."

She started to walk upstairs with the small boy, but stopped as she heard a cry from Jill. Turning quickly, she saw the young W.A.A.F. officer standing there, shaking from head to foot, her face colourless, and a look in her eyes which Celia was never able to forget.

Dropping Anthony's hand, Celia rushed back to her friend.

"Jill! Darling Jill, is it bad news?"

Jill shook her head dumbly. Dumbly she handed Celia a thin card which she had abstracted from the white envelope. Speech seemed to fail her. With a shaking finger she pointed to the printed words on that card. Then Celia's heart gave a great leap of joy for her friend. For she saw at a glance that it was a formal notice from a prison camp in Germany, and it was signed *"Tim."*

She heard Jill's voice, cracked, full of almost agonized happiness:

"Celia! Celia, he's not dead. Celia, *this is from Tim!* It's his signature. He's a prisoner, after all. Oh, Celia . . . thank God, thank *God*."

And Jill Hayling flung herself into a chair and cried as though her heart would break. All the anxiety and grief that she had repressed seemed to flow into a great torrent, taking her resistance with it. Now that the suspense was over, now that she knew that her darling was safe, she could cry. And the tears came . . . a glorious relief.

Young Anthony's round blue eyes stared in amazement.

"What's she crying for, Celia?" he asked in astonishment.

Celia, scarcely able to restrain her own tears, answered:

"She's just heard that her husband is a prisoner of war, Anthony. Run and tell Mummy. Just let Jill and me be alone for a moment."

Jill reached out a hand for her precious card and read it again, sobbing wildly.

"He's alive, Celia; he's alive. I always knew it. I kept faith. I felt he couldn't be gone for ever. Now I'll see him again when the war ends. I don't care how long it is, now I *know* that I'll see him again."

Celia knelt beside her, an arm around the quivering young figure.

"Darling Jill, I am so glad for you. You do deserve it. You've been so brave."

Jill pointed to the card.

"Look, Celia, he says that he is well. He's in Dresden. *Luft 3, Dresden,* is his address. I know all about it. I know a girl in our Group whose husband is in the Air Force and who was captured and taken there. It is where they send all the R.A.F. officers. It is in the middle of a pine forest and they are quite well treated. I shall be able to send him parcels. I can write to him now, this minute. I will get a letter from him soon. Oh, *Celia!*"

2

Celia found that the tears were falling down her own cheeks now. Jill Hayling was the only real friend she had ever had, apart from those she had made at school and with whom she had now lost touch. She could and would always be passionately grateful to Jill for championing her cause during that wretched illness which had kept her a prisoner here. Never would she forget the way Jill and her friend had helped her steal out of the Castle and take that never-to-be-forgotten bicycle ride to Cadgwith—and to Paul! She felt that she owed Jill a great deal. Not only because of these things, but because of her example. Jill had shown Celia that it did not do to be too timid, too resigned to fate, but that one should strike out bravely for oneself . . . fight for love . . . have faith in it . . . courage for it. And now Jill was reaping the reward of her own fine young character. The adored husband . . . her bridegroom of one week . . . who had been missing for three long months, was not dead but living.

The two girls, with their arms around each other, wept unrestrainedly. Then, after a moment, Jill choked between a sob and a laugh and pointed to her precious card.

"It will be washed away by all these tears if we don't stop," she said huskily. "And what the dickens are we crying for? We ought to be laughing now. My darling old Tim! Think of it, Celia . . . he's at *Luft 3*. I must 'phone Mummy and Daddy. And Tim's mother. Everybody will be hysterical. You see, Mummy and Daddy are away at the moment and our old maid must have sent this card on to the camp, thinking it was a circular or something. Printed matter! She wouldn't know what it was all about. But look, Celia, *look* at his signature. Tim's own frightful handwriting. I always told him no one could read it . . . !"

She blew her nose violently, smiling with her red-rimmed happy eyes at the other girl, and went on talking, wild with excitement.

"I wonder how long this took to get here. I wonder when I will get his first letter. I wonder if he is wounded. He says he is all right. They must have brought down his bomber and just captured the crew. Isn't it lucky, Celia? Aren't I the luckiest girl in the world?"

"You deserve to be," said Celia, blowing her own small nose.

Isobel appeared in the doorway, a cigarette between her lips and Anthony hanging on to her arm.

"What on earth is all this about?" she began.

Then Jill, forgetting how much she disliked and mistrusted Celia's stepmother, had to run to her and tell her all over again about Tim.

"That's grand for you," said Isobel.

She spoke without much enthusiasm. She was too entirely self-centred a woman to be enthusiastic about anyone else's joys or sorrows, but as she listened to the excited young voice and caught the deep note of passionate happiness throbbing behind it, somewhere in the shallow depths of her own heart Isobel felt a twinge of envy. She knew that she had missed something. She had never loved any man as this young W.A.A.F. officer appeared to love her husband. Indeed, the only person she had ever felt a real affection for was her own small son.

She had married Francis Trevarwith entirely for his money and position, sick of struggling in a film studio where she had no real chance because she had no real talent. During her life she had had one or two "affairs," but they had been entirely physical. She had experienced nothing but the momentary thrills of the flesh.

221

She had neither knowledge of, nor sympathy with, spiritual ecstasies. To her it would have been "a damned bore" to have a husband a prisoner of war and be expected to remain the faithful little wife for years. She was thoroughly bored with her own existence at the moment, resenting this war only because it cramped her own activities. She considered herself ill-used because Anthony was to inherit the Trevarwith estate and precious little money with it . . . what there was so severely taxed. She was fast making up her mind to get old Fulke to introduce her to some amusing man with cash who would be pleased to take her on. She was still good looking and only in her late thirties.

And yet . . . she saw that she had missed something rare and enviable as Jill poured out a torrent of emotion about Tim and the camp in Dresden.

"I must contact Elizabeth Cooper at once," she was saying in her thrilled, husky voice. "Elizabeth's husband, Jack, is a Squadron Leader, who was in Bomber Command with Tim at one time. He's at *Luft 3*. She'll be able to give me all the dope . . ."

"I'm very pleased for you, I'm sure," said Isobel, and then with a sidelong glance at her stepdaughter, added: "Isn't it time for Tony's rest?"

Celia pulled herself together. It was so difficult to drag her thoughts away from Jill and Tim and the R.A.F. prison camp. Those thoughts were so closely akin to her feelings about Paul. *Where was Paul?* If only she knew! Was he, too, a prisoner? Or would she see him again very soon?

Jill was buttoning up her tunic.

"I must rush back to camp and find out all I can and do all my 'phoning. I'll come again soon to see you, Celia darling. Will you be here?"

"Until Monday. After that the R.A.F. take over the Castle."

"Then I'll find you at Rachel's cottage?"

"Yes."

"You'll have had news from Paul by then. I know you will," said Jill.

The two girls embraced. Celia whispered:

"I'm so terribly glad for you, darling."

After Section-Officer Hayling had gone, Celia took Anthony upstairs for his rest. When she came down to the hall again her stepmother called her. She must help go through a chest full of curtain materials which had been overlooked.

As they worked together, Isobel, the inevitable cigarette between her lips and ash falling everywhere (Celia did dislike it so), brought up the subject of Paul, on her own account.

"Haven't you any idea where this French boy friend of yours has got to?"

"No, none," said Celia in a low voice.

"Fancy him going off in that mysterious way. A bit peculiar I call it."

"No, it isn't peculiar, Isobel. It's a hush-hush job and I can't be told anything about it. That's all."

"Is he in the Navy then?"

"More or less."

"Getting better pay than he had as a fisherman in the cove, I suppose?"

"Yes."

"And wearing better clothes, too, I hope. It's a bit 'off' for me, Mrs. Trevarwith of Storm Castle, to have my stepdaughter going around with a fellow wearing freakish sorts of jerseys and Breton trousers."

Celia coloured, and her heart began to beat fast with resentment. (How many times had it beaten that way in her life because of a sneer or a hostile act from her stepmother!)

"He doesn't wear freakish clothes. Just the clothes of a simple French fisherman," she said, quick to defend Paul.

"Well, surely you must see that you, Miss Trevarwith, can't marry a boy like that, anyway."

Celia bit her lip. It was the old argument. She was so weary of it. She said:

"For the last time, Isobel, I tell you I mean to marry Paul, if he comes back to me."

"I suppose you haven't forgotten that you are only nineteen next birthday?"

Celia, on her knees before the chest folding curtains, shook her head.

"I haven't forgotten."

"But you've so far forgotten your birth and station in life that you intend to live in a cottage in Cadgwith and let everybody think you are this man's wife in everything but name."

Celia went scarlet. Her eyes flashed at Isobel.

"It won't be true, and I don't think that anybody except those with beastly minds will think it."

"Oh, play the innocent stuff if you like, and I daresay you are both angels from heaven. You are so stupid. But it won't stop the scandal."

"If it's scandal you are worrying about, Isobel, it might be the best thing, don't you think, if Paul and I could get married?" said Celia with a set little smile.

Isobel kicked her toe against the chest.

"Your stubbornness gets me down. Why the dickens can't you choose a fellow like your friend Jill's husband? An Air Force officer, an Englishman; anything but a French peasant."

"Paul isn't altogether a peasant and I happen to love him. His father was a painter and a gentleman. You've only got to talk to Paul . . . to know what he is like . . . to see for yourself that he is an aristocrat. And whatever he is, I still love him."

"You're a pig-headed little fool."

Celia gave a deep sigh.

"You've always thought that, Isobel. But as I've come back to help you get out of here, can't we work without quarrelling?"

"Do as you like. And if you ruin your life, don't say I haven't tried to stop it."

"All right," said Celia with a smile, "I'll remember that you tried to stop me ruining my life. But I shall wait for Paul if necessary until I am twenty-one, and he is quite willing to wait, too."

Isobel digested this remark in silence for a moment,

her scheming brain busily working out a plan of action which would benefit herself. After a moment she said in a sweeter voice:

"Look, Celia, could I leave Anthony with you for a day or two while I go up to London? I've got to go on business and see your father's lawyers."

Celia raised her head and looked gravely at her stepmother for a moment. That direct look had always made the older woman feel uncomfortable and she lowered her gaze now. Celia said:

"I'd rather like to see Father's lawyers, too. Jill made a remark at lunch which has made me think . . . I'd like to know just what my position is. . . . What happens about my money?"

Isobel affected unconcern.

"What can happen about it?"

"I just want to know. I don't normally inherit Mother's money until I am twenty-one, do I? But if I marry before, is there any chance of me getting some?"

That was precisely what Isobel wanted to find out for herself, but she did not intend Celia to know it. She yawned and answered:

"I really haven't any idea."

"But aren't you and Mr. Forbes, the senior partner, my guardians?"

"We are."

"Then, if you don't know, I'd like to ask Mr. Forbes about Father's Will."

"I'll find out for you while I am in town," said Isobel, adopting a casual tone.

Suddenly Celia rose to her feet and drew near her stepmother, looking with earnest, almost appealing eyes at the woman's narrow, discontented face.

"Oh, Isobel, if only you and Mr. Forbes would let me get married soon . . . I do love Paul so much and he loves me. I'll never marry anyone else, whatever you both say. You could introduce me to all the most fascinating men in the world . . . I wouldn't be attracted by them. There is something in Paul which is just what I have always wanted. We are so well suited. Oh, Isobel, do think it over . . . please."

"I shall do nothing of the sort," said Isobel sharply. "You can't possibly marry that penniless Frenchman. Now get on with the job."

Celia, half-annoyed with herself for having lowered her pride and made the appeal, dutifully returned to sorting the curtains while Isobel made a list. Isobel returned to the subject of Anthony. Celia found herself having to promise to take the little boy back to Cadgwith with her on Monday while Isobel took her trip to town.

Later that day, Celia stole away from her stepmother and brother, and in the half-light between twilight and evening went for a long walk along the cliffs, found a place which used to be a favourite of hers as a child, and threw herself down on the green springy turf which was sweet-smelling and dry and still warm from the sun's rays.

The thunder-storm which had been hanging about all day was still threatening. The heavens seemed divided between the red glow of sunset and an ominous yellow tint that suggested thunder. From the north, dark clouds were billowing. There was not a breath of wind. Far below her the water lapped against the jagged rocks and ran upwards into the sandy cove which was sprinkled with pinkish pebbles. Sky and sea were linked by a soft violet haze. Far out on the horizon Celia could discern the outline of a ship, and her heart seemed to break with love and longing for Paul. If only he were in that ship. If only it would turn and come into harbour at Ruthlyn.

She had a swift vision of him as she used to see him, sitting down in the little harbour in his fishing-boat, mending his nets, his brown, handsome face smiling at her, a lock of black hair wet with sea-water falling across his eyes. He had a trick of shaking back that lock as he held out his hands to her and murmured:

"Ma douce cherie! Ma petite gazelle!"

What if she was never to hear his voice again, never

to know the fulfilment of their love, their perfect comradeship which had been born of sorrow and the sea?

All her young life Celia had experienced the pangs of loneliness and of yearning for a happiness denied her. This evening her pain seemed intolerable. Face downward on the cliff she lay, head on her folded arms, and wept long and bitterly.

"Paul . . . Paul, my darling, come back soon. Paul, I can't live without you."

She lay there a long time, struggling with her emotions . . . a woman agonized with yearning for her lover . . . yet still a child, lonely and afraid of the future and needing some kind of material comfort.

She was roused finally by a low growl of thunder and the sensation of heavy cold drops of rain falling upon her bare arms and uncovered head.

She looked up and saw that the expected storm was now coming nearer. The first flash of lightning made her draw a quick breath. A wind had sprung up, ruffling the surface of the sea. The tide was coming in more rapdily, breaking with sullen anger against the rocks.

Celia had experienced many storms on her native coast and they always upset her. This evening, more than ever, she felt the gloom of it all, the wild remoteness of this place. Looming up against the lurid sky stood the sinister shadow of Storm Castle. It beckoned to her as it had always done, the only home she had ever known. Yet within its old grey walls there was no comfort for her. She felt to-night that she would rather have stayed out here alone in the rain with the lightning playing about her and the noise of the thunder rolling over her head . . . anything in preference to an evening arguing with Isobel, listening to Paul being insulted.

Slowly and disconsolately she began to walk back along the cliffs towards the Castle.

3

When Celia got back to the Castle she found old Elspeth hobbling about in the hall waiting for her.

"Mercy, but you're wet through, Miss Celia. Run up and take off those things," she said in a scolding voice, much as she would have spoken to Celia when she was a little girl.

Celia brushed a hand across her forehead. Her face was wet with the rain and her clothes were dripping. Elspeth added:

"The mistress she'm gone out and left this note for you."

Celia, feeling tired and chilled, read the note:

> *Gone over to Kyland to see Fulke. Put Anthony to bed for me and expect me when you see me.*
>
> *I.*

Celia went upstairs. Anthony was hanging over the carved balustrade of the gallery waiting for her.

"Where have you been, Celie? Isn't the storm awful? Mummy will get caught in it, won't she?"

Celia reassured the small boy. Mummy would probably have reached Kyland House before the storm broke, she said. She would change into dry clothes and read to him before his bath.

He looked at her suspiciously out of his round blue eyes.

"Why is your face all funny? Have you been crying?"

Celia turned from him, wincing. Children were so brutally direct. Yes, she had been crying as though her heart would break lying out there on the cliffs. But now her tears had dried. There was just an unutterable pain in her heart and the persistent longing for Paul.

Up in her room she dried her face and hair vigorously, put on a complete change of clothes and hurried down to Anthony's nursery. It had grown dark in the Castle, which was only lit up at times by vivid flashes of lightning. The thunder rolled majestically overhead. It was all that Celia could do to quieten her jumping nerves. How she wished she had not got such a vivid imagination and did not keep on picturing her Paul at sea in a small boat . . . on such a wild sea as this one which now lashed the rocks with malicious violence. As far out as the eye could see the wind had whipped white horses on to the crest of each leaden-coloured wave.

She wondered how long Isobel would be. Well, thank goodness, she, Celia, had not been asked to go to Kyland and meet Fulke Withers. She hoped never to set eyes on that hateful leering face again. But Isobel was a sponger. Isobel hoped to fix up a comfortable billet for herself and her son at Fulke's house. Fulke was noted for his parties, even in war-time. Somehow he always managed to get hold of plenty of drink, and a crowd of old racing friends who gathered around him when they could get away from their various National jobs.

Celia managed to get through the evening, but she was surprised and a little disturbed when Isobel did not come back. The storm still hovered over the coast, now diminishing, now returning with renewed force; its darkness had become one with the shadows of night. Old Elspeth drew the curtains and lit a wood fire in the small drawing-room. The old woman, herself, hung around Celia and Anthony, apparently reluctant to leave them and go back to the kitchen, where she was alone tonight.

"Poor Elspeth, you don't like storms either, do you?" asked Celia.

The old woman shook her head. She hated them, and still more did she hate the thought of leaving the

Castle on Monday when the R.A.F. took over. But this time she was forced to go. Celia had found her another job . . . at the Vicarage, in fact . . . but to Elspeth it was like being uprooted from the place where she had lived and grown since her pathetic girlhood.

Anthony had his supper and went to bed. The little boy was good, and, unlike most children, not particularly disturbed by thunderstorms. He called the thunder "big guns" and said: *"Boom! Boom!"* after every crash, then giggled delightedly at his own wit. The summer's day having been long and tiring, he was soon asleep.

Celia sat in the drawing-room, hunched on a hassock in front of the fire and tried to read, but she kept looking at the clock anxiously. It was nearing nine, and no sign of Isobel.

Surely Isobel would not let the storm deter her from driving back from Kyland?

Then the telephone rang. Celia answered it and heard Isobel's voice, somewhat indistinctly, for there seemed to be a loud noise of laughter and other voices behind her. What she said was to the effect that she did not intend to return home tonight at all. Fulke had a party on. She had fallen straight into it. All the old crowd who used to come to the Castle were there, including Frank Curling, the Naval Commander, who was a particular friend of Isobel's. There were two women there, and all three of them had decided to sleep at Kyland House rather than turn out in the storm.

"You'll be all right, won't you, Celia? You can look after Tony," finished Isobel.

"Quite all right, thank you."

Celia spoke a trifle wryly. She knew her stepmother so well. Isobel was in an excellent mood and had obviously dined and wined well. Celia had seen some of those parties in progress here. She knew they would drink and play poker until the early hours of the morning. Well, thank heavens, *she* wasn't there.

Isobel added:

"Listen, Celia; say a word to poor old Fulke. He's

got a broken arm and he would like to speak to you . . ."

"No, Isobel," said Celia quickly. "No. Good night . . ." and she put down the instrument quickly before she could hear Fulke's voice. She was determined to have nothing more to do with him.

She read her book for a moment or two and then, conscious of extreme tiredness, put out the lights and went upstairs. Anthony was sound asleep. She dropped a kiss on the red curls with some tenderness and looked sadly at the flushed small face. Her stepbrother! Her only kith and kin . . . the only person in the world who belonged to her at all, except Paul. She realized, tonight, how much alone she was in this great Castle of the Trevarwiths. How dark and still it was in the lofty passages . . . how full of ghosts of the past.

After her bath she lay in bed for an hour or two listening to the rumbling thunder and hearing the rain spatter against her turret windows. She hardly dared allow herself to dwell any longer on the thought of Paul. It was too agonizing. If he didn't come back . . . if anything happened to take him from her . . . she wouldn't want to live.

She hid her face in the pillow, restless, hot, desperately afraid of the future. She whispered:

"Paul, you would want me to be brave. Paul, where are you? Send me some of your own courage, *mon amour . . . mon mari . . .*"

It was a bitter-sweet pleasure to speak his own language. She lay there thinking of all the lovely sentences in French that she could muster, then spoke them aloud —for *him*. Finally she fell into an uneasy sleep.

She was wakened from it by a terrific crash which roused her into a sitting position, heart thumping, eyes straining through the darkness. She heard a woman scream and then Anthony's voice, crying:

"Celie! *Celie!*"

She sprang out of bed fumbling for her dressing-gown and slippers. As she reached the door there was a second crash, and, wide awake now, she realized that it was the storm. It had come back and broken straight overhead. Torch in hand she ran into the corridor and downstairs to Anthony's floor. An acrid smell of burning wood reached her nostrils.

"Heavens!" she said aloud. "The Castle has been struck by lightning."

Anthony, in his pyjama suit, stood outside his room, crying lustily now with fear. Elspeth came running up the stairs, half-dressed, a shawl around her shoulders.

"Miss Celia! Miss Celia, we've been struck. It's the old wing. The other side of the Castle. It's burning, Miss Celia. We must ring for the fire-engine."

"I want Mummy," wailed Anthony.

The next ten minutes were, to Celia, a kind of nightmare. The left wing was burning. She, old Elspeth and Tony were alone in the Castle. She rushed to the telephone and got on to the nearest fire station. The next thing to do was to 'phone Kyland. The bell seemed to ring there interminably before anyone answered. It was three o'clock in the morning and probably the party were sleeping off the fumes of alcohol. It was Fulke who finally replied. Celia had to speak to him—no time now for personal grievances.

"The Castle has been struck. Isobel must come at once . . . and any of the men in your house . . . we must fight this fire."

Fulke for once proved helpful, shocked by her news.

"I'll get on to the R.A.F. at once. They are taking over the place, so if they want it they had better check the fire."

Celia put down the instrument. Her teeth were chattering and her body wet. She had never felt more afraid. She knew that she and Anthony and Elspeth could get out of the Castle now in time. And of course they must do so. But the very thought of fire had always petrified her. Storm Castle could not be allowed to burn. Unhappy though she had been here, it was still the home of her ancestors, and there was one ghost haunting its passages which she would not wish to banish . . .

the slender, loved, little ghost of her dear unknown mother.

It seemed an interminable period before the first fire-engine came clanging along the road and roused the sleeping village. The whole of Ruthlyn was soon awake. Every fisherman came up from the cove. A crowd of men set about trying to fight the flames with inadequate buckets of water and a garden hose. The wind had died down and it was raining hard, which helped a bit.

Celia stood out on the lawn, a coat over her dressing-gown, and looked upon the unbelievable picture of Storm Castle illuminated by the flames which were leaping from the disused wing. The dry old timbers were burning furiously. Great volumes of smoke poured up, shot with a million sparks. It was a terrifying and almost unearthly spectacle.

"Good target for the Jerries if they come over, eh, miss?" a local wit murmured to her.

She swallowed hard and tried to laugh.

"Target for To-night . . . I mean this morning . . ."

At four o'clock she was still standing there. She seemed rooted to the spot. There seemed to be hundreds of blue-clad figures running to and fro . . . boys from the local aerodrome. They were helping to bring out furniture and pictures, piling things on the lawn. There were three engines here now, and the flames were gradually being got under control. Isobel had arrived and had collapsed in Fulke's car in screaming hysterics. Anthony had been taken off by the Vicar's wife and by this time was probably snug and warm in bed again.

To Celia the whole night was fantastic and unforgettable. Many people spoke to her. She answered, hardly knowing what she said. Dozens of cars came up the drive. She scarcely noticed them. Her whole gaze was drawn as by magic to Storm Castle. Its one wing was still belching smoke, but the terrible storm had passed over. Dawn broke, casting an eerie grey light over the scene. The sea lay calm once more as though innocent of the havoc wrought in the night.

Suddenly Celia saw the tall figure of Fulke, one arm in a sling, advancing towards her. For some reason or other she felt absurdly frightened, unable to face him even in an hour like this. She turned and ran as though away from an evil thing. She ran down the drive, leaving the smoking Castle and the crowds on the dew-wet lawn.

She ran blindly on and on until she reached the gates. She was half-dazed and did not see a tall blue-clad figure coming towards her until they were almost touching. Then she stopped dead, a hand up to her throat and her heart hammering wildly. Paul! Yes, it was Paul. An apparition, of course. He was dead, and he had come here to tell her so. Celia, overwrought, near to breaking, gave a low wailing cry.

"P-a-u-l!"

All his life Paul Manton remembered that cry piercing the quiet dawn. It shivered through the very foundations of his being. He saw his love's white and desperate face framed in a tangle of silver-fair hair, a coat over a blue silk dressing-gown, bare feet in bedroom slippers, drenched by the dew. Beyond her lay the Castle, wreathed in the mists of dawn, one wing still flickering with fire. Paul wondered if he, too, was dreaming.

Then he caught the girl in his arms.

"Celia! Darleeng . . . my *darleeng!*"

Dumbfounded she heard that voice and looked up at him. He wasn't dead. It wasn't a spirit but Paul himself in flesh and blood. He had come back. He was holding her close, close. Oh, the divine warmth of his arms. Oh, the blessed relief of knowing that he was safe and with her again!

She burst into floods of tears, holding on to him wildly.

"Paul, Paul, my own dear Paul, I thought you were dead."

He covered her face with kisses.

"But no, *ma douce cherie,* I am very much alive. Don't tremble so, *petite ange.* I have you safely in my arms. I reached England late last night and came straight here. Something made me come, even before it is morning. Now I know why. There has been a fire at the Castle. You needed me. I felt it. Oh, *cherie,* are you all right?"

"All right," she said brokenly, "but, Paul . . ." she broke off. Her strength deserted her completely. She would have fallen then if Paul had not lifted her right up in his arms. She could do nothing but sob and cling to him wildly. He carried her up the drive, comforting her with his reassuring words, his passionate kisses.

4

Celia's sobs quietened down. Now, exhausted, she lay
in Paul's arms, her arms around his neck, her cheek
pressed against his. She could hardly believe that he was
back, that he was holding her, that the moment for
which she had been praying so passionately had come
at last. How warm he was! How good the feeling of a
rough sailor's jersey against her face . . . she loved her
sailor. How good the odour of cigarette smoke that
clung to him. He had been smoking French cigarettes,
she was sure. Perhaps he had bought them over there
on the enemy coast! Oh! This was a glorious dream and
assuredly she would wake from it to find him gone
again.

Paul came to the little group of people on the lawn
in front of the Castle. The fire was practically out. It
was no longer raining. In the east the sky had cleared
and was flushed with faint vermillion. The sea was
blanketed in mist. On Gull Rock the birds were rousing,
shaking their white wings in this first pearly light of the
dawn.

One or two people gathered around Paul. They
looked with curiosity at the girl whom he carried in his
arms. Old Elspeth came running towards them, filled
with anxiety for her young mistress.

"Dear life! Are you all right, Miss Celia . . . ?" and
then: "Why, Mr. *Paul!* You'm back! Mercy on us!"

Paul showed his strong white teeth in a friendly smile
at the little hunchback.

"Yes, I am back," he said. "Is it all right now that I
carry *Mademoiselle* into the Castle?"

" 'Tis all of a muddle, but now the fire is out they say —no need to fear more. 'T'will be all right in the drawing-room, Mr. Paul, and I'll light a fire, for my dear Miss Celia's shivering."

Celia stirred in Paul's arms and murmured:

"I'm all right. Set me down, darling. Let me walk."

But he would not do so. He insisted upon carrying her into the Castle. The crowd, peering inquisitively at them, chattered among themselves, most of them villagers from Ruthlyn Cove.

" 'Tis Miss Trevarwith . . . she's fainted . . ."

" 'Tis that young Paul from Hoskins' cottage who got sent away . . ."

"They'm in love, they two . . ."

Soft Cornish voices, laughing a little, friendly . . . not one person there but was a friend of golden-haired Celia Trevarwith. Not one but had liked the handsome young Frenchman who had won all hearts with his charm, his gratitude for all that had been done for him, his strong sympathies with England and the cause of the free.

Isobel, having been assured by the chief fireman that it was safe to go into the Castle now, and that her own wing had not been touched, was already up in her room making sure that her jewel-case was intact, and furiously angry because so many valuables had been taken outside. It had been a precautionary action, but it seemed unnecessary now that the fire was out.

In the drawing-room Celia lay on the sofa. Elspeth had shuffled off to fetch wood and paper and put a kettle on. Everyone was in need of a good cup of tea. Edith Hoskins, up from the cove, went to help her. There were many willing hands in the Castle this morning. Paul Manton knelt beside Celia, chafing her cold slender hands with his warm ones, smiling down into her rapturous eyes.

"It is strange, *mignon*," he said in his own language, "that I had a presentiment something was wrong when I got to Cadgwith. Rachel told me you were here and I had to come. I what you called in English 'hitch-hiked,' and found a lorry driving to the aerodrome. They put me off at the corner and I walked along the road till I saw you at the Castle gates. Of course long before that I saw the smoke and realized there was a fire. *Mon Dieu!* My heart failed me. I thought you might have been hurt."

She drew one of his caressing hands up to her lips.

"Oh, Paul, dearest Paul! It is so wonderful to have you back. I can never describe to you what a wonder it is. I've missed you so terribly and wanted you so much."

"I've wanted you, too, *petite cœur de mon cœur.*"

She made room for him on the sofa and he sat there. Slipping both arms under her slight body, he kissed her long and deeply on the mouth. She felt that she surrendered her very soul in that kiss. She could have laughed for sheer delight when he raised his head and shook back that dark lock of hair with a gesture so delightfully familiar to her.

"You look well . . . browner than ever . . . oh, tell me everything that has been happening to you," she begged him.

He lifted an eyebrow, smiling at her.

"*Mais non!* Not one word can I tell *ma petite gazelle,* because what I have been doing is very secret."

"You've been to France? Can you tell me that?"

"Yes, I have been to France."

"And rescued many people?"

"Many. Some of my countrymen who wish to follow De Gaulle. Some airmen of the R.A.F. Wonderful fellows, and it was a wonderful adventure. I wish I could tell you more about it, but I can't."

She held on to him tightly, as though afraid to let him go.

"But you were in danger all the time!"

"I suppose so."

"And you've been away so long. Were you in France all that time?"

He carried one of her hands to his lips.

"My inquisitive angel, I can tell you no more. I can

238

only say perhaps . . . perhaps not. But I saw my beloved France again, and it was an experience to shake one's soul. For a little while I was one of them again, walking amongst them, talking to them . . . and I could not say to them as I longed to do: 'Your hour will come very soon . . . your hour of liberation.' "

Celia listened with breathless attention, her large eyes fixed upon him.

"Then you must have seen *Germans* too. Oh, Paul . . . you *were* in danger."

"But I am back now," he smiled gaily, "so what does it matter?"

"But you must go back and do it again? That is to be your work. Always dangerous work."

He laughed heartily, caught her close and kissed her on the lips.

"Sweetest and most precious love, it is enchanting of you to worry about my safety, but you do not know how happy I am . . . no longer to catch foolish fish in nets . . . no longer to waste my time, but doing a real job of work for both our countries."

"You are part of our Navy," said Celia proudly, "and I shall be a sailor's wife."

He gave her a quick deep look which expressed the utmost love.

"You will be my wife, sailor or fisherman . . . whatever I am. At one time I was astonished at myself for daring to love the *petite mademoiselle* of Storm Castle, but now I have no feelings of that kind because I know that you are mine and that I am yours. We have but one soul and one heart. Oh, my Celia!"

"Oh, my darling! How lovely it is—this love we have found."

Elspeth came bundling in with hot tea. After that there was no more peace for Celia and Paul. Isobel Trevarwith, wearing slacks and a coat, a cigarette between her lips, marched into the room in a furious temper. Celia could see at a glance that her stepmother was still suffering from the after-effects of the alcholic party at Kyland House. She was not yet properly made up.

Her face was livid. Her red hair was untidy. She had every kind of complaint to utter.

Somebody had been stupid, or the fire would have been put out long ago. She couldn't go away for one night without something happening. She had been dragged out of her bed at an unearthly hour for nothing. Fulke was a fool. Celia was a fool. They were all fools.

She flung herself into a chair in front of the fire which Elspeth had just started, shivering, in her worst mood.

If all those people outside expected refreshment, they were mistaken, she declared. Tea was rationed. She wasn't going to give away anything. She hated the whole crowd at Ruthylyn anyhow, and always had.

It was here that Celia, with a sudden rush of indignation, interrupted. She stood up and faced her stepmother:

"The people are wonderful here. You just don't understand them, Isobel. They all love our family and they've always helped, and they deserve a cup of tea. They must have it."

"Who the devil are you dictating to . . ." began Isobel, and then suddenly she seemed to become conscious of the fact that Paul Manton was in the room. She cast an amazed look at the slim, blue-clad figure. Paul was rolling a cigarette between his thin brown fingers. Isobel spluttered.

"Good Lord! How did *you* get here?"

He gave a slight bow which had a suggestion of irony in it.

"Good morning, Madame."

"It is not my idea of a good morning," snapped Isobel, "and where have you come from, anyhow?"

"From France, Madame," he said with another ironic bow.

Isobel's sluggish brain did not take this in. She said:

"Still snooping around after my stepdaughter."

The fine lines of his face tautened a little.

"*Snooping,* Madame?"

Celia broke in, her cheeks flaming:

"Take no notice of my stepmother, Paul. She has no right to be rude to you under this roof . . . after all you have done for our country . . . why, she doesn't understand what you are doing . . . she doesn't realize that she owes her safety to men like you. Oh, let's get out of here . . . let's go back to Cadgwith."

Isobel flung a cigarette-end into the grate and stared from Celia to the young Frenchman.

"What the devil is all this about?"

Paul bowed.

"Do not disturb yourself on my account. I will not stay here, Madame. But when I go, Celia comes with me."

It was Isobel's turn to flush crimson. She gave Paul a searching look which held a certain amount of uncertainty in it. For the first time she began to see what it was in this young man which attracted Celia. She had to admit there was nothing gauche or common about Paul. He spoke with the pride and distinction of a gentleman, and Lord! what a dream of a figure the boy had! That slim, graceful body, and the blackest hair she had ever seen. In her extreme youth she had had an affair with a Spaniard. Paul wasn't unlike her Juan, and the said Juan had fired her blood as no other man had ever done before or since.

Isobel suddenly forgot that she was mistress of Storm Castle and the stern stepmother trying to bully the girl out of a love-affair which she considered ridiculous. She forgot to be bad-tempered. Something ultra-feminine in her . . . a wholly natural instinct in her to appear at her best before a really attractive man superseded all other sensations.

"My, oh my!" she exclaimed, imitating an American drawl. "You sure have found a honey of a boy-friend, Celia. Look how his eyes flash fire. He's mighty good looking."

Celia, tired and a little disgusted with her stepmother, put an arm through Paul's.

"If you'll excuse me, Isobel, I'm going to find some way of getting back to Cadgwith with Paul."

But Isobel had other ideas. She was reminding herself that it might pay her handsomely to be pleasant to these two. At any rate she would know more about it when she had seen the lawyers in town on Monday. She said:

"Now listen, children. I know I fly off the handle at times, but I don't mean it. You don't have to go to Cadgwith. You know I want you to look after things for me when I am in town, Celia. And if Paul would like to put up here for a night or two, he can."

Celia stared at her stepmother in a dazed way. She was bewildered by such a change of front. Paul seemed bewildered too. But whatever he thought of it, his pride was uppermost and he was not prepared to capitulate to a woman who had once insulted him. Added to which nothing that she could say or do now would make him forget the fact that she had been unkind to Celia all her life. He ignored that new look of interest in the woman's round blue eyes and gave a cold little bow.

"If Madame will excuse me, I shall return to Cadgwith."

"I'll get dressed and come with you, darling," said Celia.

Isobel protested:

"You can't walk out on me now. There is so much to be done. All those damned things the boys have flung out on the lawn have to be sorted and put back, and Anthony can't stay at the Vicarage. Don't be a little pig, Celia. You said you'd see me through."

Celia hesitated and threw an anxious look at Paul.

"I did say I would, Paul. She . . . she's going to London on Monday when we leave the Castle. I suppose I ought to stay and help. Can't you . . . if you're on leave, can't you stay in Ruthlyn for the week-end . . . with the Hoskins?"

He took her hand and kissed it like the cavalier he was.

"You shall do exactly as you wish, *ma douce cherie*. If you stay here, then in Ruthlyn I stay too. But not in this Castle."

"I understand, Paul."

Isobel, much relieved that she was not going to be left, moved towards the door.

"You two have a chat and I'll see the folks outside get their tea."

As the door closed upon her, the young couple stared at each other. Paul was frowning.

"She is . . . peculiar! *Pourquoi?*"

Celia twisted her lips.

"I think, darling, that my friend Jill is right. It is something to do with money . . . and that's what she is going to see Father's lawyer about. And if she has any luck, Paul, she may come back on Monday and tell us that we needn't wait until I am twenty-one."

"You mean that she might permit you to be married to me at once?" asked Paul incredulously.

"Quite possibly."

His face looked transfigured. He caught her close and kissed her burningly on the lips and throat.

"*Petite femme! Ma petite femme!* If only that is true."

But Celia dared say no more and gave no more hope. She was so afraid herself that her conjectures might not be correct. She clung to Paul, returning his kisses and she thought:

"Whatever happens now . . . we shall have had this morning. Nobody can take this hour away, or any of the hours which we have had together."

And so that fantastic night ended. The fire was extinguished. The half-burned wing of the Castle, charred and dripping with water, looked as though a bomb had shattered it in the night. But the rest of it stood unharmed, inviolate, strong and indestructible against the morning light.

The last pages of the history of the Trevarwiths of Storm Castle had yet to be written.

5

On the day that Isobel Trevarwith went up to London to see her late husband's solicitors, Celia had what she described to old Rachel as a "fit of the jim-jams." (A word she had not used since her school-days!) But she was filled with a restlessness which she could barely control; bubbling with excitement. Somehow she had a premonition that Isobel was going to come back from London with news that might alter the whole of life for her, Celia . . . and Paul.

The whole week-end had been exciting. Paul had stayed down at the harbour with his old friends, the Hoskins, and his young compatriot, Jean, who would scarcely leave his side. He and Celia had seen as much of each other as they possibly could, and then on the Monday the Trevarwiths left the Castle, the R.A.F. took over. Celia went back to Cadgwith, taking her little stepbrother with her, as arranged. Isobel (accompanied by Fulke Withers, who had business in town) caught the Penzance express at Helston. And Paul, more than reluctant to leave Celia, returned to his ship.

His leave was over. He was returning to his secret and hazardous work with the Navy. But this time, he consoled Celia, he would not be away long. He expected to be back within forty-eight hours.

Young Anthony was amused and pleased with the change from life in the Castle to the simple existence which he led in Cadgwith. He and his stepsister spent most of that sunny summer's day down on the rocks or on the beach where Anthony was allowed to paddle. Celia bathed for the first time since her illness.

She felt vigorous and well—hardly recognized herself. She had not felt so strong or so happy for months. And all day she kept thinking:

"What will Mr. Forbes tell Isobel? Will they allow me to marry? Oh, *what* is going to happen?"

Paul had been so marvellous to her all week-end. She was more in love with him than ever. They were spiritually one and nothing could separate them. But she knew that he longed for that other closer union with her and she shared his longing. She had but one ambition . . . to become Paul's wife and devote the rest of her life to him.

Jill Hayling cycled over from the aerodrome with the exciting news that she had had her first letter from her husband. She was the happiest girl in the world, she told Celia. Naturally Tim had not been able to tell her much, but he had said he was well, studying languages in order to pass the time, and aching for news from her. She was going to write to him as often as she could and send him parcels whenever allowed to do so. This letter from Tim had brought him close to her again.

"We had our honeymoon in Cadgwith, and for a while I couldn't bear to come back," Jill told Celia, "but now it is marvellous to see all our cherished places again. He is coming back to me, Celia. We shall have another honeymoon in dear little Cadgwith. Isn't it heavenly?"

Celia agreed that it was heavenly. The two girls, both in a state of half-suppressed excitement, spent the afternoon together, knit by a bond of love and memories.

"I've got to wait a long time perhaps," sighed Jill, "but your Paul is still here. You don't know how lucky you are."

Celia agreed.

That following evening, Isobel arrived from London and telephoned to Cadgwith Post Office, leaving a message for Miss Trevarwith to ring her up at once. Celia answered this call with some trepidation. It would be so awful, if it was only to hear that Isobel had not changed her mind and was still forbidding her marriage.

But Isobel seemed in the best of humours. She would say nothing definite over the phone, but declared that she had something to tell Celia which would interest her.

"You'd better drive over to Kyland and bring Anthony with you," said Isobel.

Celia hesitated. She had determined never to set foot in Fulke Withers' house, but Isobel added:

"You needn't worry about that silly fool, Fulke. I've left him in London. He's got a broken arm and a broken heart, and I don't think you've got anything more to fear from him."

So Celia drove Anthony over to Kyland that clear summer's night, and sitting in Fulke's handsome library listened to the proposition which her stepmother put up to her.

Isobel did not speak too bluntly. She was a little ashamed to do so, having stood in Celia's way so remorselessly up to now. But she gave Celia to understand that according to the terms of her father's Will she would receive a half portion of her money on the day of her marriage (providing it was with the approval of her guardians) and the other half when she came of age.

"This being so," Isobel said, smiling sweetly at Celia, "you would not need to be so very poor as Paul Manton's wife. You could afford quite a nice home of your own."

Celia, trembling, flushing, and with a hammering heart, said:

"Paul wouldn't want my money . . . he only wants me . . ."

"Quite so. But you would have it all the same."

"Then you mean . . . you mean you won't stand in my way any more. You'll give us permission to marry?"

Isobel cleared her throat and lit a cigarette to cover her embarrassment. Hardened though she was, she felt a twinge of shame as she looked into the girl's honest, beautiful eyes. She knew she had behaved badly to Celia and she knew she had been a fool, too. She had never had any interest in legal matters and she had not really gone into the details of her husband's Will. Whatever she had thought about it, she had determined to marry the girl off to one of her own friends. To Fulke! Now she was forced to realize that *that* match would never come off, and that if she wanted financial assistance she would have to get it through bribing rather than thwarting her young stepdaughter.

"I might do," she said. "As a matter of fact I told Mr. Forbes about your love-affair, and when he asked what I thought of Paul Manton I said that I reckoned, in spite of his humble origin, he was an exceedingly attractive and presentable young man."

Celia gasped.

"You said that?"

"Yes. I did what I could for you," said Isobel, feeling quite heroic. "And Mr. Forbes said that as your stepmother I was to make the final decision."

"And you've made it?" Celia could scarcely breathe.

"Well, I said I thought I'd let you marry Paul—young though you are, Celia."

Celia rushed to Isobel's side and for the first time in their lives the two embraced. Celia hugged the woman whom she had feared and detested as a child, and despised when she grew older. She kissed both Isobel's well-rouged cheeks a dozen times.

"Isobel. Isobel . . . you *angel!*"

Isobel Trevarwith gasped and extricated herself from the feverish young arms. She was beginning to see that she had missed something by antagonizing Celia so bitterly all these years. She might have had this warm, impulsive affection and been the richer for it. She said:

"Don't lose your head, you silly goof."

"But I've lost it!" cried Celia, flinging her arms above her head. "I've lost my heart, too. Oh, Isobel, if you KNEW what this means to me! Why have you changed your mind? Why . . . just because I'll have some money?"

Isobel coughed and looked away from the girl.

"Well, my dear . . . you know my own affairs are none too bright, and Anthony's future is not particularly rosy. Your father left us poorly off considering all the taxation and the upkeep of Storm Castle, etc. You were the lucky one, and of course, if you and Paul don't need a lot of money, Anthony and I . . ."

She paused, clearing her throat again and her face and neck were actually scarlet.

Celia could not now misunderstand the base motives for Isobel's change of demeanour. But she was too thrilled and ecstatically happy to care. Money meant so little and Paul and their marriage so much. She said breathlessly:

"I'll help you and Anthony, Isobel. I'll share my money with you gladly. You don't need to worry. I'll pay all your bills. It's just your permission to marry Paul that I ask for in return."

Isobel sighed with relief. She felt almost sincerely fond of Francis Trevarwith's daughter in this moment. She said:

"That's a deal. Then we'll both be okay. Better tell your boy-friend to get a special licence. You might as well be married in St. Ruthlyn's whenever you want."

"You mean *at once?*"

"Why not?" said Isobel, thinking of her many debts, and knowing that it wouldn't be long before she fell out with Fulke Withers, and would be asked to leave Kyland. And she was planning to go back to London, pose as a wealthy widow and catch a husband with some kind of position. Tony could go to a day-school in town this winter if he were strong enough. If there were bad air raids, she might even put him in a nursery school in the country. It would leave her a free hand. Thank goodness she was still good looking. With a few new clothes and some money in her pocket she would soon impress some idiot . . . perhaps a rich Colonial or American.

Celia's happy voice cut in on this selfish reverie.

"Oh, Isobel . . . it's the *most* wonderful news. I can't wait for Paul to get back."

Anthony came into the room. He looked downcast.

Mummy, how long are we going to live here? I

248

don't like this house. I want to go back to Rachel's with Celia."

A few months ago Isobel would have been mad with jealousy of Celia. This evening she smiled.

"So you can if you want, duckie. But sister is going to be married soon, then you will have to live with Mummy again."

Anthony's blue eyes stared at his stepsister.

"Are you going to be married, Celia?"

"Yes, darling . . ." she swept him into her arms and kissed his red curls. "And you shall be my little page and hold my train. I shall wear my mother's white satin court-dress and her wedding veil. I've got everything. It fits me perfectly. I shall have the loveliest wedding and the handsomest prince for a bridegroom that any princess in a fairy-tale has *ever* had . . ."

"You and your fairy-tales," said Isobel, yawning. "What a girl! You always were crazy about them when you were a kid. A bit queer, I call you."

"But fairy-tales come true, sometimes," said Celia with shining eyes. "Anthony knows that. And this princess from the Castle is going to marry her sailor prince and live happily ever afterwards."

It was a week later, on a September morning of golden mist over a translucent blue-green sea, and with the merest touch of autumn coolness in the air, that Celia Trevarwith and Paul Manton were made man and wife.

Everybody for miles around turned out to see the wedding in St. Ruthlyn's church, which stood in the middle of the little village a quarter of a mile back from the harbour. It was a day of days for Ruthlyn Cove . . . when the daughter of the Trevarwiths of Storm Castle took a husband . . . and the bridegroom was so glamorous and romantic a figure as the handsome young fisherman who had once belonged to the Franco-Belgian fishing colony here.

Rich and poor alike flocked to the church. The rich . . . some of whom had known Angela and Francis Tr⸺

varwith in the past . . . out of curiosity, because the romance between Celia and Paul had become almost legendary in the village. The poor, because they all loved Celia and knew and liked Paul.

And if it was a great day for Ruthlyn Cove, it was for Celia as though the gates of paradise itself opened to let her in.

The vicar's wife had insisted upon putting her up in the Vicarage the night before. The aged vicar had known Celia's mother before her. Neither he nor his wife had had much to do with the second Mrs. Trevarwith, but they had always been extremely sorry for little Celia, and glad now to do her a service.

Isobel was pleased to present herself in the role of kind and doting stepmother today. In blue, with fox furs, floral toque and veil, she took Celia up the aisle. She was the only relative whom Celia had in the world to give her away.

Paul was waiting there at the altar steps . . . a Paul whom none of them had seen before in his smart new uniform of a petty-officer in the Free French Navy. A uniform which he had just been given the right to wear and which suited his slender darkness extraordinarily well.

Old Rachel and her sister from Cadgwith were present. The Hoskins, in their Sunday best. Elspeth, weeping sentimental tears, remembering her young mistress who had died. Section-Officer Hayling in her best uniform, buttons shining, eyes wet, with memories of her own wedding in her mind. Many of the R.A.F. from Storm Castle, including Flight-Lieutenant Simon Pierce . . . as many as could crowd into the church were there, too, to see the wedding of Miss Trevarwith. But Fulke Withers was conspicuous by his absence.

The sun slanted through the lovely stained-glass windows and enriched the beautiful carved woodwork in the old Norman church. The altar was a mass of flow-

The organist, Miss Smithson, who had also known mother, played her very best. And, as the music l and swelled, up the aisle came the bride, a

Celia so lovely that Paul, watching her move slowly toward him, wondered if this could be his *petite gazelle,* his Celia of the well-worn cotton frocks and sandalled feet and flying tangled curls.

This was a glorious bride indeed . . . in the court dress which her mother had worn before her . . . shimmering satin, train embroidered with silver lovers' knots . . . tanned young face almost colourless with emotion, and veiled in rich Mechlin lace . . . that same veil that had covered Angela Trevarwith's face when she had come up this same aisle to marry Celia's father twenty years ago.

Celia carried a great bunch of lilies. Behind her, young Anthony (in a white page's suit hastily bought by Isobel) held up his stepsister's train. The light through the rich stained-glass windows turned his red curls to fire. He looked proud and pleased, feeling that he was, indeed, taking part in a fairy-tale, and that sister Celie was a real princess.

Outside could be heard the muffled boom of the naval guns from beyond Land's End . . . the faint droning of planes overhead . . . the sudden sharp crack of machine-gun fire. . . . The R.A.F. were practising, sending the sea-gulls screaming up from the rocks with a whirr of white agitated wings.

Outside there were many such evidences that there was a war on, but in St. Ruthlyn church there was peace, and a happiness in the hearts of Celia and Paul which exceeded anything either had ever experienced before.

Perhaps in this hour, as Paul's dark tender eyes watched his lovely bride draw near to him, he thought sadly of his native land and wished that his mother and sister Yvonne could be here. But the day would come, he knew . . . the day he was working for . . . when he could take Celia back to France to see them both. That was a time, perhaps not so far ahead, when all France would be free.

Celia reached Paul's side. She slipped a cold, nervous little hand into his, but in a moment his warm reassu

ing clasp had brought the blood back to her cheeks and steadied the trembling of her limbs.

The service began:

"Dearly beloved, we are gathered here together . . ."

Celia felt as though she were in a dream. In this hour it was hard to believe she had ever been so unhappy, so desolate, so wild with grief and pain throughout her sad young life. Now she was being married to the man she loved more than anything or anybody in the world. There could be, and must be, no more tears.

The scent of the lilies became almost overpowering. She shut her eyes. The service went on:

"Celia Angela Trevarwith, will you take this man . . ."

Vaguely she heard the words and then her own voice answering:

"I will."

And afterwards Paul's voice, strong and serious, making his responses, with his slight French inflexion:

"I will."

The little ring slid on to her finger. Her hand remained clasped in Paul's. They knelt to receive the final benediction.

In her pew, Jill Hayling put a handkerchief to her eyes and prayed passionately for the husband who was a prisoner of war.

Old Elspeth whispered to her next-door neighbour:

"Dear lil maid! She'm a beautiful bride . . ."

Later on, down the aisle, with veil swept back from her golden hair, came Celia Manton on the arm of her sailor husband. A flushed, glowing Celia, smiling happily at her friends. There were cheers for her outside in the sunlight; a shower of confetti . . . many Cornish men and women to wish her luck and bid her *adieu*. There was to be no reception. Because of the war, this wedding was to be a very quiet one, and Celia and Paul were going away immediately. They were to spend honeymoon in Devonshire in a hotel on the fringe moor, which they had both chosen because they change from the sea, and because they both loved the wild moorland at this time of bracken and heather.

First, back to the Vicarage for a glass of wine and where the bride could change. Good-byes to Isobel, to Anthony, who promptly burst into tears, loath to part from his beloved Celie. Good-bye to Jill. Finally, the newly-married couple found themselves alone in the car which was driving them to Helston station.

Paul, his voice husky, held his young wife's hand tightly in his own and said in his own language:

"It was a truly beautiful wedding, *mon ange,* but I do not wish to go through another. I feel I have no breath."

Celia laughed and answered:

"I hope you'll never have occasion for another, my darling Paul."

Then quickly she turned her head to take a last glance at Storm Castle before they rounded the headland. There it stood, grey and indomitable as ever, filled with hundreds of young airmen who were to be trained as pilots. Good-bye to Storm Castle! . . . to her old home . . . her old life, and she had no regrets. Not one.

She was Paul's wife now. *Madame Manton.* The thought of that made her smile a little—it sounded so strange, so sweet. When Paul went back to sea she would wait for him in Cadgwith. No matter what money she had, she would not wish to spend it at the moment. She wanted to remain with Rachel while Paul had this job and until it was possible for them to set up a home together.

Paul said:

"Of what are you thinking, *ma douce cherie?*"

"Of everything—and most of all of how lucky I am to be your wife."

He drew away from her a little and his dark eyes looked gravely at her. The dream-like girl in the church in her bridal finery had changed back to the Celia he knew . . . just a simply-dressed girl in a tweed suit, with a felt hat on her fair young head. His gaze travelled to the luggage at their feet . . . their two suitcases . . . and his thoughts winged to the week which lay before them and all the ecstasy which would be theirs.

Deepest emotion shook him. Slipping an arm around Celia he drew her to his side and kissed her lips.

"Petite femme. Je t'aime. Je t'adore. Ma femme— yes, you are mine, really and truly now!"

The car moved on down the white road between the tall hedges. Cheek to cheek sat Celia and Paul, their hands clasped together, their eyes fixed on the rich bright countryside before them.

THE
SUPERB
GOTHIC
EPIC

A TOWERING MANSION
AND ITS TANGLED LEGACY
OF EVIL AND DESIRE

THE STORMY ROMANTIC SAGA BY

FLORENCE HURD
ROMMANY

It began with Eustacia, first mistress of Rommany, whose love for Duncan Blackmore was not to be denied. But the innumerable rooms and sins of Rommany drew her into the grip of a sinister plot that spread its evil stain across seven decades. . . .

Until, in the life of Constance, her granddaughter, three generations of mystery converge in a fateful decision to love the hypnotic Leonard, a man cruelly linked to the shadowy past.

Suddenly, the gloom of Rommany is punctuated by ominous thumpings in the night, and Constance must pierce the veil that enshrouds her hopeless passion—so the ultimate secret of Rommany can be unmasked at last!

 28340/$1.75

ROM 6-76

THE BLAZING, TUMULTUOUS NOVEL
OF A LOVE AS OLD AS TIME,
AS TIMELESS AS FOREVER . . .

JOYCE VERRETTE

DAWN OF DESIRE

*In a faraway time, by the shores of the ancient River
Nile, they stand, possessed by a single naked desire,
in the dawning light of their eternal love. The un-
bounded passions of the incomparably beautiful
Princess Nefrytataten and the tawny-skinned Prince
Ameni sweep across the torrid landscape of Egypt
as the two lovers, wrenched asunder by treacherous
events, must brave peril, degradation, and intrigue
before their twin desires can find release once more
in a surging tide of full-blooded joy!*

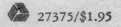 27375/$1.95

DOD 6-76